APOCALYPSE
2012

FORGE BOOKS BY GARY JENNINGS

Aztec

Journeyer

Spangle

Aztec Autumn

Aztec Blood

Aztec Rage
(with Robert Gleason and Junius Podrug)

Aztec Fire
(with Robert Gleason and Junius Podrug)

Apocalypse 2012
(with Robert Gleason and Junius Podrug)

Visit Gary Jennings at www.garyjennings.net.

GARY JENNINGS'

APOCALYPSE
2012

ROBERT GLEASON
JUNIUS PODRUG

A TOM DOHERTY
ASSOCIATES BOOK
NEW YORK

This is a work of fiction. All of the characters, organizations, and events portrayed in this novel are either products of the author's imagination or are used fictitiously.

APOCALYPSE 2012

A Forge Book
Published by Tom Doherty Associates, LLC
175 Fifth Avenue
New York, NY 10010

www.tor-forge.com

Forge® is a registered trademark of Tom Doherty Associates, LLC.

Library of Congress Cataloging-in-Publication Data

Jennings, Gary.
    Apolcalypse 2012 / Gary Jennings, Robert Gleason, and Junius Podrug.—1st ed.
        p. cm.
    "A Tom Doherty Associates book."
    "A Forge book"
    ISBN-13: 978-0-7653-2259-3
    ISBN-10: 0-7653-2259-5
    1. Indians of Mexico—Fiction. 2. Prophecies—Fiction. 3. Quetzalcoatl (Aztec deity)—
Fiction. 4. Mexico—History—Fiction. 5. Code and cipher stories. I. Gleason, Robert
(Robert Herman). II. Podrug, Junius. III. Title. IV. Title: Apocalypse twenty-twelve.
    PS3560.E518A86 2009
    813'.54—dc22

                                                                            2009012864

First Edition: June 2009

Printed in the United States of America

0 9 8 7 6 5 4 3 2 1

For Joyce Servis

ACKNOWLEDGMENTS

Many people helped bring this book to fruition. We particularly wish to thank Sessalee Hensley, Tom Doherty, Linda Quinton, Christine Jaeger, Eric Raab, Ashley Cardiff, Katharine Critchlow, Jerry Gibbs, Elizabeth Winick, Hildegard Krische, and Maribel Baltazar-Gutierrez.

PART I

DOG PEOPLE

1

ONE-WORLD, 1001 A.D.

I sat on a large rock on a hillside and fought my rope restraints. The task was next to hopeless. My captors had wrenched my elbows up behind my back, shoved a pole between them, then lashed my wrists so tight across my stomach, my elbow joints and wrists screamed in agony. Hobbling my feet, they roped me to a tree.

Nonetheless, I struggled to turn sideways, hoping to use the tree trunk to push the pole out from between my elbows. Free of the pole, I would then cut my binds on a jagged rock.

An angry commotion announced Tenoch's return. The leader of our party, he was notoriously ill-tempered. He hurled a deer to the ground perhaps twenty paces from my feet. Little more than bones and parchment, the shriveled deer wouldn't even satisfy our twenty hunters much less the hundreds of our clan, who camped by a waterhole a day's walk to the north. Kicking and thrashing several hunters with his wrist-whip, he thundered obscenities at them for not flushing a fatter deer or stealing the corn, peppers, and beans he'd wanted.

Then he turned his wrath and his whip on his slave, Desert Flower, and for the ten thousandth time in my life, I swore I would kill that devil.

Young and attractive, Flower was a poor woman whom Tenoch had forced into the expedition to attend to his physical needs, despite the elders' prohibitions. Tenoch had spurned their counsel, insisting that he needed her to dress out his kills, cook his meals, carry his gear—and endure his violently depraved debaucheries. Tenoch's abuse of her hurt me worse than his assaults on me. Born, like myself, during the first year of the Great Drought, we were each going on our sixteenth summer, and we were each Tenoch's property. Both of us suffered under his whip, but she had it infinitely worse. Shy and small of frame, she was compassion incarnate with a virtuousness that infuriated our master. Her large, dark eyes and tiny sensitive mouth expressed her caring nature quickly and unmistakably—her pleasure at sudden acts of kindness and her displeasure at deliberate cruelty. Tenoch despised such displays.

When he saw her so moved, he flogged her like a fiend freed from Mictlantecuhtli's hell.

He was still screaming about the scrawny deer and the failure to find produce. Of course, the food shortage was no one's fault. There was little food to be found. The weather had been drier than old bones for more seasons than I could remember. The crops had withered, and the emaciated game was increasingly scarce.

Even worse, our Aztec people now paid for that scarcity in blood. Increasing their annual blood-tithes tenfold, Toltec priests roamed our countryside, abducting anyone they could get their hands on, dragging them back to Tula, where they immolated them en masse after cutting out their hearts. They emptied their victims' blood in scarlet torrents down the temple troughs and hurled their severed heads down the pyramidal steps . . . none of which brought back Tlaloc, our bloodthirsty thunder god, or watered our maize fields.

Our people were starving, and hunger had forced us into Toltec land to poach that deer. Fierce bands of Toltec hunters were everywhere, but Tenoch had reasoned he could offer me to those warriors as recompense for the deer and thus escape their wrath. Content with the gift of a sacrificial prisoner, they'd haul me back to Tula and deliver me to their bloodthirsty priests.

Whatever the case, we'd had no choice but to poach on Toltec land. I was also an obvious choice for the sacrificial victim. An orphaned babe, found in a reed basket by a river bank, I was a slave with no rights. So here I was: I would either starve to death trussed to a tree or die on a pyramid under a priest's black blade.

Before I could curse my fate, however, hell exploded. Half of our twenty hunter-warriors collapsed before me, arrows impaling their heads, torsos, and necks. One lay writhing on the ground, clutching at an arrow that skewered his throat, gore gushed from his wound. Another stared sightlessly at a feathered shaft sunk deep between his eyes. Four others were mortally pierced through the chest.

Another near-simultaneous arrow-volley took out six more of our men.

Eight attackers erupted from the tree line, dispatching the survivors with obsidian-bladed axes and black knives. Like ourselves, these loinclothed men were stripped down to their heavily tattooed torsos, and limbs; and, like ourselves, they sported nose, ear, and lip ornaments. The resemblance, however, ended there. Our warriors wore simple, coarse-cloth maxtlatl loincloths made of fibers worked from maguey plants; these soldiers were dressed in bright loincloths, with higher-ranking warriors wearing mantles and headdresses. While this enemy attacked with shocking swiftness, rigorous teamwork, and unerring precision, our few surviving warriors panicked like children, either fleeing or cowering, each man looking out solely for himself.

At their head, three paces in front of his charging men, was their leader. There was no mistaking his high status—even from where I stood I could see that the maxtlatl between his legs was made of costly dyed cotton. The mantle that was tied at his shoulders and draped down his back was covered with images of wild animals, skulls and bones, and demonic gods.

Unlike our skinny soldiers, these were powerfully built killers—men with rocklike biceps, block-like shoulders, massively muscular legs and chests. Nor were their weapons tipped with coarsely chipped flint, as were ours, but ebony-hued, sharply honed obsidian—blades now glistening with the blood of my adopted people.

A severed head lay beside a pair of headless shoulders. Another warrior lay on his side with a javelin protruding from both chest and back. Only one victim still moved, writhing in his death spasms, his limbs convulsing, blood pumping from his neck and stomach. Another, who had tried to scale a tree, was now affixed to that sought-after sanctuary, a lance pinning his chest to the trunk, his feet dangling a handsbreadth above the ground.

Of our entire band, only two others survived: Tenoch, who lay on the ground unconscious—thanks to a towering, muscular warrior who had clubbed him into bloody oblivion—and Desert Flower.

Emerging from the forest, a ninth man walked through the camp—an elderly dignitary who had not participated in the fray.

His clothing confirmed his importance among his people. His loincloth was richly embroidered in vivid shades of red and green and yellow, with sparkling gems delicately weaved into the cloth. Hanging from knots were tiny bells of gold.

His mantle was long, falling from his shoulders almost to the ground. As colorful as his loincloth and as costly, it was lavishly decorated and fringed with gold.

He was at an age in life when most men no longer marched with an army unless their role was planning as opposed to leading warriors into battle.

As he stood over me and stared down, I knew what he was looking at: the star patterns tattooed on my lower belly and painted with black dye on my white loincloth.

"Who put these drawings on you?" he asked.

He spoke Nahuatl, the same language as the Aztecs, though his diction and accent were different from ours.

"I painted the ones on my loincloth."

"Why?"

The question stumped me. I had never thought of why I had drawn them. I gave him the answer that came to my mind. "It's what I see in the sky at night."

Kneeling next to me, he examined the scars on my abdomen, fingering the pattern of scars.

"Where did you get these designs?" he asked.

The words were spoken almost in a whisper.

"I don't know," I told him, truthfully. "They were on me when they found me."

"Who found you?"

"The Clansmen—"

"Dog People found you? Where? When?"

"I was found when I was a babe. In a basket, next to a river."

The nobleman stood up. "Do not hurt this one," he announced to the warriors.

Suddenly I felt a chill, and a shadow fell over me. A startlingly tall, shockingly muscled warrior had come up beside me silent as the grave. Possessing a hawk's nose, wide flaring cheekbones and blood-streaked shoulder-length hair, black as a raven's underwing, he was an imposing specimen.

He wore the close-fitting loincloth and white padded-cotton shirt of a warrior, but his shield and helmet told me he was far more important than a mere commander of what appeared to be a small force—only eight soldiers plus the elderly nobleman. The warrior's shield bore the image of a jaguar, and his headdress included the actual head of a jaguar as well as the brilliant green and red plumes of rare birds.

Jaguar Knight.

I had never seen an actual knight, but I knew from cooking-fire talk that the Toltec had three orders of knighthood: Jaguar, Eagle, and Coyote. The Coyote Knights were in charge of the Toltec forces that guarded its northern border, the one it shared with us Dog People. The Jaguar Knights guarded the king.

What was a Jaguar Knight doing so far from his king?

Who was this man?

Glancing up at him, I was surprised to find his eyes were . . . kind.

He was the man who had subdued my tormenter, Tenoch.

"What is happening, Citali?" he asked.

Citali. *Stargazer.* So the elderly nobleman was a shaman, like my adopted father. A very important person in any Clan—often the most important.

"He bears a sign of the stars," Stargazer said. "I have placed him under my protection."

The Jaguar Knight glared down at me. "He's of the Dog People. Probably the son of a village shaman." The knight kicked me. "What's your name, Aztec?"

"Coyotl," I said.

I hoped it would be offensive to the gods for a Jaguar Knight to kill one who bore the name of a brethren order.

Stargazer chuckled. "The writing, the scars, the name—Chimalpopoca, this young man is not fated to die this day . . . or end up sacrificed. Not yet . . ." he said to me.

Chimalpopoca—Smoking Shield.

Smoking Shield appeared as puzzled about the significance of the scars as I had been . . . but was just as frightened of the unknown as I was to question what the gods had written.

Even if neither of us understood what it meant.

He stared at my bare, tattooed abdomen.

"Relax, young friend," he finally said, raising his eyes. "I was only admiring your body art along with Stargazer." Turning to the old man, he said: "We don't murder the young, do we, old man?" He slashed my bonds, freeing me from the tree. "Come to dinner with us tonight. Enjoy your venison. We will simmer it in a pot of ripe maize, plump red beans, succulent onions, and scorchingly hot chilis even as we wash it down with octli. Afterward, you will get a good night's sleep. We leave at dawn."

"I'm going with you?"

"Indeed."

"Where do we travel?"

"Who knows? All of life is an adventure. Tonight, we will eat, and drink to the gods. Tomorrow we face the far horizons."

2

Smoking Shield was true to his word. He equally divided the rations—the corn, beans, wild onions, rabbit, and venison, all of it stewed, spiced with chili, and rolled up into thin flat corn cakes. He and his killers were surprisingly pleasant and unfailingly polite.

A generosity of spirit that Tenoch failed to pick up on.

As soon as dinner was served, he shoved Desert Flower and myself aside, and began gorging himself on our rations.

At that point our host's face darkened. Again, he hammered Tenoch into unconsciousness. Yanking Tenoch's elbows up tight behind his back, he then shoved a thick tree limb between them, lashing Tenoch's wrists across his stomach and tying the rawhide thongs painfully tight. Afterward he divided Tenoch's stew evenly between Desert Flower and me.

When he sat back down between Desert Flower and myself, the young woman trembled so furiously she could not even hold her wooden bowl of stew. Smoking Shield's anger instantly subsided. Putting an arm around her, he said quietly:

"Do not fear. With us, no one will harm you. Here. Eat up. You are safe."

He took a large chunk of venison loin from his bowl and held it to her mouth. He then offered her a taste of corn beer from his drink-sack.

"The venison is peppery. Take some corn beer to wash it down."

Staring at him shyly, she accepted the meat and, after drinking the corn beer, began to slowly chew.

"Why don't you harm us?" she asked.

The question popped out of her so quickly I was astonished at it—Flower was too, I believe. I, of course, understood her mystification totally. She and I had suffered so much abuse during our short lives, we weren't used to the kindness of strangers—particularly professional soldiers. I didn't understand their indulgence of us either.

I think we both assumed they would laugh at her question. We were wrong. Smoking Shield answered her in precise detail:

"As I said before, we don't hurt the young and innocent—particularly when they're civilians. And there is the matter of this young man's belly designs. That old man over there is the Royal Astronomer and much respected by King Quetzalcoatl. He finds that young man's star tattoo somehow significant and has placed him under his protection. Since you are with the boy, we're extending you the same privilege. So eat, drink, relax."

He then offered me the potent brew. I accepted but drank carefully, never having tasted spirits. To my surprise, I did not choke or even wince. In fact, I found it pleasant.

"Tell me, young warrior," our host asked, "what's your name?"

"Two Ollin Fire Coyotl."

"You were named for your birth date?"

"On the second day of our Aztec calendar—the second day of Ollin—an old shaman found me in a basket on a riverbank when I was an infant. No one knows when I was born."

Ollin was motion, a powerful sign because everything that moved had ollin. The wind that blew, rivers that flowed, rain that fell, the leap of a jaguar and the flight of an arrow, all had Ollin.

"Fire Eyes, the old shaman, also called me Coyotl," I said. "He told me that I was gaunt and quick of foot like the desert dog." Our host smiled. "Others in our village believed that a she-coyotl with litter had suckled me in the wild."

At that line our host laughed.

"And what of your third name, young Coyotl?"

"Fire. Because no one looked more to the stars that fire the night sky than I did—not even the old shaman who had taken me in, and he had studied the star-gods all his life. 'The stars don't just light the night sky,' he used to tell me, 'they reveal their secrets to those who can see. Despite your young age, you see more than others, and you carry a map of the stars in your head. Any starwatcher knows where to look in the night sky to find this god or that one, but none I have ever met or heard of had your ability to know exactly where stars would be—day or night, summer or winter—without even looking up.' Cutting his finger, he anointed me with blood as a sacrifice to Ollin. 'From now on, you are Two Ollin Fire Coyotl,' he'd said."

. . . My eyes had always been drawn to the night sky. My fascination was more than fired by the marks on my body that reflected a celestial shrine. I never told Fire Eyes but when I looked to the stars I experienced a great sense of comfort and warmth . . . as if I had made a connection between the canopy of stars overhead and the time I had spent in my mother's womb.

My mother was a shadowy ghost in my mind—I had no remembrance of the physical person, nor shared remembrances from others who had known her and could have told me about her.

While Fire Eyes boasted of my extraordinary eyesight and memory of the routes the gods and other sky spirits took on their daily journeys, I learned much from him about the relationship between mere mortals and the eternal gods.

Fire Eyes pointed out to me patterns of stars that formed celestial creatures in the sky that names had been given to—a scorpion, serpent, turtle, jaguar, bat, skeleton, thirteen signs in all.*

---

* Translator's Note: Although only twelve signs are used in modern horoscopes, there is actually a thirteenth zodiacal constellation sign, Ophiuchus, the serpent bearer.

The Sun God, Moon God, and principal star-gods moved along a path in the sky that went through the thirteen signs. Without conceiving the form of animals in the boundless sky, it would have been impossible for most people to image the routes of the gods.

As I got older, I began to draw the patterns that I saw in the sky. At first it was just scratches made with a stick in the dirt. After Fire Eyes showed me how to make colors, I painted rocks, the walls of our hut, and anything else I was permitted with the patterns I saw in the night sky.

When I had nothing else to draw on, I painted images on my clothes and body.

When I turned five, Fire Eyes died. Cast into slavery, the brute, Tenoch, became my master . . .

"Eat and drink your fill," Smoking Shield said. "At first light we journey, and you will need your strength."

"Who knows what the dawn will bring?" I asked.

Ruffling my hair, he treated me to a great belly laugh.

"Indeed, young friend, tomorrow is a *new* day."

PART II

3

We arose at first light and breakfasted on maize cakes. Since Tenoch was still bound tightly to his back-pole, Smoking Shield dropped his breakfast at his feet. Tenoch would have to kneel and devour it like a dog.

Faithful to whatever demented code drove him, he refused to bend his knee, not even for sustenance. Remaining erect, he scowled at one and all, even Smoking Shield. He glowered at me in particular with unconcealed hatred, and when he turned to Desert Flower his eyes blazed with an even more virulence.

Why he so despised a young woman who had done nothing but suffer his abuse and serve him obediently, I could not fathom. I was even more surprised when she put down her corn cake and plucked his from the ground.

"We journey far," she said. "Who knows where? If you do not eat, you will not make it."

Locking his jaw, he glared at her. I arose from my own breakfast, less interested, I must confess, in nourishing Tenoch than in supporting Desert Flower.

But Smoking Shield beat me to her side.

"Here," Smoking Shield said, "this is how you feed a Tenoch."

Pinching off Tenoch's nose between his fingers, he shoved the corn cake down his open jaws as he inhaled.

"Chew, Tenoch, chew, or we shall humiliate you further. Eat, enjoy, and—who knows? Perhaps we shall all live to see tomorrow."

I sidled up beside Smoking Shield. I spoke Nahuatl with an accent different from his, but he still understood my words.

"Quetzalcoatl, the Feathered Serpent, has not promised us tomorrow," I said.

He smiled and clapped my shoulder.

4

By noon the next day we were entering the canyonlands to the south. Scoured smooth and slick by wind and water, the arroyo floors and reddish sandstone walls wound into an interminable maze of twisting chasms, now dry as sun-scorched rocks. The only signs of life in those deadlands was an occasional darting fly or the hissing buzz of a diamondback, the only shade the black flash of a buzzard's shadow. Wheeling endlessly overhead, waiting for one of us to fall, when that death-bird's shadow passed over me, it chilled me to my marrow.

The twisting canyons intersected endlessly, until I feared we were walking in circles. Stargazer, the wizened old shaman, however, seemed to know the way. I initially feared he was not up to the long trek, but though he was ancient he was also wiry and fit. In fact, I thought at times he would walk me into the ground, and I possessed strength and youth.

Having hung back during the attack, the old relic had not participated in the annihilation of our hunting/raiding party; later that night he had eaten by himself. As we walked, however, Smoking Shield kept the ancient shaman at his side, seeking his advice continuously.

Still, he and his adviser sometimes joined Desert Flower and me. Once Smoking Shield asked:

"Tell me, young Coyotl, if you could return to this blighted, benighted world as any animal on earth, which would it be?"

"A vulture," I said, glancing at the dozen or so carrion birds that circled overhead, keeping their lethal vigil.

Stargazer laughed.

"Was I funny?" I asked politely.

"More than you will ever know. Tell him, Smoking Shield. In your dreams," the old man said, "you often see yourself as a vulture, no?"

"In my *nightmares*, you mean. I see myself as one, gliding on the thermal drafts, and I fear I might come back as one of those blood-crusted, death-reeking fiends."

"You obviously disagree with Smoking Shield," Stargazer said to me. "Why do *you* find them so attractive?"

"Wheeling overhead, aloof, alone, with no enemies, they lead lives of inviolable peace."

"Why are you sure they have no enemies?" Desert Flower asked.

"Why would any creature fight them?" I said. "They circle in peace, on the high thermals, far out of reach, nourishing themselves almost solely on those who fall—but seldom, if ever, on the living."

"Peaceful intentions protect you from nothing here," Stargazer countered. "Look at the animals here—scorpions armed with stingers, snakes with venomous fangs. And the plants? They're covered with thorns and spines. Nothing is safe here—until it is dead."

"The vulture is safe," I disagreed. "Nothing wants to eat a vulture."

"Except other vultures," Smoking Shield countered. "They will attack, kill, and devour their own kind. Have you ever seen a swarm—like those above—descend on a fallen animal and battle over the offal? They will rend and tear each other to pieces when their foul-stinking sustenance is at stake."

"The male vulture will cannibalize his offspring," Stargazer said, "if the mother cannot protect them, and, yes, they will kill and consume one another if the offal runs out."

"The most self-destructive of the beasts is us," Smoking Shield agreed. "We kill our own kind en masse."

"Nothing here is safe," Stargazer agreed. "Nothing."

"Until it is dead," Smoking Shield reiterated.

5

Later that night Smoking Shield summoned Desert Flower and me. He and his men sat around the big campfire, eating dried meat and tortillas. The blaze reflected off the surrounding rocks and sandstone, illuminating the pass. Men's shadows writhed and twisted across the canyon walls, and the fire's warmth cut into the biting cold of the desert night. In the distance an owl hooted, and a cougar roared.

Other than that, there was silence.

"Young Coyotl," Smoking Shield said as he took a place next to me at the desert campfire, "explain your cicatrice to us, if you can."

He pronounced it "sick-a-treese"—a word I did not know—and I stared back at him, bewildered.

"He refers to your tattoo," Stargazer explained.

I stared up into the desert sky. A clear, cloudless night, across the sky blazed a broad white swath of dense stars—"the World Tree" or sometimes "the Crocodile Tree," Fire Eyes, my old shaman spirit-guide, had called it—that illuminated the desert as brilliantly as a full moon. Out of the thousands of stars overhead, I fixed on six, which framed the center of the Underworld Road's Dark Rift.

I pointed the six out to Smoking Shield and Stargazer.

"I think of my cicatrice as those six stars guarding the Dark Rift—the entrance to the Underworld Road."

Smoking Shield stared at me a long moment.

"Who taught you the stars?" the old man finally asked.

"My spirit-guide and teacher instructed me on the Road and its Rift."

"Did he inscribe those stars on your belly?" Smoking Shield asked.

"When Fire Eyes found me in a thatched basket in on a river-bank, I already had them."

"Did he point out the six stars to you?" Stargazer asked.

"I pointed them out to him," I said, "and he explained they guard the road to Mictlantecuhtli's Hell, a dark and bloody realm where evildoers go."

"The road and gate go both ways, young Coyotl," the old man said.

"When our world ends," Smoking Shield said, "the hounds of Mictlantecuhtli's flood that road, storm your gateway stars."

"Tezcatlipoca—the black god of death and the everlasting night—will loose those hounds and shatter those gates," Stargazer said. "He and his diabolic dogs will raze the Black Road and ravage the earth—and that will be the One-World's Last Day."

"It will be everyone's Last Day," Smoking Shield said.

"And you spotted them among thousands upon thousands of stars?" the old astronomer asked.

"The pattern seemed obvious to me."

"I believe you," Smoking Shield said.

"Coyotl knows not only the secrets of the stars, he deciphers dreams," Desert Flower said, looking Smoking Shield in the eye for the very first time. "Fire Eyes told me, and it is so. Coyotl has read my dreams."

"Is he any good?" Smoking Shield asked.

"Fire Eyes said that Coyotl knew not only dreams and stars but the secrets of the heart," Desert Flower said.

"That is, no doubt, why the brute called Tenoch—whom my lord has so wisely trussed to a stout staff—hates him so vilely," Stargazer said.

Smoking Shield looked away for awhile, then said absently, "For the life of me, Stargazer, I do not know why I let the wretch live."

"Because you will take Tenoch to the priests, who will sacrifice him to the gods," Stargazer said.

Smoking Shield shrugged. "So Desert Flower says you know the secrets of the heart and you read dreams. Read *my* dream for me, then. The one in which I effortlessly ride the mountain thermals on motionless wings—a vulture keeping my everlasting deathwatch, waiting for those who fall."

"The vulture is of two natures," I said, staring him straight in the eye. "On one hand, he exults in his godly view—seeing all, knowing all. Still he is not content. Against his will, he must descend and nourish his flesh.

"He also knows that he will one day descend, never to return to the skies. A slave to the earth forever."

"And what does that say of me?"

"In your soul you ride the high thermals, but your life is bound to this earthly plane . . . against its will."

"You read dreams well, Cicatrice. We shall talk further on this journey."

"Sick-a-treese," I repeated, trying to pronounce my strange new name.

"We will have many days to walk, talk, and ponder these matters. Now, however, we must break camp."

I leaned forward and studied Smoking Shield. "And after this journey, what awaits us?"

"I thought you knew. The most magnificent city on earth: the great city of Tula."

A sudden chill ran through my bones. What I knew about "the most magnificent city on earth" filled me with dread.

"What happens to us there?"

"Who can say? Important persons dominate Tula. Priests and warlords swarm the emperor, vying for power, working their wicked ways."

"What are their ways?" I asked.

"The high priest wants to spread-eagle prisoners faceup on his sacrificial stone. The warlords may seek them for their deadly battles and games. The quarry-master desires them for his pit, hewing stone and breaking rocks."

"Anything can happen," Stargazer said. "What do your six stars tell you?"

He pointed to the six-pointed cicatrice on my belly, then to its bright likeness in the star-filled sky.

"The stars echo your words," I said to Smoking Shield. "Tomorrow's another day."

"Yes," the Stargazer said, "but as *you* have said, the Feathered Serpent has not promised us tomorrow."

6

That night I awoke from my sleep, rose from my resting place on the ground, and hobbled down-canyon to relieve myself. I could have untied the short rope between my ankles that kept me from running, but I had no place to run to even if I possessed the speed of a deer.

A dark figure was waiting for me when I started back to the camp. Stargazer stared up at the sky and said nothing for a moment.

"Tell me, Coyotl, how many stars do you see in the House of the Jaguar's Paw?"

The question caught me by surprise, but I immediately looked up. Thousands of stars filled the sky, sharing the night with the Moon God. Stars were the gods and demons that dominated our lives, some providing us the miracle that made maize grow, others sending down terrible diseases that gave pain and took lives. The most important star-gods had names all people knew. But the Jaguar's Paw was not a star-god, but a place.

I knew from my Aztec father that some stars grouped together to form patterns in the sky, what we called celestial houses. There were the thirteen celestial houses named after animals. The House of the Jaguar's Paw was not directly overhead at this time, but to the south.

"I see nine stars," I said.

"Mark the pattern of the stars on the ground with a stick," he said.

The request was strange, but I didn't dare question it. Taking a stick, I marked the pattern on the ground. When I was done, he nodded. I realized I had pleased him in some way.

"The number of stars that can be seen depends on how clear the night is and how bright the Moon God shines. On a night like this with a bright moon, most people would see five or six stars in the Paw. A person with eyes that saw farther and clearer than most would see six or seven. In my lifetime, I have known only one other person who could have seen nine stars in the Paw."

I knew my eyesight was exceptional. Fire Eyes had relied upon it when his own sight eventually waned. I realized that Stargazer had me scratch the pattern in the dirt to ensure that I had actually seen the stars, rather than just reporting what I had been told.

"Where is Quetzalcoatl, the Feathered Serpent,* now?"

Finding the Feathered Serpent in the night sky was much simpler than finding nine stars in the Jaguar's Paw. I pointed up.

"The Feathered Serpent is the brightest star-god in the sky. Only the Sun and Moon gods cast a greater light. Right now the Feathered Serpent is in the House of the Tortoise."

"Where is the Dark Rift?" he asked.

The words flew out of my mouth before I could stop them. "In the House of the Magician."

"Who told you that?"

I stepped away from him, blown back by the harshness of Stargazer's words. I withered under his stern gaze, realizing I had made a terrible mistake, but mystified as to why I did it.

I knew my statement was nonsense—there was no celestial House of the Magician. The Dark Rift was a dark area of the night

---

* Translator's Note: The star-god called Quetzalcoatl, the Feathered Serpent, was the planet Venus.

sky.* It was the most frightful and menacing area of the sky, the opening from which the world was birthed and from where the destroyers of worlds emerge. My shaman father called it the Dark Road to Xibalba, the terrible Underworld of the Dead that lies to the far south. That I had the marks on my body had saved my life as an infant and had gotten me selected for sacrifice as a young man.

"You said the Dark Rift was in the House of the Magician. Who told you that?" Stargazer spoke in a normal tone of voice, but his eyes appeared to me as burning embers in the moonlight.

"I don't know. I know there's no House of the Magician in the sky. It's just something that came to me."

"You never said this before?"

I shook my head. "No."

"Are you certain the shaman who raised you didn't say it?"

"No, he never said that. He taught me the thirteen signs in the night sky, but he never said that the Dark Rift was in the Magician's House."

We walked together back to where our campfire was still smothering. I could see that Stargazer was deep in thought so I kept my peace. It was obvious that this skywatcher was a great man of state in Tula. That made him equal in rank to a high noble in the One-World's mightiest empire.

Why this important man was concerned with me was a puzzle.

"What do you know about the Book of Fates?" he asked me.

I took a breath to answer. Everyone knew about the Book of Fates, so it puzzled me as to why he would ask a question that could not test my knowledge.

"The destiny of each of us is predetermined by the day and time of our birth. The Book of Fates is consulted to determine each person's destiny."

---

* The Dark Rift is created by interstellar dust that runs along the middle of the Milky Way. An opening to the heart of the galaxy, modern astronomers have discovered a black hole at the galactic core.

The Book of Fates was a 260-day sacred calendar a shaman consulted to gain an indication of a person's fate. Only the patron god of the day upon which you were born knew your true fate, but with knowledge of the date and time of your birth, a shaman able to open a channel to the gods could divine some of your destiny.

"Is that the only Book of Fates that you know?"

The question was whispered and once again Stargazer caught me by surprise. Of course it was the only Book of Fates that I knew—only one existed.

※

Back on my place on the cold, hard ground I stared up at the glowing night sky, to the Dark Rift, my personal celestial house.

As I lay and could not find sleep, I went over in my mind everything Stargazer had said and how I had replied. Why had he reacted so violently when I spoke of the House of the Magician?

The stars gave me no answers, but I acknowledged one truth about Stargazer that I would not have dared speak aloud: When he looked to the Dark Rift in the celestial heavens he had been off a tiny bit from its location. His eyesight was not good.

For a skywatcher to lose eyesight was as serious as a warrior losing his arms.

I wondered why that phrase had slipped out of my mouth when Stargazer had posed the question of where the Dark Rift was located.

And I wondered about Stargazer. Why was he treating a Dog People captive with the sort of courtesy he must reserve for high-ranking Tula lords?

I had lied when I told Stargazer that I knew nothing about the words I spoke which placed the Dark Rift in the House of the Magician. There was something else I knew, something I didn't understand myself and could not have shared with him even if I had wanted to reveal it.

When I spoke the words I had felt a warm glow inside and I remembered something—not words or a person, but a feeling. A feeling of being in the arms of someone warm and soft who cradled me with love and tenderness.

The person holding me was a woman. And I knew that I had once been part of her. She was my mother.

I didn't have a name or a face, but just a feeling of love and warmth.

I tried to put her out of my mind, but she would not go away.

Who was my mother? I wondered.

And why had she floated me downstream in a reed basket to drown?

PART III

7

Seated at a long mahogany conference table, Monica Cardiff looked around the empty room and waited for her colleagues. She felt ill at ease. The leather-padded recliner-swivel armchairs didn't discomfit her, nor did the mahogany paneled walls—she admired the dark wood, even if computer monitors, television screens, and portraits of past presidents obscured most of the paneling. She liked the three sterling-silver coffee carafes, pristine bone china cups and saucers; the pitchers of iced orange juice; the Avian and Perrier bottled waters; the ice buckets with sterling tongs flanking the glasses bearing the presidential seal.

No, it was her colleagues who aggravated her, specifically: President Edward Raab himself; Special Defense Adviser and former Chairman of the Joint Chiefs, General Richard H. "Hurricane" Hagberg; and the CIA's former Director of Covert Operations, Bradford Chase. New to the team, Chase was the third addition to the newly created Presidential Scientific Advisory Board.

From Cardiff's point of view, these were the kinds of people who mired the U.S. in Iraq, sank the world economy, and now that the planet faced the gravest crisis in human history, they were in charge. In these desperate hours, she did not like depending on those whom she privately derided as Washington hacks. She was used to dealing with world-class scientists—people with real brains who worked round-the-clock on groundbreaking scientific projects.

A world-renowned astrophysicist, Cardiff had also made a name for herself as an expert on global catastrophism—a specialty she'd almost single-handedly invented twenty years before and which encompassed everything from megavolcanism to Global Warming–induced drought and wildfires, from sunstorms to suboceanic methane vents, and from nuclear terrorism to asteroid and comet strikes. She sometimes referred to herself as a partisan of the apocalypse.

An academic star at Berkeley and CalTech, she'd reluctantly taken a job at NASA only because NASA had granted her unlimited access to Goddard's space telescopes. Otherwise, she found government employment too boringly bureaucratic. Unfortunately, her astronomical discoveries *there* had landed her *here* . . .

She was not an easy person to deal with. As a former student of hers, President Raab knew that. He had witnessed her tirades upfront and personal. That they had remained friends all these years was a mystery to her—particularly after he'd been elected president of the United States.

She'd been here less than a week, and so far they'd only had a single, preparatory meeting. She'd spent most of that session skewering that fascist four-star general, "Hurricane" Hagberg, with her limitless fund of inventive invective. Well, at least she'd made that bastard miserable.

Looking back on their encounter elicited a small smile.

His stream-of-consciousness scatology had immediately put her off, and she began to badger him.

"Tell me, General Goebbels," she asked, "have you considered electroconvulsive therapy for your Tourette's? Or perhaps intravenous thorazine?"

"Is a metastasizing brain tumor provoking that flood of filth?" she asked politely after his next obscene outburst.

"I say, Reichsmarshal Goering, excremental expletives are no substi-

tute for trenchant analysis," Cardiff said pleasantly after another foul-mouthed fusillade. "Or perhaps they purge your brain like a plumber pumping out a septic tank."

When he tried to ignore her, she shouted: "What's the matter, Herr Himmler? Gone deaf? Can't hear me?"

By meeting's end, she had broken him of the habit, but he wasn't happy about it. Every so often she caught him glaring at her.

These Washington operators, from Cardiff's point of view, were all pimps, pandering for a coven of transnational conglomerates, Wall Street loan sharks, oil oligarchs, and medical industry Draculas.

She'd even come to despise the way the way they dressed. Struggling in the salt mines of science and academe, her lifestyle had been Spartan, her clothing budget ferociously frugal. Her best attire—until her recent sales of a book and a TV documentary—had been purchased at consignment shops. These people, however, paraded the halls of power in eight-thousand-dollar suits, thousand-dollar shoes, nine-hundred-dollar shirts, and ten-thousand-dollar watches.

More and more, Cardiff felt out of place . . . a K-Mart frock in a high-fashion whorehouse. She blamed it all on the financial freebooters, petro-pirates and high-line lobbyists polluting DC.

The hallways were fashion-show runways for thousand-dollar footwear—Gucci, Dior, Ralph Lauren, Zegna, and Brooks Brothers—and stodgy thousand-dollar solid-color neckties. Shirts for the most part were Michael Bastian pimas or Ralph Lauren Purple Label Contrast-Collar shirts, plus an endless array of Armanis, Dior Hommes, Hickey Freemans, Brooks Brothers, and Savile Row.

Brioni clearly ruled the DC suit world. Presidents, vice presidents, senators, congressmen, cabinet officers, staffers, oil sheikhs, despots, movie stars, procurers, lobbyists, lobbyists, lobbyists, and more lobbyists—anyone who was anyone at Washington's pinnacle of power sported a Brioni. It had become le couture de rigueur.

Dark blue was especially sought-after. Navy tailored, customized Brionis—"bespoke suits," as they were known among England's

Savile Row tailors—were the favorites . . . every one of them boasting the signature Brioni collar roll.

Suddenly, there they were strolling into the conference room, the president leading the way.

"Dr. Cardiff," President Raab said, "I see you're prompt."

"I see you're late," she said.

President Raab's Brioni Pure Escorial Jet Black—she had seen it priced at eleven thousand dollars. Cardiff immediately dismissed it as "the Executive Moron Model" since George W. Bush had sported one similar to it, and VP nominee Sarah Palin had reportedly hondled a couple like it for her husband.

General Hagberg, on entering the room, flashed his diamond-studded rose-gold Rolex Oyster. That four-star fascist, no doubt, did the same for his Washington power-broker clients and third-world dictator drinking-buddies, as if his glittering timepiece was the keys to the kingdom.

Well, at least the president's timepiece was simple. He favored a Cartier Santos-Dumont, modeled after the aviator timepieces of the early 1900s. Its blade-shaped hands and outsized Art Deco Roman numerals—all contained in a simple steel case—had seemed to Cardiff the quintessence of modesty and good taste . . . until she learned that the "simple steel case" was white gold and that it retailed for over ten grand.

Now former CIA Director Bradford Chase strode through the door. A hulking bear of a man with a thick shock of iron-gray hair, he had a face like a catcher's mitt, a nose like a badly busted knuckle, and eyes that bore into you like power drills. His perfectly tailored Brioni Navy Minicheck accentuated his barrel chest and ox-like shoulders. His huge gnarled hands looked like they could straighten cold horseshoes and hammer fence posts into hard ground.

Then there was the limp. President Raab recently told her that Brad had worked as an undercover NOC (no official cover) in Asia, the Mideast, and Africa for thirty years, which was the most dangerous undercover work there was. Fighting behind enemy lines in four shooting wars, he'd been blown up, stabbed, and shot a dozen times.

Sick of the agency's bullshit, he'd cashed in his chips and headed to Hollywood. Selling parts of his life's story to three top studios, he'd initially signed on as a technical adviser but quickly became a scriptwriter and executive producer. Between films, he hid out in Palm Springs and wrote his own series of mega-hit spy flicks, the first of which was titled *Out of the Night*. Selling the series to a fourth studio, it had already netted him over $100 million, and bred an infinite string of sequels and TV spin-offs.

None of which stopped President Raab from dragging him back to DC.

Why he was so important, Cardiff could not say. This was only the second time she'd met him, and the first time they hadn't had a chance to talk—only to shake hands.

She wondered why he never smiled or talked, or why—against her will—she actually . . . *liked* him. She found her reaction . . . alien.

Prior to this meeting, the president had asked her privately to "lighten up on the general," and she was starting to think the president was right. If her calculations proved correct, the world was coming to an abruptly horrendous end, in which case maybe they should all be out baying obscenities at the moon, like hydrophobic hounds, instead of hanging around conference tables, technobabbling the crisis to death.

Maybe she should join the general in his scatological expletives.

Still, she thought with a bitter grin, she couldn't wait to get her tingling talons into him again.

Finally they were seated, and the president rose solemnly to speak.

PART IV

8

ONE-WORLD, 1001 A.D.

By noon the next day we were entering the slickrock canyons to the south. Reddened with desiccated clay, the arroyo floors and wind-scoured walls wound into an eternal labyrinth of twisting barrancas.

As I walked beside Stargazer, Smoking Shield told the astronomer that he first visited the area when he was a boy.

"As with myself, my father had been commander of the Jaguar Knights in the region. Sometimes he would take me along on ma-neuvers, even though I was too young to be a warrior. This region was different back then, green enough to grow maize, though you could see that the rain gods were already abandoning it."

Stargazer nodded. "Much blood was fed to the gods, but they still refused to nourish the land. It wasn't long until people had to leave, moving farther south as the land dried up behind them. This was once land that could be farmed. Look at it now—scorpions sporting stingers, snakes with spitting fangs, and thorn-covered plants."

"A land of death," Smoking Shield said.

Stargazer waved his hand at the land that had been abandoned by both the gods and people. "If the gods keep being stingy in the rain they give us, someday Tula itself will be as dry and blighted as this."

Stargazer said to me, "You watch the vultures. You find the creatures interesting?"

"Not interesting, Noble One, but frightening. They are messengers of death. You don't see them unless something—or someone—is dying."

"They only kill when they absolutely have to," Smoking Shield said.

"Is that good or bad?" I asked.

"Ask those who tied you to the tree," Stargazer said, "and left you as fodder for their blood-starved gods."

"They're all dead, except for Tenoch," I said.

"Does that answer your question?" Smoking Shield asked.

He walked on ahead of us before I could offer an answer I did not have.

9

For two days we trudged up and down steep slopes. The farther south toward Tula we went, the greener the land became. My earliest memories of the land we Dog People occupied was of riverbeds that were drying more each year, and of cactus—prickly pear, spiny ocotillo, thorny bushes of every size and shape—sprouting where maize stocks once stood.

As the dirt between our toes grew drier, we were pushed farther and farther south in search of life-giving water. And as we pushed south, the conflict between my people and the Toltec grew more frequent and bloodier.

Listening to Stargazer and the Jaguar Knight talk, I learned that the Toltec had been forced back, not just from pressures from my people, but from the changing conditions of the land. As the land became drier and dusty winds blew in from the north, the Toltec moved back, abandoning farmland that no longer produced sufficient crops.

That the rain god had not been generous to the Toltec came as a surprise to me. Among my people, the land of our cousins was thought of as a green and gold paradise where maize stalks soared high into the sky, the ears growing to be as tall as a man, while beans were the size of a child's head.

When I mentioned this to Stargazer during a stop for the midday meal, he laughed.

"In comparison to your people who grub for worms, the people of Tula live as gods. No other people in the One-World are as rich as the Toltec, though all civilized peoples, too, would appear to be inhabitants of paradise to your miserable, barbaric Clans. You will see that—"

He stopped as we heard Smoking Shield curse at Tenoch. Tenoch had refused food again and butted the warrior who tried to feed it to him. His rudeness earned him a severe beating.

"He would rather die than be humiliated," I told Stargazer in a tone low enough so the Knight would not hear me.

"He will die soon enough. He's only being fed to ensure that he survives long enough to be sacrificed."

I noted respect in Stargazer's tone.

"It is good that he has been captured. Strong blood like his will not only nourish the rain god, but his sacrifice will rid us of a vicious beast and an eventual enemy."

❧

Trees gradually materialized—not the short, scrawny ones that were common in the higher altitudes in the arid region, but medium-sized pines and some stands of cottonwood, along with clumps of thorny but hardy mesquite.

We came out of the hills and I got my first sight of the occupied land of the Toltec, the first clear sign that we had left the wilderness of the Dog People and were upon civilization.

The land before us was not a lush tropical forest as I had imagined my first sight of Tula would be, but a place where something valuable and useful was grown: endless rows of tall, green, heavily spiked maguey plants. In between the maguey were rows of maize and periodic rows of beans and peppers.

"The land here is still thirstier than the field nearer Tula," Stargazer said, "but well suited for maguey. As we get nearer the city, from a hill you can see fields of maize and beans spread out as far as even your exceptional eyes can see. But even our vast fields are not able to produce enough food for our city. The gods have not only been stingy with rain, but the city has grown more than twice the size it was ten years ago."

Maguey was not as prized a gift of the gods as sun, water, and maize, but it provided dozens of things that we used every day: the stalks were used to make shoes, roofing for the houses of farmers, and to create fiber weaved into rope, cloth, and containers; the sharp tips were used for needles and to draw blood from one's own body when making sacrifices.

Maize was a goddess and so was maguey, but the godliness of maguey transcended its practical uses—from its heart at the core of the plant came octli, which became the nectar of the gods when fermented.

I watched workers tending the plants as we marched through the field. The core of plants that had reached their full growth were being stabbed dozens of time.

Stargazer saw the question on my face and explained the process.

"When the plant is about to flower, it is stabbed with a dagger to keep it from flowering. It is called castrating the plant. Plants that have been castrated give more of the liquid than those that flower."

"I have tasted the sacred juice just once," I said. "It made my head spin."

Stargazer chuckled. "Indeed, it is said octli opens our minds to the gods. But it is said as well that octli takes over our minds and makes us act like stupid children when we drink too much of it. The liquid you see being taken from the plant is not the nectar of the gods yet. It must be put into large clay jars and aged so the spirit of Mayahuel enters it."

Mayahuel was the goddess of the maguey. Our people depicted

her as having many breasts with which to feed her children. We called the children the 400 Rabbits and it was they who entered our bodies and made us drunk when we drank too much of the sacred juice.

As we crested a high hill, the sea of maize and other foods was laid out before us. But it was not the richness of the supply of food or the two rivers that met and flowed among it that caught my eye, but my first sight of Tula.

In the distance, it glittered and sparkled like the reflection of the midday sun off a pool of pure water. Its sloping pyramidal temples, with their heaven-piercing summits, soared high above the city's high white walls.

I shivered with excitement, with anticipation and fright. I had never seen anything in my young life so inconceivably intimidating. To my untrained eye, the pyramids seemed massive as mountains, their supernal peaks taunting the clouds, teasing the stars and tantalizing the gods. Nor was Tula a hollow, defenseless work of artists and craftsmen—perched on a rise, the walled city was a formidable city-fortress.

It would swat away an Aztec raiding party like smashing a mosquito. I could not even imagine the city falling to an army of all the Clans of Azteca.

A wide road that was occupied by people coming and going from the city stretched out before us. We paused by a building with mud brick walls and no roof.

"If you need to relieve yourself, that is where you do it," Stargazer said.

I gaped at him. "Relieve my body wastes . . . inside a house?"

"It's not a house to live in, but one for comfort."

I found the concept inconceivable. I waved at the world around me. "But there is a whole world to—"

"That is for animals. And you are no longer one. From now on, you must act and think like a Toltec. We do not relieve ourselves where we eat, sleep, work, or walk."

"I understand, Noble One." I didn't understand, but knew better than to display my ignorance. But another question slipped by my tongue. "What happens when the . . . the house of comfort is full?"

A sigh told me that it was not the most insightful question I could have asked.

"We relieve ourselves in jugs for that purpose. The jugs are taken out and emptied into the fields. The same is true for the waste of the entire city. It is carried out of the city to the farms."

I understood now. Tula farmers must not be favored by the gods. "Ah, then the farmers must wade in this waste."

He shook his head. "The waste is worked into the ground. You have heard tales about how the crops grow to an extraordinary size? Now you know the reason."

Ayyo!

As we walked toward the city, he went on to tell me that clear, clean water was brought into the city by clay ceramic pipes.* And confirmed what I thought was a tall tale: the people of Tula bathed *every day*.

I was speechless. When I found my voice again, I said, "The gods must truly bless Tula."

His features became grave and I held my tongue from further comment. I had not seen Stargazer so somber.

We walked a thousand paces toward the city before Stargazer spoke to me again.

"To your eyes it is a blessing, but the green once extended out half again as far. I told you earlier that we no longer produce enough food to feed our people."

He stopped and locked eyes with me. "Coyotl, you must grasp something before you enter the city. It may save your life."

"Yes, Noble One."

---

* Translator's Note: Tula had a water and sewerage similar to that of Rome when Rome ruled the Western World. At the time Coyotl saw Tula, Europe was in the Dark Ages and sewage was thrown from dwellings into the stinking streets. The Aztecs, who envied and copied the Toltec, later used a similar system for their magnificent capitol, Tenochtitlán.

"Tula is not as favored by the gods as you imagine—but you must never speak this or even whisper it."

"Yes, Noble One." But I understood nothing.

"Our great king Ce Acatl, One-Reed, has taken the name of the god Quetzalcoatl, the Feathered Serpent. He says the god has permitted him to take the name. And all went well after he did. But now the rain has dwindled. There is not enough for our crops." Stargazer looked away from me, pursing his lips. "What you see when we enter the city will surprise you. No . . . it will terrify you. Learn now to keep your thoughts and your fears to yourself. Expressing them can cost you your life."

10

We paused a hundred paces from Tula's city walls. Gessoed with dissolved riverbank gypsum to a gleaming alabaster, those imposing barricades seemed insurmountably high—as tall as four grown men. The bloody ball of the late afternoon sun descended beneath those walls like red doom.

Glancing to my rear, I noticed that Stargazer, Desert Flower, and I were alone, the rest of our band having slipped away. In the distance I saw them—with Tenoch in tow—heading toward the other side of the Tula.

"Where are they going?" I asked Stargazer.

"To the eastern gate," the old man said, "where soldiers always return from battle. They leave by way of that gate too."

"Why that gate?"

"It is nearer to the House of the Sun, where noble warriors while away eternity. Soldiers believe that gate is blessed. *This* gate is for common folk."

I personally believed Smoking Shield had abandoned us.

We were passing hundreds of sentries in tight-fitting loincloths, short tunics, and quilted body armor, all of whitest cotton, their hide sandals laced up to their knees. They shouldered javelins and battle-axes, and long, lethal knives hung from braided agave-fiber belts dyed charcoal-dark. All of their weapons were bladed with black, shiny, wickedly sharp obsidian. A hard lot, their expressionless eyes barely flicked over us, as if an ancient man and two callow youths weren't worthy of their consideration.

I saw now that the wall was of one piece, composed of heavy, whitewashed, sun-dried brick more than two spear-lengths thick. As-wide as three spear-lengths and as tall as two men, it was a rectangular tunnel, rather than an actual gate, and the front wall's only entrance. Rather than breaching the wall, the tunnel-gate ran under it.

The soldier manning the crenellated wall-top recognized Stargazer.

"Old man, how goes the fight?"

"Three prisoners, much information, and no casualties."

"Go with Quetzalcoatl."

"Always."

"Pass through," he yelled down to us. Then he crossed the wall-top and yelled down to the other side, "Passing through."

Entering the dark passageway, we emerged into the blazing sunlight on the wall's other side. Hundreds of large sunbaked bricks were stacked and stored beside it. Piled lumber was also nearby with which to fashion braces. In the event of an attack, they would be used to seal off the city.

The passageway opened up by the front edge of the great square. I was first struck by the sheer immensity of that plaza. Two hundred paces on edge, it contained a surprising number of bushes, flowers, and trees—cottonwoods and piñon pine flourished in particular. The hard-packed earth beneath our feet seemed as unarable as the wall's gessoed bricks, and drought had plagued us all for years. How they survived was unclear.

In the center of the square was the explanation. An enormous fountain-pool, it was one of the many wonders of the Tollans—as Tula's citizens were known—and proof that Tula had its own internal water source. From a spout in the shape of the water goddess—Chalchiuhtlicue, "She of the Jade Skirt"—geysered sparkling agua.

"Chalchiuhtlicue had once brought about the destruction of the One-World," the old man said, "by flooding it with fifty-two years of rain. Changing the people into fish, she saw to it that the waters would not drown us."

I waved at the buildings at the sides of the square. "Are these palaces of the notables?"

He shook his head. "The palaces are nearer the city's ceremonial center. Common people live in these buildings. A family may have only two or three rooms in one of these large buildings."

They appeared to be palaces to me.

"How many people live in Tula?"

"Over fifty thousand within the walls, five times that in the towns and villages within a day's walk. It would take an hour just to walk across the city."

Our entire Clan was less than a thousand Aztecs.

Taking a deep breath I finally forced myself to look at the great temple-pyramid looming over us. A sacrificial ceremony was already under way, and a maniacal mob had assembled at the pyramid's base. Enraptured, their eyes were fixed on the black-robed, bloody-haired priests at the temple's summit. Shouting their encouragement, they waved their arms and shook their fists.

With Stargazer leading the way, we threaded our way through the packed, screaming, hysterical crowd.

In my whole life I'd never seen more than fifty people assembled or a building taller than a thatched village hut, which a man typically had to stoop to enter. Desert Flower—who'd come from a village only slightly larger than mine—confided to me once she had never seen more than one hundred people at one time. The courtyard held at least a thousand people, and I was gape-jawed at . . . *everything.*

The clothes alone stunned me. Where I had lived, the men seldom wore more than a thin white loincloth of agave fiber, which our women gathered and separated out of the maguey bush, then wove our loincloths and their skirts of the rough but sturdy cloth. Unlike the men, the women typically went topless. Our waist garments were tied off in the front.

In Tula most waist garments were fashioned out of triangular cotton cloth, a corner of which ran between their legs and was then tied off. Only the poorest wretches wore coarse agave, which currently covered my loins.

Even poorly clad Tollans, however, fringed the edges of their garments with fur or stitched colorful stones into the cloth, so Flower and I were indeed shabbily dressed. She seemed especially self-conscious. She kept her eyes on the ground, ashamed of her crude garb.

"If it's any consolation to you," I whispered, "I look a lot worse than you do. You look great, if you want to know the truth."

My words seemed to cheer up the young girl. Smiling, she lifted her eyes and squeezed my hand.

In truth, Flower did look better than I did. While Smoking Shield had covered Desert Flower's naked chest in a white cotton shawl, I was stuck with my shoddy loincloth.

Tollans clearly wore their wealth and power on their bodies, and even the poorest of men wore a white mantle. To flaunt their status, many men wore multiple mantles despite the late afternoon's uncomfortable heat, the topmost cape elaborately embroidered.

The wealthier women wore ankle-brushing skirts and straight-line blouses with armholes cut out at the sides, elegantly embellished with swirls, stripes, squares, triangles, and other fancy shapes and designs, the most striking of which were woven directly into the fabric.

Here in the courtyard gaudily dyed clothing was everywhere. True, we knew about coloring dyes in my primitive village. We could crush and dissolve the cochineal insect, which clung to the prickly pear, and when boiled with the setting agents, such as urine and alum, our women could make what had seemed to me a miraculous crimson. We also could extract yellow from the mora tree, blue from acacia leaves mixed with black clay. However, such dyes required countless insects, leaves, and plants—and unending labor. A practical people, we instead relied on simple attire, and what dyeing we did was rudimentary compared to the exotically hued attire surrounding me, much of it accentuated by all the garish hues of a gaudy rainbow: brilliant vermillions, lurid purples, flaming yellows, midnight blacks, lush verdant greens.

Men and women not only sewed flamboyant feathers into their clothing, they sported headdresses of eagle, hawk, and parrot plumes. They favored necklaces, bracelets, jeweled ear- and nose-piercings of gold and silver, festooned with crystal, amber, shell, tiny bells, and jewels; bead- and gold-decorated leatherwork; ornamentation of every description and dimension, as well as intricately wrought tattoos.

While our impoverished villagers went barefoot, here cactli sandals with soles of tough hide or maguey fiber were ubiquitous. Fastened to the feet with straps, some, like those of the soldiers, were laced crosswise up to the knee.

I was so intent on the crowd I missed the high priest's initial harangue. Whatever it was, it got the crowd roaring and raging as if all the demons in Mictlantecuhtli's Hell were fighting to get out.

"What's that roar for?" I asked Stargazer.

"It's a welcome-home celebration," the old man said back to us.

"For us?" I asked him.

"For the soldiers," he answered.

Tula throbbed again with the throng's ear-cracking roar.

The temple-pyramid was so immense I could barely take it in. Its square base was two hundred paces on edge with hundreds of steps cut horizontally into its slopes—steps so numerous I lost count after two hundred. Its summit featured a sanctuary consecrated to Quetzalcoatl, a turquoise mosaic emblazoning his likeness on the front wall.

And of course the summit also swarmed with fire-breathing priests.

The crowd surrounding the pyramid thundered:

"Blood for the gods! Blood for the gods!"

Draped in capes of human skin and crested with headdresses of intricately woven featherwork, burnished gold, and gleaming gem-stones, these gore-splattered priests whipped up the multitude even as they dragged another victim to the altar.

I noticed Stargazer standing beside me.

"I have seen sights atop that pyramid," Stargazer whispered sadly, "that made the sun veil its eyes and the rocks weep."

Throughout the One-World, sacrifice victims were described as delighting in their deaths, as if honored by the downward-plunging blade. Not today. The man whom the priests dragged to the altar was scared witless. He was not the only one who sobbed, screamed, and shook—queued up along the pyramid's sloping steps, a long line of conscripted victims waited, their faces and limbs trembling.

Five priests were required to drag the half-naked man across the summit and bend him backward over the blood-drenched altar— one clutching each limb, the fifth restraining his head. Only then did the head priest ululate his bloodcurdling incantations and drive his black blade into the screaming man's pumping chest. Sawing open the central cavity, he tore the rib cage open and plunged both hands into it. Pulling out the throbbing heart, he waved it high overhead.

The mob screamed orgiastically.

Hurling the dripping heart into a chest-high heart-crock, he commenced hacking at the man's neck. Dropping from the man's shoulders, the head fell with a sickening *crack!* onto the stone sum-mit. Retrieving the severed head by the hair, the priest raised it high overhead.

Again, the mob around me detonated. Flung down the temple's terraced slope, the head bounced and bled step by step to the pyramid's base, where other priests deposited it in another capa-cious crock with those of several dozen other victims.

His assistants then held the hemorrhaging man upside down over the edge of the triangular slopes like a slaughtered deer. The man bled out into one of the downward-flowing blood-troughs cut into each of the slope's edges, the frothing crimson stream cascading down the gutter.

Now the priest and his henchmen dragged another hysterical victim to their sacrificial stone.

Averting my eyes in disgust, I noticed that Desert Flower was looking away and trembling, her eyes tearing over. Instinctively, I put an arm around her while her body convulsed in mute sobs.

I was always amazed that Flower, who'd suffered so horribly under Tenoch's whip, could be so genuinely concerned about others.

Nor was Stargazer pleased with the bloody ritual. I noticed he also turned his head in disgust.

"Stargazer," I asked, "does the sight of blood make you queasy? Like this girl here?"

"Watch your tongue, Cicatrice," Stargazer said. "We are no longer on the trail. You observe a different decorum in Tula. The priests hear you address your superiors—including me or Smoking Shield—in that way, they'll stuff avocadoes in your mouth before they cut out *your* heart and bounce *your* head down the pyramid's steps. Watch how you look at them as well. They will extract your eyes with hot knives, then stuff the bloody sockets with burning coals."

"Does Smoking Shield have any influence here?" Desert Flower asked. "Can he save us from the priests?"

"Your chances are vanishingly small. The king is unapproachable."

As if to confirm his judgment another head banged down the pyramid's steps.

I was terrified by his words, but Desert Flower's discomfiture was infinitely worse. Again, I put my arm around her shoulders, hoping to comfort her, saying, "Do not despair, Young Flower. We will show these barbaric people what we're made of."

"I wish Smoking Shield were here," Desert Flower said.

"The prince always sends his adjutant here to inspect the new prisoners," Stargazer said to Desert Flower. "That fiend from Mict-lantecuhtli's Hell will approach us shortly. Smoking Shield is wise to avoid him."

"But you're still here," Desert Flower said, grateful for the old man's support. "Smoking Shield could have stayed as well."

"He is not old and worn like me. He still harbors the illusion that life is worth living."

"You don't fear death?" I asked.

"My death will come as a grace."

"You're sure the hellish fiend will come *here?*" Desert Flower asked.

"This night in particular. As the head of our king's Praetorian Guard, he must examine the prisoners."

"Perhaps if I begged him for mercy?" Desert Flower asked.

Stargazer's derisive laughter was painful to the ear.

"If you show fear, he won't simply send you to the stone. He will cut you into a thousand pieces, hang you from your hocks over a slow-burning fire. While you are still breathing—but well-seared—he will . . . *eat you.*"

Desert Flower was now sick with terror, and I took her hand.

The old man was relentless. "You must convince this demon you're brave as jaguars."

Desert Flower fought to pull herself together, even as another gore-streaking head hammered down the temple slope. Stopping at our feet, the eyes stared up at me, vacant and sightless as dead suns. A be-robed acolyte trotted up to fetch it.

"Oh, curse us now," Stargazer said. "The devil himself approaches."

The screaming mob went silent as a tomb, then parted in terror, making way for the king's adjutant.

Desert Flower and I started to bend our knees as well. Stargazer jerked us upright.

"Stand like warriors," he counseled even as every nerve in my body screamed at me to genuflect.

The adjutant was also the head of the Jaguar Knights, and while he favored a long black-hooded robe, he was flanked by a retinue of Knights. Dressed in the cat's black-and-yellow-furred skins and lavishly feathered headdresses, they carried battle-axes of black-bladed obsidian over their shoulders.

He and his warriors walked purposefully toward us.

"He's come to inspect his spoils," Stargazer whispered.

At those words, Flower and I again started to kneel, and again Stargazer straightened us.

"You must show defiance, not deference, and martial courage."

Martial courage? I felt mortal terror. Still I whispered to Desert Flower:

"Just don't let him see you flinch."

I could feel her backbone stiffen. Raising her chin, she even stopped trembling. Her example gave me heart. I squared my shoulders, threw out my chest, and fixed my eyes on the face of the brutal Inquisitor, which was concealed in the shadows and folds of his heavy black hood.

"You are my hero," Flower whispered to me, and oddly enough, her words lifted me up.

He moved toward me, his head still down. When he was chest to chest with me, he raised his head and threw back his hood.

And smiled.

We stared unflinchingly into the eyes of . . . Smoking Shield.

Giving me an even greater smile, he then gave each of us a rib-cracking hug.

PART V

11

Smoking Shield and his jaguar-clad retinue continued to the palace by themselves to meet with the king. Stargazer, meanwhile, took us through the city, explaining:

"We will visit the palace when the king finishes his other meetings."

Everything about Tula overwhelmed me—from its bloodstained pyramids to its innumerable buildings to the thousands of people packing its broad streets. I had never encountered more than fifteen or twenty dwellings at one time, all of them thatched-roofed huts whose thin walls consisted of vertical maguey stalks interlaced with branches, fronds, maguey leaves, and dried mud. Here, however, were thousands of solidly built structures—sturdy enough to withstand anything short of flood or fire. One- and even two-story dwellings were spread in all directions as far as the eye could see, their rectangular walls of sunbaked, whitewashed brick glistening in the setting sun. The backs of almost all the houses opened up onto flower-filled patios.

"Most of these houses have cramped living and sleeping quarters," Stargazer said. "The larger the homes, the wealthier the occupant."

He pointed to one of the bigger dwellings, a house almost twice the size of its neighbors. "The owner is clearly prosperous."

"Which means he grows much maize?" I asked.

"Young friend," Stargazer asked, "do these people look like farmers to you? Do you see any maize fields within the city?"

"What do the people here do?" I asked.

"They're storekeepers, city and temple employees, craftsmen and officials."

"Where do they get their corn?"

"Much of our goods and services are paid for in corn, vegetables, sometimes even turkeys and ducks."

"Turkeys and ducks?" I said, amazed.

"You think having a pen full of birds makes a man prosperous?"

"Doesn't it?"

"Our king has turkeys and ducks by the thousands," the old man said.

"He must be a mortal god," I said softly.

"Some say he is."

As we continued on our tour, I realized the old man was right. We entered an even wealthier quarter of the town, where the dignitaries and officials lived. Their homes had five and six rooms, and several were three stories high. One house not only had turkeys, ducks, and edible dogs in its courtyard, but two parrots were tethered to a garden tree, their plumes so green they seemed eerily unreal.

"Green parrots!" Desert Flower whispered. She, like myself, stopped, spellbound.

Even an ignorant Aztec such as myself knew that green parrot plumes were prized beyond measure.

"Our king has thousands of them," Stargazer said.

"There is not so much wealth in the world," Desert Flower said.

"Are you sure about that?" Stargazer said.

Turning the corner, we entered Tula's central marketplace. Again, the old man was right. I had never dreamed such bounty existed in all of earth, the House of the Sun, the southern hereafter and Tlaloc's paradise combined, let alone in a single market—not even one as immense as Tula's.

Here was a universe of plenty: ropes of braided rawhide and maguey; towering, tottering piles of maize, sweet potatoes, onions, peppers, and cocoa; skinned and smoked rabbits, peccary pigs, turkeys, ducks, venison, roasting dogs, frogs, and fish, all ready for the table; maguey and bark paper; agave syrup and fresh honey; dyes, particularly indigo and cochineal; obsidian knives, flint spear blades, copper axes; bamboo smoking pipes; chairs and sleeping mats; braziers; pottery; salt; building lumber; charcoal; resin-soaked pine torches; green parrot plumes as well as eagle and falcon feathers; herbal medicines, poultices, oils, and ointments; drums, conch trumpets, flutes, calabash rattles; lengths of elaborately dyed, elegantly embroidered cloth; gems, precious stones, shells, even silver and gold; every kind of necklace, earring, and bracelet; even stalls that served as tattoo parlors and barbershops.

Women knelt in front of stoves, cooking bean- and pepper-stuffed tamales, tlaxcalli corn cakes and tortillas, grilling, then stuffing them with meat and fowl.

At the far end of the market, I even espied a half dozen slave cages, where quarry bosses and sacrificial priests could examine captured soldiers and convicted criminals sentenced to bondage or the sacrificial stone.

I quickly spotted Tenoch. He was caged by himself, his face, bare chest, and filthy loincloth bloodied from beatings. His head unbowed, his eyes were still uncowed.

The same old brute, he glared at me murderously, and when his gaze fell on Desert Flower his eyes filled with blind rage.

"He will go for a good price," Stargazer observed. "He has a strong heart and well-developed muscles. The priests and quarrymasters will vie for him."

"The gods will vomit up his bile," I said.

"The quarries may be preferable," the old man concurred.

Standing directly in front of the encaged Tenoch, we spoke of him as if he wasn't there, infuriating him even further.

"Why were Flower and I spared the quarries and the stone, but not Tenoch?" I asked Stargazer as we walked past the prisoners' cages.

"You have a keen eye for stars and a retentive memory for both imagery and words. I am old; my eyesight and memory are both fading. I need a young assistant to help me with my work."

He pointed up at the night sky. The moon was full, and thousands of stars brightened the blackness. The broad, densely starred band known as the World Tree blazed across the obsidian sky.

"I need you," Stargazer said, "to study the star-gods and crack their code. To unveil the secret of the Dark Rift and divine our destiny."

"And Desert Flower?"

"If I sent her to the stone or sentenced her to the quarries, you would never forgive me. To finish our work, I need your total commitment."

"You're sparing her to keep me happy?"

"We will also need a young woman to shop, mend, clean, grind corn, and cook our maize-cakes. You and I have will have no time for such things."

"There are many star-gods to observe," I agreed.

"They are infinite and immortal, and we are minute and transitory."

"I do not know where to begin."

"With your six small orbs."

"My belly contains the secrets of the gods?"

"No, but they mirror those which guard the World Tree's Dark Rift—the gateway to the Underworld Road."

"The old shaman called that blazing band 'the Crocodile Tree' and the Dark Rift and my six stars 'the Crocodile's Mouth.'"

"Then you shall open the Crocodile's Mouth."

"To what end?"

"Our journey's end."

"And where do we journey?"

"Through your stars and into the Rift. Young Cicatrice, you and I together, we shall walk the Underworld Road."

12

Rounding a corner, we approached the city's Pyramid of the Sun. Walking toward its base, I stared down its bottom edge. Both star- and moonlight were unusually bright, and along with the hundreds of torches surrounding the temple, lining its steps and illuminating its summit, the edifice was well lit. Even so, it was so massive that staring down at its base, I could barely see the end of it, as if the pyramid stretched as far as the eye could see . . . as if it went on forever.

Why shouldn't it go on forever? I thought. *Its summit all but touches the stars.*

If I thought the first pyramid by the gate was awesome, it shrank to an anthill compared to this one. Surrounded by square terraces on each of its four sides, it was barricaded by serpent-headed crenellated walls; dominating its truncated top were twin sanctuaries.

Standing at the farthest edge of the terrace, I could observe the massive monument from base to peak. Each sanctuary was crested with a tall stone-carved roof comb, mounted on a stepped platform. Gessoed white and embellished with portraits of Quetzalcoatl, ornate jaguar masks alternated the carved effigies of the Feathered Serpent.

Several hundred steps were carved into each slope, but the slope I stared at also featured a raised stone staircase. The blood-drenched priests were already mounting the staircase, their cowering victims in tow.

When I was finally able to take my eyes off the towering temple, I noticed the assembling crowd. The chant was rising up again:

"Blood for the gods! Blood for the gods!"

Desert Flower, who had suffered so much in her young life, was sickened by the suffering of others—even strangers. She trembled so hard I again had to put an arm around her.

The sacrifices bothered me, too, but my concerns were more practical. One wrong move, and I knew Tula's rulers could make Flower's and my life a living hell. True, both of us had eluded the slave cages, thanks to Smoking Shield's and Stargazer's intervention, but I viewed our salvation as only provisional. Goodwill can change overnight due to a grim whim or a vicious caprice. I'd learned that lesson when Fire Eyes had died, and here we lived on other people's sufferance, nothing more. One wrong move or a simple change of heart and we could find ourselves climbing that staircase toward the knife-wielding priest.

In no way was I sanguine about our fate.

"We've seen this before," Stargazer finally said. "There'll be refreshments at the palace, and I'm famished. Let's go."

"We're going to the palace?" Desert Flower asked.

"Why not? They're celebrating our return home."

13

To get to the palace we had to pass through the religious quarter where the priests and their thousands of underlings lived. Religious stalls and tents were all around us: penance pavilions where the righteous knelt while the priest or his votary slashed your arms and legs in expiation, the flowing blood ostensibly feeding the gods; prayer tents where religionists taught chants that allegedly charmed the gods into providing sun or rain; soothsayer and sorcerer tents where priests claimed to enrich and enrapture their customers by reading their stars and casting divine spells; sacrifice tents where priests tore their flesh with thorns and implored the gods to accept their tithe of human blood and living hearts. One could apply for immolation on the temple summit at these tents, but I never saw an applicant, only blood-streaming priests, emaciated from fasting, rending their sallow flesh.

In one of the sacrifice pavilions, scores of sacrificial skulls lined tiered platforms, before which black-robed priests—gore-streaked and emaciated, with long, straggly, blood-stained hair—knelt and wailed. One cleric held a particularly vile death's-head above his head, then lowered it beneath his waist, while the lugubrious wails of his votaries rose and fell with his gesticulations. While they wailed, they too plunged maguey needles into their arms and legs, shedding their own blood, supplicating the gods, imploring them on behalf of humanity for a few more drops of rain, a little more sun, another day of life. Reaching into a large pot laden with amputated hearts, two of the black-robes lifted them high overhead, again. Chanting hellish incantations, as indecipherable to me as the dark between the stars, they dropped abruptly to their knees and lacerated their flesh with maguey thorns until great gouts of gore covered the pavilion's earthen floor.

People were lining up at both the penance and sacrifice tents to shower the priests with valuable trade goods. In return, the clerics promised—on behalf of their clients—to placate the gods and protect them from the deities' wrath.

When Desert Flower cringed at these bloody sights, I took her arm.

Priests were everywhere, going in and out of every building we passed; and for a long time we walked in silence.

"There are a lot of priests," Desert Flower finally said.

"This is the religious quarter," Stargazer said. "These people are either priests or their servants or their staff."

"Why so many?" I asked.

"They run the One-World as much as our king."

"Why does the king allow that?"

"Times have been dry," the old astronomer said. "Without the priests and their human sacrifices, without heads banging down the pyramid steps, without cataracts of blood cascading down the temple troughs, people fear the sun will not rise, the rain not fall, night will not end, and Mictlantecuhtli's Hell will rule this hard land. What do you believe?"

"What I or Desert Flower believe does not matter. We are slaves."

We continued our stroll, passing legions of priests going to and from their sprawling three-story homes, their bathhouses, their administrative offices, and their schools. Passing a dozen massive structures, far bigger than any other buildings I had seen, I asked Stargazer what they were.

"Granaries," he said, "for corn, beans, squash, and peppers. Two of them are arsenals stocked with bladed lances, javelins, bows, arrows, atlatls, knives. The priests oversee many such storage sites throughout Tula."

Another spectacularly huge building came into view. "That's the biggest building I've ever seen," Desert Flower gasped.

As big as the four biggest buildings we'd seen thus far.

"What is it?" I asked.

"The public treasury," Stargazer said.

"What's it hold? Gold, gems, treasure?" I stared at it awe-struck.

"Yes," Stargazer said, "but also vast stores of maize, beans, peppers, bales of cloth, coils of agave-fiber rope, hide and fiber sandals, obsidian knives, sewing needles, dried fish and meat, animal skins, rich plumes, and lengths of cloth—most of which our lord takes from his subjects in taxes."

"The priests control everything, it seems," I said.

"Much of Tula's food, goods, weaponry, and, especially, the people's allegiance," Stargazer said sadly. "They even control our blood."

"They are a world within a world?" I asked, their bloody vision and brutal power making me uneasy. "A power within a power?"

"In many respects," Stargazer said, "they *are* the power."

"Is that true?" Desert Flower asked.

"Do you fear the black-robes?"

"I'd be insane not to. So would you."

"They have too much power," I said.

"Never forget that, young friend," Stargazer said. "And never cross them."

PART VI

14

Rising to his feet, President Edward Raab faced the three people sitting before him.

"Brad, since you missed our first meeting, I thought I ought to explain how I got to know Dr. Cardiff and General Hagberg. As you may be aware, I served under General Hagberg in Nicaragua and in Operation Desert Storm before wisely abandoning my military career for a less strenuous life. Little did I know I was out of the frying pan and into the fire. Attending Berkeley on the GI Bill, I took a seminar on global catastrophism under Dr. Cardiff—a more arduous ordeal than my Special Forces training at Ft. Bragg. In fact, people routinely compared her to the sadistic drill instructors we had there, usually invoking the DIs in films like *Full Metal Jacket* and *An Officer and a Gentleman*. She didn't just grade papers, she broke them on the rack. 'Dr. Torquemada' was one of her standard nicknames.

"I've kept in touch with her ever since, and when she contacted me four weeks ago with her latest scientific findings I assembled this group. I obviously have total confidence in her. I have equally strong feelings about you and General Hagberg. Not only do I think each of you will offer judicious counsel, the need for iron-clad secrecy has forced me to keep the group unavoidably small. I know from personal experience all three of you are inviolably discreet and will honor that commitment, which is another reason I'm relying on you three to tell me how to proceed with this grim situation. Dr. Cardiff, I yield the floor."

Dr. Cardiff rose. "Thank you, Mr. President. At our last meeting I alluded to some of these crises, but we mostly discussed the need for secrecy—a need which I again point out is paramount. News leaks could topple stock markets, and the world economy is desperate enough already. They could even destabilize some of the world's more troubled regions. The resulting chaos would radically undermine our ability to ever address these problems globally.

"And we have another reason for discretion. As you shall see, multilateral efforts to deal with our newly discovered megadisasters are probably doomed. Not only has the world economy gone to hell, the world's most violent trouble spots are running out of food, water, energy, and money. These rapidly failing states and their predatory neighbors and patrons have not worked all that well together in solving even minor geopolitical problems, let alone problems of this magnitude.

"Leaking of this information will not only subvert U.S. attempts at disaster prevention and consequence management, it will impede our need to act—unilaterally, if necessary—in our own best interests. It will sabotage any and all efforts at self-preservation.

"I've jotted down some notes. Read them here, then return them to me for immediate shredding." She handed out her notes.

15

Covert action in four shooting wars had filled Bradford Chase's body with enough shrapnel body to set off—some said short-out—metal detectors. Still, Cardiff's report was making him uneasy. Her notes made his counterinsurgency wars look like *Rebecca of Sunnybrook Farm*.

Before going into my most recent findings, we need to examine several of today's other problems and consider how they will affect the crises to come.

One of global warming's most disastrous—yet least reported on—consequences has been global drought. Transforming one-half of the planet's semiarid cropland into irretrievable desert, this desertification has at last created serious food and water shortages, destroying almost half of all crop- and rangelands—altogether an area larger than all of China—and depleting water supplies for two billion people. India's 1.3 billion people are officially out of potable water; its major rivers are now little more than fetid sewage. Water scarcity is already fueling serious conflicts on the subcontinent, in South Asia, the Mideast, and Africa.

Of Africa's fifty-one nations, only twelve feed their people without assistance.

Another by-product of climate change, the worldwide wildfire plague, has aggravated drought and desertification even further.

The aridity crisis fuels the global wildfire plague most dramatically in the Amazon Basin. More Brazilian rainforest is now consumed each year by fire than by loggers. More CO_2 is pumped into the atmosphere by wildfires than by internal combustion engines, the pandemic fire plague thus exponentiating the Greenhouse Effect. And the wildfire plague mounts annually in size and frequency eroding and ruining even more land.

The first of the megafires, Cardiff went on to say, was Yellowstone's 1988 forest inferno. Since then the numbers of such fires had also skyrocketed, and the total increase in their devastation had a multiplier effect: the fires pumped out incomprehensible quantities of greenhouse gases, accelerated drought, increased desertification and impeded the rainforest's ability to process CO_2 and other greenhouse gases.

These natural infernos were now ten times the size of anything people had seen previously. Ten years ago a hundred-thousand-acre fire would have been massive. According to Cardiff, wildfires in the U.S. alone routinely ran five times that size.

Bradford had seen some of the California fires on TV. He noted at the time that overhead night-footage of those megafires resembled that of Tokyo's World War II firebombing.

Firestorms increasingly consumed the Amazon rainforest. During one recent year satellite photos had documented over 350,000 Amazon forest fires. Previously that rainforest had been impervious to such conflagration.

The drought and the fires, Cardiff noted, had even dried up many of the Amazon's tributaries. An irreplaceable transportation system for the rainforest's interior, the disappearance of these waterways had isolated hundreds of riverside settlements, forcing the Brazilian military to air-drop thousands of tons of food and scores of tons of medicine into these areas.

Christ, Bradford thought, even Antarctica was not immune to the firestorms' destruction. After the rainforest fires propelled their nitrogen oxides and methane into the stratosphere, southbound jet streams carried these highly reactive gases over the South Pole, where they ate colossal holes in the ozone shield—the irreplaceable shield that had protected life on earth from ultraviolet radiation for almost a billion years.

On earth, the shrinking forest canopy has also diminished the rainforest's assimilation of CO_2 and other greenhouse gases, sabotaging its cleansing of the atmosphere as well as undercutting raincloud development over the desolated jungles, reducing precipitation even further.

These multiple disasters—shrinking farmlands, pandemic wildfires, food and water scarcity, compounded by dwindling energy reserves—are destabilizing the world's most violently troubled nations, most glaringly India, Pakistan, China, Africa, and the Mideast oil states. By destroying peoples' livelihoods, aggravating poverty, and fueling terrorism, these shortages increase the likelihood of extremist takeovers. Racked by terrorism and a financial black hole, resource scarcity could easily turn nuclear Pakistan into a failed nuclear state and a spawning ground for drug-financed nuclear terrorism.

She underscored that a major cause in any civlization's decline and fall—as documented by such scholars as Arnold Toynbee, Oswald Spengler, and Edward Gibbon—was the wealth inequity, exploitation of the populace, and the violent rise of poverty-inspired class warfare.

She finished by stressing the need to keep her findings tightly classified, reiterating some of her opening remarks.

The crises I have outlined preclude any hope of multilateral so-lutions to the megacatastrophes we are about to examine. Con-flict, not cooperation, is the world condition. In this new crisis, the U.S. must not seek to protect the planet but instead look to its own self-interest. If we are to have any chance at disaster-prevention or consequence-management, we must act quickly, decisively but covertly. The coming catastrophes will exacerbate the current conflicts. We are looking at the ultimate zero-sum nightmare. UN resolutions, multilateral consensus, and world opinion will do the U.S. no good. We must take what we need and do what we can without regrets.

So this was it, Bradford thought: The final Hobbesian nightmare had arrived—"the war of all against all" . . . abetted by all the hor-rors of hell.

Turning the page, Bradford Chase stared into that hell—the first of Cardiff's newly discovered megadisasters.

16

The first of Cardiff's imminent super-disasters made Bradford feel physically ill. He'd always known that something eerie seethed beneath Yellowstone's surface. He'd remembered visiting Yellowstone as a kid and marveling at its Dantesque steam vents, bone-jarring tremors, soaring geysers, hot mud flats, slurping mud pots, and steam-haunted fumaroles. He thought of Yellowstone, however, as surreal, as Nature According to Disney—a geological fairy-tale, designed to thrill children.

Thanks to Cardiff, he now knew he was wrong.

He had not known that Yellowstone was a 1,400-square-mile volcanic caldera, created out of a supervolcano that had gone nova 640,000 years ago. Groaning, sobbing, roaring, incessantly erupting, the pressure inside its magma chamber had mounted exponentially until the chamber's roof detonated, and the volcanic mountain blew apart with the force and velocity of a crashing asteroid and a hundred thousand thermonuclear bombs. Melting, demolishing, and devouring the surrounding mountains, the explosion had formed a cauldron-shaped volcanic crater, thirty-four by forty-five miles. This vast depression was eventually called the Yellowstone Caldera—or by tourists, Yellowstone Park.

Bradford had not known as a visiting child that the Yellowstone supervolcano had ejected one thousand cubic kilometers of flaming hell into the atmosphere, which, coming down, had buried North America in two meters of smoldering debris. Nor had he known that the detonation had effectively exterminated most of the world's life forms and plunged the planet into black, volcanic winter.

There were a lot of things Bradford had not understood until he read Cardiff's hair-raising report. He had not known about La Garita Caldera in the San Juan Mountains of Colorado, which had been formed 27.8 million years ago when its supervolcano blasted 5,000 cubic kilometers, Fish Canyon Tuff into the heavens and across the earth . . . or Indonesia's Lake Toba supervolcanic detonation, which 75,000 years before had blanketed the world with 2,800 cubic kilometers of smoking rubble while shrouding the planet in a perpetual black veil. The biggest volcanic detonation of the last 1.8 million years, it launched a thousand-year Ice Age and exterminated most of humankind, leaving only a few thousand survivors to wring a wretched existence out of that ash- and smoke-choked hellworld—a bleak moonscape of ash, mud, and everlasting night.

Nor had Bradford heard of Greece's Thiran disaster—the Santorini eruption of 3,500 years ago that engulfed Greece and its islands with towering tsunamis and destroyed the legendary Minoan civilization, which some believed inspired Plato's lost civilization of Atlantis.

Nor was Bradford familiar with Indonesia's Mt. Tambora eruption, which in April 1815 lofted seven times Krakatoa's debris: thirty-six cubic miles (150 cubic kilometers) into the air—the largest volume of volcanic ejecta ever witnessed and recorded. Dropping temperatures globally, 1816 became known as "the year without summer."

On an infinitely smaller scale, Indonesia's Krakatoa eruption in the late nineteenth century shattered a volcanic island, triggered 120-foot-high tsunamis, and blasted five cubic miles of fiery rubble fifty miles into the stratosphere. The loudest blast ever heard by homo sapiens, its upwardly rocketing rubble obscured almost 90 percent of the world's sunlight for the next year—a black volcanic veil that plummeted temperatures worldwide.

Compared to Yellowstone, it was a baby's burp.

While detonating with the force of five hundred Hiroshimas, the 1980 Mt. St. Helens eruption launched 1.2 cubic kilometers of ejecta skyward. It only brought down half a mountain instead of obliterating the Pacific Northwest.

Compared to Yellowstone, it was a spent cartridge, a burnt-out light-bulb.

As big as its descendents were, Yellowstone's supervolcanic detonation dwarfed them all, its devastation many times greater than all those subsequent megaeruptions put together . . . a portentous devastation which, according to Cardiff, was coming back for an encore.

Being a scientist, she of course backed up her case with a supervolcano of facts. That last year alone over two thousand earthquakes had convulsed the caldera, averaging over five per day, Cardiff reported. Many were minute but the rate, strength, and amplitude were mounting. Hebgen Lake had registered an 8.1 temblor, which had fissured the earth and buried nearly one hundred tourists under a landslide. Borah Peak and Norris Geyser Basin hit Richter numbers almost as high, and over forty people perished. During the first two months of the preceding year, an earthquake swarm shook the caldera, which produced over three thousand quakes—almost six per day.

Cardiff recorded a USGS geologist who had sonared a volcanic bulge under Yellowstone Lake a half-mile long and one hundred feet in height. Lake temperatures shot up twenty degrees, leaving dead fish floating on its surface and washed up on its shores.

Cardiff concluded humanity's fate might mirror that of the stricken fish—especially when the supervolcanic eruption emitted its superabundant sulphur dioxide. For decades geochemists had documented its disastrous effect on the earth's stratospheric ozone layer. The SO2's erosion of that already fragile ozone shield would inflict on humankind irreversible gene damage and skyrocketing cancer rates worldwide—a veritable cancer pandemic. Simple sunburn would prove a mortal injury.

Cardiff reported that the area around Old Faithful's pressure was already seven-hundred times the world average, and beneath the caldera, thirty to forty times greater a sign that the melting of the magma chamber was well under way. In the magma chamber, tests showed that the heat was now fifty times that of the world average, a thermal intensity that was hastening the chamber's meltdown. Swollen with a mother lode of magma—ten times the amount it had already discharged—it was primed and pumped, locked, and cocked. Balanced on a hair trigger and distended at its seams, the swelling chamber was ready to blow.

She described the caldera's valley floor as sobbing and groaning, rising and falling, like the mountains that once writhed in labor. The caldera's elevation was increasing a foot per year.

Cardiff reported that the Norris Geyser Basin's temperature had shot up 120 degrees—from eighty to two hundred, annihilating trees and other plant life, forcing the fauna into migration, turning the surrounding area into an apocalyptic deathscape.

Overnight, countless new steam vents and exceptionally hot springs opened up. These new springs were so boilingly hot that their adjacent trails scorched the feet of booted hikers. Rangers were forced to shut the trails down.

The Norris Basin bulge—twenty-eight miles long and seven miles wide—had risen over half a foot in a dozen years and was still swelling upward. Meanwhile, the volcanic bubble beneath the Yellowstone basin had shot up over one hundred feet in less than a day. An overinflated balloon, it was ready to blow like a geological Big Bang.

"Who else has seen this report?" Bradford asked, breaking the long silence.

"Thirteen science teams contributed to this report," Dr. Cardiff said. "I was the only individual to read and process more than one of the reports. The team-leaders are still waiting for my conclusions."

"They must be impatient," Bradford said.

"I get some nervous e-mails," Dr. Cardiff acknowledged.

"How do you handle them?" Gen. Hagberg asked.

"I report back that their findings were aberrations."

"What can we do about Yellowstone's magma chamber?" Bradford asked. "It's about to go critical, according to your report."

"I've discussed it with seismologists and geologists," Dr. Cardiff said. "Hypothetically, of course. Since no one has ever tried to suppress a supervolcano or relieve its pressure, we have very little data on the subject. One geologist who specialized in oil deposits speculated that long-distance slant-drilling might relieve the pressure. Another scientist feared it would do more harm than good."

Dr. Cardiff collected the papers and ran them through the conference-room shredder.

"Let's discuss disaster prevention and consequence-management at the next meeting," the president said, "after we've had time to discuss your thoughts on the subject privately with each other and particularly with Dr. Cardiff. Continue, please."

"Part two of my presentation is serious enough that I've not committed it to paper," she said. "I will describe my findings to you orally."

Bradford took her reluctance to write up her notes as a bad sign.

PART VII

17

ONE-WORLD, 1001 A.D.

We were now approaching two long parallel walls, half as high as a man, their tops lined with torches. Between the torches people leaned over the walls, yelling excitedly at young men running up and down a field.

"What's going on between those walls?" Desert Flower asked.

"I've never known anyone who did not know of tlachtli or its ball court," Stargazer said, astonished.

The two of us stared at him, silent.

"The game of life and death, it is said to foretell the future, solve the riddles of the universe, and embody the meaning of life."

"Why don't the priests run it?"

"They run as much as they can, but the game is so vast, so universal, so popular even they cannot control it."

"It sounds like octli," I said.

"There are similarities. Obsessed with the game, some men abandon their work and their families, gambling and drinking themselves into perdition. Priests and princes, scientists and scholars—believing it holds the secrets to power and war, to our deities and destinies—sometimes lose their souls to the tlachti madness."

"How so?" I asked.

"They see in the court, the sky; in the ball they divine the sun, the moon, the sacred stars. In the sky the gods themselves play tlachtli, the heavenly bodies their balls. The games of the gods foreshadow our fate."

"You are hopefully immune to this lunacy," I said.

"Stronger men than you and I have lost themselves to the game."

Stargazer led us around one of the walls, and we looked out over the ballpark. A game was in progress. Men ran up and down the court chasing a ball the size of a man's head, hitting it with their knees and hips. Well-to-do men, many of them officials and dignitaries, leaned against the wall, where they cheered the players on.

"Only important people are allowed to play. Those on this court are royalty. Watch."

I could see the court and the players better now. Several hundred paces in length, the court flared out at both ends. The players wore tight loincloths and were otherwise naked except for heavy leather pads on their knees and hips, and leather gloves on their hands. Some of them wore masks.

The game made no sense to me, but Stargazer did his best to explain it to us.

"They begin the game at midcourt and fight to keep the other side from invading their half of the court with the rubber ball. They can only hit the ball with their knees and hips."

"Rubber?" Desert Flower asked.

Stargazer stared at us, astonished. "A thick brownish liquid we milk from trees in the hot lands and mold into a ball like the one on the court—hard enough to hurt when it hits, even kill players, which happens with some frequency."

"How do you know when you've won?" Desert Flower asked.

"See the two rings on each side of the midcourt?" Stargazer said. The rings were mounted on posts that jutted out over the field. Only slightly larger than the ball, these twin hoops were as tall as two men. "If a player drives the ball through the ring, his team wins automatically. It's hard to accomplish and seldom happens. Otherwise you have to drive the ball through those crosspieces at each end of the court."

A crossbar was mounted on posts at each end of the field.

"The game sounds difficult," Desert Flower said.

"You should see the skull games," Stargazer said. "One of the losing players has his head cut off, his brains removed, his skull stuffed and encased in rubber."

"Players play tlachtli with skulls?" Desert Flower asked, stunned.

"Only the most important players and only in the most important games."

"People think the game is . . . divine?" I asked, skeptical.

"Emperors have been known to bet cities on it, to risk war and gamble their empires on their religious interpretation of tlachtli's game-play and its outcome. They think the game possesses the power of divination."

"And they sometimes play it with skulls," I said, my face a mask of blank incredulity.

"It is not called 'the game of life and death' for nothing."

"Does our king play tlachtli?" Desert Flower asked.

"He's one of the game's finest players," Stargazer said, smiling.

18

Beyond the ballpark stood an enormous edifice, which dwarfed any building I'd so far seen—except for the temple-pyramids. Glowing braziers and resin-soaked pine torches illuminated its entrance, which was at least as wide as the ball court. The building was as long as two ball courts.

"What is it?" I asked Stargazer. "Another city?"

"The imperial palace," the old man said. "Where our ruler holds court."

"They must have an awfully big court," I said.

"Priests, officials, magistrates, generals, warriors, musicians, concubines, family members, servants, cleaning women, cooks—yes, it is a very big court."

"I'm afraid," Desert Flower said quietly.

"What's to fear? Smoking Shield?"

"Are we his friends?" Desert Flower asked.

"You would not be here, if you weren't."

"He will not send us to the priests for their temple sacrifice?" she asked.

Stargazer smoothed her hair. "Is that what you thought? You

could not have been more wrong. Come, relax. This is a celebration. You will have fun. Enjoy yourself. We've had a long journey."

We walked up the brick pathway to the great, draped-off doorway, pushed aside the gorgeously embroidered, crimson tapestry, and entered the city-within-the-city.

19

Stargazer led us through the palace—through dozens of interconnected rooms and passageways. On the first floor we went past council chambers for Tula's civil and criminal courts, its military/political tribunals as well as offices for its officials and military commanders. Purely functional, the offices were furnished with low wooden chairs and platforms. Rolled-up sleeping pads also served as chairs, although tonight no one worked late. The pine torches bracketing the walls were unlit.

The official public treasury took up much of that first floor. Many people paid their taxes in dry food and self-manufactured goods, and we strolled past huge storage rooms. Pallets and huge thatched baskets were piled high with tax levies—great stores of maize, beans, chili peppers, cocoa beans, smoked and dried meats, agave-fiber rope, sandals, knives, amal paper, fancy feathers, gemstones, bailed cloth, and piles of expensive apparel.

We passed the workrooms, housing the king's craftspeople, who chipped obsidian, chiseled jade, created feathered mosaics, molded gold and silver. Their work platforms were strewn with their partially finished but artfully fabricated handiworks.

As we approached the courtyard, we encountered troupes of singers, musicians, and dancers. They served at the royal court's pleasure, and when some royal personage required entertainment, they had to be ready. In large rehearsal rooms, they practiced their instruments—their drums, gourd rattles, conch-shell trumpets, chimes, bells and reed flutes—even as beautiful, licentiously attired woman worked on their vigorous, voluptuous dances.

Stargazer continued our tour up to the second floor. The king's apartments—as well as those of his closest friends, warriors, staff, attendants, and concubines—occupied that floor, and they contained more wealth than Desert Flower and I had seen in both our lifetimes . . . room after room of priceless treasures.

Fastened to many of the walls or propped up on low platforms were turquoise mosaics adorned with lignite, pyrite, shells, pearls, copper, silver, and gold. The most elaborate were fashioned into decorative masks or shields, festooned with hawk, eagle, and parrot feathers. Constructed of burnished copper, the most ornate masks and shields glittered with gemstones, pearls, shells, obsidian, silver and, gold as did the ornate helmets, scepters, and crowns beside which they sometimes were placed. Mirrors of pyrite and obsidian were also propped up on platforms or hung on the walls.

Many of the low platforms featured leather-lined human skulls embellished with mosaics of lignite and turquoise. In several cases the eye sockets scintillated with sparkling pyrite. As I examined one of the more meticulously designed death's-heads, Smoking Shield approached me. Clad in a simple black loincloth with matching cloak and hide sandals, he wore his long hair loose and without ornamentation—no feathers, jewels, earrings, or piercings . . . not even a tattoo.

"You have good taste, Cicatrice," Smoking Shield said, clapping me on the shoulder. "That skull belonged to a close friend and comrade. A tlachtli captain, he was as good a player as any I ever teamed up with, as well as a superlative soldier. I was going to fill and cover his skull with rubber, then return his head to the game he loved, but in the end I could not bear to part with him. Come, though, you are a guest. Let's get you some refreshment."

He led us through another succession of hallways into a spectacular courtyard, brightly lit not only by the moon and stars but by a blazing array of torches and braziers. Spacious as a dozen tlachtli ballparks and built around a small lake, it teemed with the wonders of nature—glimmering gardens redolent with brightly hued flowers, intertwining vines and vociferous birds. Caged pumas, jaguars, anacondas, rattlesnakes, iguanas, and alligators populated its menageries. In its fountains and waterfalls geese, swans, ducks, and egrets splashed. Its ponds boasted fish, turtles, and alligators, its wooded groves tame rabbits and deer. Tethered hawks, eagles, and falcons perched on blocks and on tree limbs, their feet fettered but their fierce eyes untamed.

A massively intricate maze lay to my right, made up of intersecting passageways of impenetrable bushes, each twice as tall as a man. When I wandered toward to it, curious, Stargazer took my arm.

"Do not enter, young Cicatrice. I would have to go in, find you, then lead you out. You do not know the palace ways . . . or its people."

At the front of the courtyard an endless assortment of delicacies was arranged on low platforms: maize cakes floating in honey; tamales stuffed with meat, beans, hot chili peppers, wild onions, and tomatoes; cocoa from the jungle Hot Lands, flavored with vanilla, chilled in pitchers, and sweetened with maguey syrup; platters of grilled venison, turkey, wild boar, roast duck, rabbit; piles of smoked fish; frogs in pimento sauce; white fish and freshwater shrimps with red pepper and tomatoes; pots overflowing with beans, maize, squash, peppers, wild onions, and tomatoes.

"Go easy, Cicatrice," Stargazer warned me, pointing to the beverage platforms. "Many drink-jugs are laced with the infamous octli—including the chilled chocolate."

Smoking Mirror's attitude was clearly different. He was handing us ornately crafted cups inlaid with turquoise and obsidian, brimming with straight undiluted octli. He offered a toast:

"To those who fall."

With those words, he threw back his drink, and as if on cue, troupes of singers, musicians, and dancers flooded the courtyard, their voices harmonizing, their seed-filled gourds and calabashes rattling. Four of them pounded bass drums with flat-handed ferocity, even as the conch horns, bells, and long reed flutes rendered a rhythmic yet strangely melancholic refrain . . . all the while beautiful, exotically attired women spun and whirled, gyrated and writhed with sinuous sensuality.

While I nursed the octli, which the warrior had handed me, Stargazer led me away from the endless platters of food and pitchers of drink.

"Our lord's palace is a snake's pit—not a place for drunkenness. To survive in this hard land, you will need all your wits. Watch the octli."

Glancing at the warrior, I said, "Smoking Shield freely imbibes."

"Oh, you're a Jaguar Knight now?"

I smiled at the jibe.

"Do you even know what octli is?" Stargazer asked.

"A poison brewed in hell by devils with fangs and horns?"

"It comes out of the maguey in your own fields."

"We used maguey stalks to prop up our hut walls," I said.

"Yes, and you sewed your clothes with its needles. You braided its fibers into rope and thread. You wove those fibers into cloth."

"We planted it in rows between the corn and beans and peppers. We sometimes made syrup from its juice, but mostly we turned it into medicine."

"Octli's not that hard to make," the old man said. "Cut the stem at its base, bleed the juice in the plant's heart, collect it in skins and calabashes."

"We also used it as a sweetener."

"Around here people ferment it into tino octli, the demon juice."

"It suits him," I said, nodding toward Smoking Shield, who was throwing back another cupful.

"It will rob you of your already diminished senses, young friend, and the people here are not your friends."

"I noticed no one's spoken to me."

"Perhaps it's your stylish clothes," Stargazer mocked.

A loincloth was all the clothing I wore—and everything I possessed.

"You will have all the fancy cotton clothes you want," Stargazer said seriously. "Smoking Shield likes you."

"Do you like me?"

Stargazer gave me a long, meditative stare. "Cicatrice, I asked you to assist me, did I not?"

"So?"

"Yes, that means I like you."

We were now in front of a platform filled with reed and clay pipes. People picked them up, lit them in the nearby braziers or the pine torches propped up on stands, inhaling, then exhaling the pungent smoke.

"I suppose I should stay away from that stuff too," I said.

"The smoke is as dangerous as the drink, perhaps more so."

The warrior's guests did not seem to think so. They eagerly drank octli and lit pipes—men and women both. Our Knight was especially fond of the octli.

Several of the male guests joined the female dancers. They danced slower than the professionals, and soon some of the men and women ceased dancing altogether and drifted into secluded corners and groves, where, I noticed, some of them . . . embraced.

"In my village such public displays were forbidden," I said.

"Men back from expeditions or soldiers who have proven themselves in the wars, have a special dispensation to . . . indulge."

"Our village elders would not have cared."

"Cicatrice, you are in the palace of power. With it, you can do *anything.*"

"Including drinking, debauchery, and dream-smoking?"

"Why do you think all those palace apartments contained sleeping mats? Officials, warriors, dignitaries often take the auianime back to their offices and apartments."

"Take the *what* back?"

"The auianime—unmarried women who become consorts to our soldiers and dignitaries."

"Why don't the women marry the men instead?"

"When husbands learn their wives cannot bear children, many summarily divorce them. In some cases men violate women, then refuse to marry them. Such women seldom find husbands. Left without means, they may become consorts . . . if they are attractive enough."

"The beast, Tenoch, violated Desert Flower. Will she become one?" I said, noticing how Flower shivered as she watched a woman being pawed and groped by a drunken dignitary.

"We will look after her as long as you wish . . . for as long as we can."

Now I studied him, curious. "You *are* a friend, Stargazer."

"Are you surprised?"

"I've never had a friend before."

We were standing by a drink platform lined with full cups of octli. The old man, having drained his cup, helped himself to another one.

"I'm old and can kill myself however I will. You are a coyotl pup who must watch himself." With that admonition he tossed off a full cup.

I picked up a second cup myself. "I hate to see old men drink alone."

I turned and watched the auianime. Like most of our village women, many of the courtesans went bare-breasted. Favoring lavish, even lurid makeup, they lightened their skins with an ointment called axin or with yellowish tecozauitl earth and covered their arms, throats, and breasts with indigo tattoos. Some reddened not only their mouths but their teeth with cochineal. Wearing their hair loose, almost all of them chewed tzictli and doused themselves with erotic scents. Many of them smoked from the long reed pipes and imbibed straight octli.

Smoking Shield came up behind us.

"Note the prevalence of skull tattoos on our women," the warrior said, "particularly on their breasts. They even string small ceramic skulls—painted and burnished bright cerulean or stark carmine— from their necks."

The Jaguar Knight was right. On closer inspection, I saw that many of the women had strung miniature skulls around their throats.

"Don't men find skulls . . . repulsive?" I asked.

"Were that true, our consorts would not wear them. They live off their allure and find that the men are amorously aroused."

"And you? Does death not repulse you?"

"Death is with a soldier always, perched on his shoulder like a bird. I often find its prospect comforting and long for . . . the endless night."

"If the night never ends, you cannot return as a vulture."

"That was a dream. Death is real."

"Death never frightens you?"

"A soldier takes war as a lover, Cicatrice. Valiant death is the soldier's driving vision. To the soldier, such a death is his wisest adviser and a sublime gift."

"A death with a noble purpose," I said.

"Exactly so."

"What about death on the stone?" Desert Flower asked.

Our warrior studied her thoughtfully. "If the man or woman goes willingly, perhaps."

"They saw a sacrifice today," Stargazer said. "The prisoner was hardly . . . willing."

"How you die determines your future in the Afterlife," our warrior said carefully. "If that man was not ready, Mictlantecuhtli will not be kind. Taking a person's life when they are not ready is a sin."

"The man on the stone was not ready, yet the priests and the people reveled," I said.

"We honor the gods by choking on each other's blood," Stargazer said, "by devouring each other's flesh, by sacrificing our daughters to these vile, unseen deities? There is a curse on our blood . . . a blackness in our hearts."

"Did you ever notice how black our people's eyes are?" Smoking Shield said. "How ancient their sadness, how bottomless their despair? That is why we drag men to the stone and women to the fiery pit."

"I thought we slaughtered each other for the gods?" Stargazer said, his tone ironic.

"Our priests advocate ignoble death—even venerating suicide."

"Venerating suicide?" I repeated, realizing now how little I knew about the Tollan religion and its gods.

"Most of us go to Mictlantecuhtli's Hell," Stargazer explained. "Our suicides go to Tlalac's Paradise—a land of eternal spring and bright flowers, of food in abundance, of soaring mountains, blue rivers, and towering trees."

"That is insane," I said.

"I have warned him to watch his tongue," Stargazer said to Shield, shooting me a disapproving look. He then gave Shield the same stare. "He does not understand the ways of Tula and its priests." Stargazer whispered the last three words.

"Listen to him, Cicatrice," Shield said. "He's telling you plain. They worship death for death's sake—the more vile the better. To suggest otherwise is to spit on their power."

"What do *we* worship?" I asked.

"This old man is our last and greatest astronomer," the warrior said, pointing to Stargazer. "He will teach you the star-gods' riddles—and perhaps you will help him finish his Long-Count, End-Time Calendar. One day you will share his reverence for the star-gods as well."

"I do not know enough to reverence them," I said.

"He will teach you."

"I wish I knew more about this calendar."

"The Long Count Calendar, begun so many sun cycles ago, is ancient as the stars and incomprehensibly complex," Stargazer said.

"The only astronomer capable of calculating its genesis and its End-Time stands before us," Smoking Shield whispered.

"There is no one else to assist you in your work?" Desert Flower asked Stargazer.

"Today's priests disdain honest stargazing," the old astronomer said, shaking his head. "For them the star-gods are a scheme to defraud the ignorant—nothing more."

"Terrorizing the populace out of their possessions, they invoke the star-gods only to expand their power," Smoking Shield whispered.

"Why do the priests then allow Stargazer to study the heavens?" Desert Flower asked.

"Because our king has commanded that he do so," Smoking Shield said.

"Why does our king court the priests' wrath?" I asked the warrior.

"So the truth will not vanish forever . . ."

"Forever?" I asked.

"Like a virgin in volcanic fire," the warrior said.

Suddenly, I smelled a sickening, charnel odor, then fear. The crowd parted, and the ugliest human being I'd ever seen approached: a black-clad, blood-smeared, long-haired emaciated priest draped in a foul-smelling human skin.

His companion, on the other hand, was blindingly, achingly, breathtakingly . . . *beautiful*.

Tall and slender, dressed in simple unadorned black, she wore her dark hair long and loose. Sporting neither tattoos nor piercings nor ornaments, she had no need of them. They would have only diluted her radiance—her full, generous mouth, her flashing smile, her flaring cheekbones framing blackfire eyes . . .

"Who is she?" Flower asked Stargazer.

"The Dark Goddess of Mictlantecuhtli."

"*What* is she?" I asked.

"For you, a walking apocalypse," the old man said.

"She's Princess Zyanya—the king's sister," the warrior whispered in my ear.

She was moving toward us with the feral grace of a prowling puma.

"My brother's dearest mentor," she said, staring at Stargazer.

I had not realized he was an intimate of King Quetzalcoatl.

"It has been so long," she said. "I missed you too, Shield. You must tell me everything that happened. I am so pleased you are both back and in one piece."

"I am pleased to see you as well, my lady," the Jaguar Knight said.

"Tell me about your journey," she said.

She and Smoking Shield drifted over to an octli table.

Taking my arm, Stargazer eased me away from them.

"What do you think of her?" the old man asked.

"She is the most beautiful thing I have ever seen."

"And?"

"She terrifies me. Even our Knight seems . . . timorous."

"We should all fear her. Anyone whom her brother favors is her hated prey."

"Who was the foul-smelling man with her?"

"Tezcal, the High Priest. Her closest ally, his allegiance to her makes her doubly dangerous."

"Why?"

"We will talk later."

"Where is the king?"

"We will talk later."

While she and the Knight conversed, her eyes flickered indifferently over the people assembled. Suddenly, in midconversation, blazing eyes fixed on me, raking me with a hard stare. Breaking off the conversation, she headed toward me.

"So you are the crude young boy they call Coyotl," she said. "Are you a sly, treacherous, murderous beast like your namesake?"

"I am your faithful servant and subject," I said, bowing my head.

"You'll bow to my stone and my black blade," the death-reeking, vile-eyed priest said, joining us.

"But you won't have your way yet," the sister said, smiling, stroking my hair. "Not if the pup does my bidding." She turned to the high priest and said sternly, "My brother and this old stargazing fool favor him. They think he can help with their idiotic calendar, so you'll leave the youth alone. Understand?"

The high priest treated the sister to a mean, mirthless smile. "He'll come to grief with me."

"Hurt the youth, you answer to me," she said coldly. She turned and stroked my cheek with blood-chilling tenderness. "You will do my bidding, won't you?"

"If I can be of service."

"He did not answer yes," the blood-reeking holy man observed.

"This coyotl pup has pride. I give you that. But never fear, malodorous cleric. I'll bring him to heel."

Tugging at my cheek with a playful display of mock affection, she pinched it so hard it almost bled, and I almost yelped . . . but I didn't. Instead I locked my eyes on hers, silent, unblinking, my features impassive.

"Just remember, pup," she said, still pinching the tortured flesh. "Pride precedeth the fall."

"He's had a hard day," the Knight said.

"You'll have hard days and harder nights to come," she said. "If you're up to it, pup." She returned her attention to the Knight. "Now tell me more about your travels."

Taking his arm, she escorted him to the octli platform and helped them each to a cupful.

"Well, Cicatrice, you've met the sister," Stargazer said. "What do you think now?"

"I've never seen such eyes."

"What did they remind you of?"

"Thunder, lightning, war."

"You were staring into the grave—your grave, if you are not careful."

"But she's so stunning."

"For a pit viper."

"When she touched my hair I almost fainted."

"Beware the bloodthirstiness of great beauty."

"I can't take my eyes off her," I said, watching her at the octli platform.

Stargazer studied me in silence. "I'm trying to educate the fool out of you," he finally said, "but I fear it's buried too deep."

Desert Flower appeared at my side.

"That woman scares me," she said.

"You're the only one with any sense."

"And she's not going away," I said. "That's a fact of life."

I tossed off another full cup of octli.

"But I am," Stargazer said. "Since you ignore all my advice, I have nothing more to teach."

Out of the corner of my eye, I saw the king's sister begin conversing energetically with the bloody priest. Our Knight used that diversion as an excuse to slip away.

"I heard you say you have nothing more to teach," he said to the old man. "Here endeth the lesson?"

"Night falls and my bones are old."

"Those bones held up well on the trek."

"But now they need rest. You young people must deal with this den of degenerates."

"What do *you* want after a long, hard trek?" Smoking Shield asked me. "Drink, food, peyote, women?" He helped himself to a long pull from his octli cup. "Come, Cicatrice, the night is young."

"I wish to see my six stars."

20

"I want to see his stars too," Smoking Shield said, and to my astonishment he followed us out of the palace. I had no idea where we were headed nor did I, as yet, know the city. To me, Tula was still a blind labyrinth of intersecting streets, alleyways, and avenues, surrounded by thousands of buildings, surmounted by towering temples.

Our torches, the street braziers, and even the stars above provided some light, and slowly the streets became more familiar. In the distance, the Pyramid of the Sun finally loomed over the rooftops.

Smoking Shield continued to imbibe octli from a drinking skin fashioned from a peccary bladder—which he slung from one shoulder by a leather strap—while Stargazer directed us toward that destination.

Every so often Stargazer helped himself to Shield's octli supply.

We were approaching the slave cages close by the pyramid. Escorting Flower and me up to Tenoch's cage, Smoking Shield pointed to our former master, who lay prone on the cage floor, bloodied and beaten. His loincloth was shredded, and he had lost weight. Shield picked up a small stone and tossed it through the bars. Bouncing off Tenoch's head, it woke him.

"Awake, slave," our warrior-knight said.

Tenoch opened a livid bloodshot eye.

"I can't say I'm sorry to see you in your fallen state," Shield said. "You are a dog, you know. Torturing and raping defenseless slaves, tormenting anyone and anything less powerful than you—to you it's a way of life. In fact, your behavior is worse than any dog's. You still spurn and spit on us, a mad dog attacking its master. Do you know what we do with mad dogs here, Tenoch?"

"We put them down," Stargazer said.

Tenoch stared at us in silent defiance.

"I see three possible destinies for you: death in the stone quarries, death at the stone, or Death by Knife and Fire," the warrior said.

Tenoch looked puzzled at that last possibility.

"Oh, the beast has never heard of Knife and Fire," our warrior-knight said. "Well, one of our priests scalps and flays you, then slowly carves you into little pieces. While your heart still beats, he cuts out your tongue, tears out your finger- and toenails, trusses up your arms and legs, stuffs your amputated genitals into your bloody mouth, then hangs you by your pain-racked feet from a pole-tripod over a slow-burning fire."

"One good thing," Stargazer said. "The fire will cauterize your scalpless head."

"The one priest who specializes in this ritual," the warrior continued, "takes singular pleasure in it. Do you know why?"

Tenoch stared at our warrior-knight, silent.

"Tell him, old man," Shield said.

"He enjoys eating the man's roasted flesh," Stargazer said, staring unblinkingly at Tenoch, "in front of the man before he dies. Yes, Tenoch, given the wickedness of your life, Death by Knife and Fire is the most poetically just possibility. Were it up to me, that fate would be a foregone conclusion, but that decision belongs to this warrior, not me, since he captured you."

"Think on your options, beast," Smoking Shield said. "I'm leaning hard toward the blade and the flame." He treated Tenoch to a scintillating sneer.

"We all are," Stargazer said.

The old man and Shield led us away from the slave cages and Tenoch's fiery stare. The two of them were up front, laughing hysterically at Tenoch's fate. I stayed back with Flower, who silently shook. She bit her lip to keep from sobbing.

I would never understand how or why she cared so deeply for others when so few people in our Clan had cared for her. Nor would I understand why she cared what Shield and Stargazer did to the foul fiend, Tenoch, who had abused her so viciously and deserved whatever misery he got.

But perhaps, I thought idly, *gratuitous cruelty is easier to fathom than unrequited compassion.*

21

We stood at the base of the Great Pyramid of the Sun. If earlier, from the terrace's edge, the temple had seemed big as a mountain, up close it was vertiginously vast, of almost preternatural proportions. The slope to the summit stretched many hundreds of paces—greater in length than the tlachtli ballfield—the upward angle impossibly steep. When Stargazer unexpectedly began his climb, I did not believe he would survive those steps, nor did I expect him to maintain a running monologue.

While the rest of us panted and gasped our way to the top, Smoking Shield talked.

"Young Cicatrice, at the temple's summit sits not just a sacrificial altar but the finest observatory in all the world."

"We need to keep it up there," Stargazer explained. "In case you haven't noticed, Tula is not well suited for stargazing. A city of smoke and flame, it is ubiquitously ablaze with torches, braziers, and stoves, to say nothing of our innumerable religious fires. To fuel these countless conflagrations—these ceremonial, sacrificial, celebratory, revelatory, birth, marriage, and death fires—our priests have stocked this city with mountainous lumber piles. You want to study the stars in Tula? Be my guest. But the whole place is choked with smoke. Only on these hallowed heights can you transcend the haze."

"In other words," I said, "you've turned the Feathered Serpent's temple into your own private observatory."

"With our king's blessing," Smoking Shield said.

"What of Quetzalcoatl's blessing?" I asked. "The god Quetzalcoatl, that is."

"Is he not the god of learning, science, writing, drawing, language, numbers, and mathematics?" Stargazer said.

"As well as travel, curiosity, compassion, adventure, the wind, and the sea," our warrior grunted breathlessly. "To say nothing of the stars."

"Wherever Quetzalcoatl resides, he is pleased," Stargazer said.

"A toast to Quetzalcoatl," our warrior-knight said, lifting his octli skin.

"I could do with a drink," I said.

He handed me the drinking sack, and I helped myself to a pull.

"It tastes like buzzard piss drunk out of boar tracks," I said.

"It has been too long in that peccary bladder," Stargazer acknowledged.

"Our fault for not drinking faster," Smoking Shield said.

"I think you have a problem," Stargazer said, pointing at Shield's octli skin.

"I sure do, old man. I'm hollow to my heels."

"Maybe you should give it up," Stargazer said, attempting to wrest the octli sack away from Shield.

"We have four hundred gods consecrated to drink and drunkenness," the warrior said. "We have to honor them."

"Four hundred?" I repeated, skeptical.

"An unfortunate fact," Stargazer said, shaking his head.

"They feel slighted if we do not toast them all," the warrior said, raising his peccary drink-bladder, and offering up another toast: "To the gods of drink!"

"Let me help," I said. Grabbing the sack, I took another swallow, saying, "Again, to Quetzalcoatl."

The warrior had another drink in honor of the Feathered Serpent.

The old man shook his head wearily.

"Why so many steps?" I asked.

"The builders constructed 360 steps—one for each day of our solar calendar, the Haab," Shield said.

"That's 360 *official* days," Stargazer corrected.

"What are the unofficial days?" I said.

"Five more days added on to the year's end," Stargazer said. "We call those the Wayeb', the nameless days. We consider those a dangerous time, the period during which the portals between the mortal world and the Underworld fade. It is a time when deleterious deities roam the earth."

"Why don't you make it 365 days and abolish the Wayeb'?" I asked.

"That number is not divisible by the number of our months," Stargazer said.

"That's no answer," I said.

"The number's inconvenient," our warrior said.

I stopped in midstep and stared at both men.

"What's the real reason?"

The two men stopped, stared at each other, and shrugged. They started back up the steps.

I stopped again. "Well?" I asked.

"Don't ask me questions I can't answer," Stargazer muttered under his breath.

"You're here to answer questions, not ask them," our warrior said.

Desert Flower had begun to giggle. I suddenly realized that our warrior had been sharing his octli with her as well.

An inconvenient number . . . I mused.

I helped myself to another drink.

We were now standing before the last flight of five steps, which was nearly vertical. Nonetheless, the warrior, octli bladder in tow, still managed to clamber to the top. Reaching a hand down over the side, he helped to pull Stargazer up while I pushed from below. Desert Flower went next, and I took up the rear.

When everyone was on top, I turned and surveyed Quetzal-coatl's domain. From this god's-eye view, Tula was even more magnificent than it had first appeared—thousands of alabaster buildings, hundreds of straight wide thoroughfares joined by intersecting streets and alleys, the magnificent ball court, the treasury buildings, the palace, and scores of temples, many of which were toweringly pyramidal.

And, yes, I saw now that Stargazer was right. An infinity of fires lit up Tula, like miniature stars searing the earth.

I finally turned to study the summit. Massive turquoise and pyrite mosaics, featuring the Feathered Serpent's likeness, fronted the twin sanctuaries.

"Look inside," Stargazer said.

He escorted me into the first sanctuary. Skulls hung on most of the walls and were mounted on racks. In between the wall-skulls hung the priests' sacrificial obsidian knives. The far wall was empty save for two poles—each an arm's length long—notched together in an X-pattern, the X's joint tightly secured by a rawhide thong.

Crossing the room, Stargazer removed the wooden X from the wall and escorted me out of the sanctuary.

"Come," the old man said, leading us around the building.

The far side of the sanctuary was edged with a series of sculpted stone serpents, bas-reliefs featuring eagles and jaguars and more Feathered Serpent mosaics. All of them served as hand- and footholds, which allowed the four of us to scale the wall. The warrior ascended first, and I went second. Ironically, it was easier to climb than the stairway's final flight of near-vertical steps.

The stone roof was empty and flat save for a single upright pole at its center, which I'd assumed to be decorative. Stargazer walked us over to it. A mount with a hollow cylindrical base fitted over the pole's top. The mount had a notched top of its own, and I now saw that through a series of pole holes the top mount could be raised and lowered. A peg inserted into the holes, braced the mount, and determined its elevation.

When Stargazer rotated it in one complete circle, I saw that the pole top could be adjusted for sighting.

"So the young man wishes to spy on the gods," our warrior-knight said to the old man. "Give him a look."

Stargazer adjusted the star-viewer until he had bracketed the World Tree's Dark Rift.

"Step up," the old man said, and I took his place on the viewing stone.

Locked between the poles were my cicatrices, focused hard and sharp, possessed of an almost blinding clarity—a clarity never achieved on the earth below with the naked eye.

A clarity so stunning it weakened my knees.

"So what do you think of your stars?" the warrior said. "You've carried them on your belly your whole young life. They convinced the old shaman to let you live."

"They are me," I said.

"But what are they to us?" Stargazer asked.

"They frame the Dark Rift," I said. "They're the entrance to the Underworld Road."

"Some say they are the pathway to Mictlantecuhtli's Shadow-land, where the hounds of hell howl perpetually," Stargazer said.

I said, "You told me that on the Last Day Tezcatlipoca—the black god of death and the everlasting night—will free those hounds and smash those gates. He and his infernal beasts will scorch the Under-world Road and scourge the earth—and their final scorching scourge will be our Last Day, the One-World's Last Day."

"I've bad news for you, young friend," Stargazer said. "The prophecy of Tezcatlipoca's wrath is coming to pass. I have seen him emerging out of your six stars, out of the Dark Rift and the Under-world Road. I have seen him twice."

"He is coming for us," Smoking Shield said. "Tezcatlipoca and his hounds of hell."

"Why?"

"Tezcatlipoca," Stargazer said, "defeated the Divine Quetzalcoatl—the white god of learning and compassion, of divine wind and life-sustaining sea—in the heavens long before humankind was born. But on earth—especially among our people—the peace-loving, knowledge-seeking Feathered Serpent holds sway. An envious and vindictive deity, Tezcatlipoca will no longer be placated by our throbbing hearts and life's blood. He comes to slay Quetzalcoatl, his emissary, the god-king and his devoted votaries. He will not rest content until he kills the Feathered Serpent's incarnation and obliterates us all—until we are all consigned to the everlasting void, the infinite night, and the One-World is erased from the earth."

"So can we," Smoking Shield asked, "break the code, crack the conundrum, and stave off the eternal wrath of the black god?"

"You must," Stargazer said.

"I shall," I said.

"I wish I had your certitude," the old man said.

"I'm different, Stargazer. As you say, I carry these orbs not only on my belly, but in my bowels, in my balls, in my brain, in my heart, in my soul."

"The stars are *you?*" the warrior asked.

"They are my . . . destiny."

"Then what do these stars say to you?" the old man asked.

"They say that my destiny cries out."

"Cicatrix," the warrior said, "I fear now they are our stars too; that we are all in this together."

"Then *our* destiny cries out," I said, helping myself to the octli skin.

Our warrior raised his drink sack to Quetzalcoatl. Stargazer, Desert Flower, and I joined in the libation.

"Now we have a tale for you, Cicatrix," Smoking Shield said. "You have an amazing memory—the finest I have ever seen. We want you to apply it now. Eventually you will learn the sacred glyphs and commit this tale to amal paper and the urn, but in the meantime listen."

"Remember everything we tell you," Stargazer said. "When you and I complete the calendar, you will know your glyphs, and you will record for all time what we will tell you tonight. Though the calendar will tell our people the *when* of the End-Time, even the exact day, it will not tell the *how*. To correct that omission, the Feathered Serpent—in his divine wisdom—has spoken to his god-king, our lord, Quetzalcoatl. Without that sacred vision of the end, the calendar does the world no good."

"We are entrusting you with his vision," Shield said to me.

"The calendar as well," Stargazer said. "Write them with all your skill and protect them well—with all your might."

"Why me?" I asked.

"You are young and strong and may just survive the violence to come," Stargazer said. "I, on the other hand, am old, my days numbered."

"What of you?" I asked Shield.

"I am a soldier surrounded by enemies," Shield answered. "And I am sworn to protect and stay with my king at all times and at all costs."

"Shield is also much hated by our priests," Stargazer said. "And as adjutant to our king, his life is even more precarious than mine."

"But why *me*?" I asked, still confused.

"Ask your six stars," the old man said. "Your six stars command your fate, Cicatrix. Not us."

"Your fate is to transcribe the god-king's prophesy of the Last Day and the Long Count. Carry these codices to safety and protect them for all people and for all time," Smoking Shield said.

"From this day forth, you shall be Coyotl—Bearer of the Word," Stargazer said.

"Whom must I protect these works from?" I asked.

"The priests," Smoking Shield said.

"We are at war with the priests?" I asked.

"They will want the god-king's vision, his sacred calendar, his very memory erased from the earth," Smoking Shield said.

"Why?"

"Our lord, Quetzalcoatl, plans in the near future to outlaw human sacrifice, to abolish the priests' reign of terror with a single decree," Smoking Shield explained. "They will not surrender their bloody power without a fight."

"They will whip up the multitude till blood inundates the streets, and Mictlantecuhtli's hell reigns," Stargazer predicted.

"But enough questions," Shield said. "Open your ears and remember. Prepare for Quetzalcoatl's tale."

"Listen well," Stargazer said. "You must carry this first in your heart and brain, in your bowels and blood. Then you must record it in your sacred book."

"Here," Shield said, offering me a libation from his octli skin. "Pig piss or not, you'll need this. It is hardly an edifying tale."

The old man took a deep breath. "Thus the tale begins. . . ."

PART VIII

22

I woke up with a start. A room in the astronomer's quarters was my
new home. I was on the second floor and through the window I
could see the courtyard. I had the room to myself—an incompara-
ble luxury among my people—as well as new clothes and possessions, which were stacked neatly near the window.

My head still spun with King Quetzalcoatl's fiery vision, the one
which our god, the Feathered Serpent, had vouchsafed him. It still
rang in my ears, and I would be with Stargazer atop the Pyramid of
the Sun listening to him, the words blazing and smoking in my
brain . . . always. No longer Coyotl, the wretched Aztec slave, he'd
renamed me *Coyoltl, Bearer of the Word*. The six stars blazoned across
my belly had saved my life as a babe and now made me a scientist
and a scribe. I would learn the sacred glyphs, record the blazing vision. Finding a permanent repository for it, I would hide and protect it from our innumerable enemies. I would begin my study of
the sacred glyphs this very day.

Also my brain rang and my bladder groaned from the prodigious
amount of octli I'd consumed. Luckily I remembered a closed corner
pot that Stargazer had placed in my room for urination. Staggering

up to it, I lifted the lid and made generous use of it, then limped back to my sleeping place. I was indescribably exhausted.

But as soon as I lay down, my head rang again—this time with all the horrors of Mictlantecuhtli's hell. The most portentous sound any Aztec can hear was searing me to my soul: *An owl was calling my name.* The night owl was dreaded above all other beasts, not only for physical fearsomeness but because his presence presaged death. Fire Eyes, the old shaman who'd raised me, warned me of this fiend, telling me to shun the owl above all beasts, that the owl despised me, was my lifelong nemesis, and was determined to take my life. I feared the owl above all the creatures of the earth.

Shrieking my name again, he sounded so close he seemed in my room, almost in my bed. I was too frightened to fight off his attack. Burying my face in my sleeping mat, I tried instead to hide from him, my entire body convulsing.

But then a guardian goddess entered my room and lay down with me on my mat, her arms embracing my body as she whispered:

"It's all right. You can go back to sleep now."

"It was no nightmare," I whispered. "The owl called my name."

"Was it the hooting of an owl or the mourning of a dove?" she asked.

A mourning dove? Their cry was similar to the owl's, but I was positive the shriek had been an owl's. Rolling me over, however, Desert Flower pointed to my window, and there on the ledge perched a mourning dove. As if to dispel my fears, the gentle bird emitted her mournful call again.

"You see, master, it was only the gentle dove."

She continued to hold me close even after my tremors subsided. Her arms, body, and soothing voice were palpably pleasurable, unlike anything I'd ever experienced before—but then I'd never experienced a woman's embrace. Not since my mother had held me to her bosom before placing me in a reed basket and entrusting my fate to the god of wind and water, to my own personal savior and deity: Quetzalcoatl, the Feathered Serpent.

I turned to gaze on my benefactress.

And she'd called me "master?"

"Desert Flower," I said, "I'm not your master."

"You've sold me to another man?"

"Of course not."

"Smoking Shield and Stargazer both told me I am your slave, that I was to . . . take care of you."

"I've been a slave. No one should ever own another person. I will never own another person."

"Do not tell that to Smoking Shield or the astronomer. Promise me."

"Why?"

"Believing I do not please you, they will sell me to someone else."

"They would have to sell me too," I said. Turning to face her, she continued to hold me.

Now I could see she was trembling.

"If I am not your slave," she said, "what am I?"

"I hope I'm your friend."

"As I am yours."

She placed one hand behind my head, her face on my neck, and her other hand . . . between my legs. I'd never felt so much electric pleasure in my life.

"You don't have to do this," I said. "I know Tenoch brutally abused you, and it was terrible."

"But you too have been beaten and abused, and you are not cruel."

"I don't own you, Desert Flower. You can do as you wish."

"And I wish to please you, master."

"The experience would bring back memories of Tenoch."

"Your gentleness will erase those memories, will heal me at the broken places and make me whole."

"I don't want to hurt you."

"Hurt me? You do not know the meaning of hurt."

"I've been hurt, Flower. You know that."

"I don't think so. Here, I'll show you what hurt is like." Glancing around the room, she spotted a new pair of sandals with tough rawhide soles. She jumped up and brought them over to me. Throwing herself over my lap, she said, "This is what hurt is. Go on, hurt me. See what it is like to hurt someone."

I gave her bottom a couple of gentle pats.

"I said to hurt me." I gave her two more. "Are you a baby?" she said, her voice raspy. "Hit me like a *man*, like a master."

Her tone was urgent. She'd grown rigid, almost angry, so I did as I was told. I walloped her a half-dozen times—not as hard as I could, but hard enough to turn her bottom red. I then lifted her up and sat her on my lap. Her eyes were brimming with tears, and her face looked forlorn.

"Hurt?" she said. "You still think you hurt me."

"Yes."

She stared at me in silence. "You know *nothing* about hurt," she finally said.

What was she getting at? Did she want to be the master? Did she want to find out what that was like? Suppose I let her have that experience? Would it purge her of Tenoch's shameful abuse?

"Do you want to show me?" I asked.

She stared at me, unbelieving. "I am a slave. I am a victim."

"Then see what it's like to abuse. Would you like to?"

Tears still flowing from her eyes, she nodded twice. "Yes, just once."

I climbed over her lap. Pulling my loincloth down around my knees, she rubbed my bottom curiously.

"I have wondered what it would be like."

She gave me tentative pats, each one a little harder than the last. Clearly, however, she was afraid to hurt me. Believing her incapable of inflicting true hurt, I decided that in order to let her experience part of what it might feel like to be the master, I'd have to provoke her.

"Oh, I don't think Tenoch ever hurt you unless you deserved it," I said, baiting her.

"It isn't true," Flower said.

"You're just a whiny, self-pitying little girl looking for sympathy. You don't really care about other people."

"Don't say that."

"You don't care about anyone but yourself. You're making all that up. You just want to wallow in self-pity."

"Don't say that," Flower said, becoming increasingly frustrated.

"If Tenoch really hurt you, show me. Pretend I'm you, and you're Tenoch," I said. "Show me how your former master did it."

She said nothing, but I could feel her rage building.

"You can't show me anything, because Tenoch never did anything to you."

I could feel the fury seething in her.

"You need a man like Tenoch to keep you in line. Perhaps I shall whip you every night."

I could hear the steam coming out of her ears.

"From now on I'll be Tenoch and punish you every time you're an ungrateful, dishonest, deceitful, whiny, sniveling—"

Her eyes were now flooding tears of rage. She could not believe that her gentle master was treating her so cruelly. She needed no further exhortations. Turning into a hound of Mictlantecuhtli, she hit my bottom like she was possessed—until my own eyes teared with the pain. Nor would she let me go. When I tried to break loose, she flung a leg over the back of my legs, clamped her ankles together. Gripping with a leg-lock, she grabbed my hair and shouted:

"I'll show you what Tenoch did! I'll show you what *hurt* is!" She then hit even harder—until her arm would no longer move.

We lay on our sides, facing each other, our faces streaked with tears. She'd beaten me so badly my face and chin trembled. She was coming to her senses, and, realizing what she'd done, was scared out of her wits.

"You are no longer a slave," I said after I got my voice back.

"Anything I do to you, you can do back. You are in charge as much as I am. You have the power."

"I can do *anything* I want?" she whimpered.

"You have the power."

"Then I want to do *this*."

Eyes still tearing, she caressed my ears, throat, chest, and stomach with her tongue, lips, and torrid breath. Pausing at my navel, she probed and palpated that minute enclave in a curious foreshadowing of coitus. Over my abdomen her tongue and lips traversed, then languidly worked their way over the inside of my thighs, then with infinite indolence peregrinated back up.

When she finally reached the immensity of my member, she held it with both hands. Staring at me with expressive ebony eyes, she said in a quavering voice:

"It's so huge . . ."

Its enormity did not deter her. Tonguing it assiduously, her mouth circumnavigated its tingling extremity.

To my utter shame, my ungrateful friend began drizzling and spurting immediately—so much so even her agile mouth could not contain his emissions. Nonetheless, she persevered, even as my lust streamed out her mouth and down her chin.

Now I'd reached a fatal conundrum: I was ready to explode, and I'd promised not to hurt her. Painful as it was, I began pulling him out of her mouth—with every nerve in my body resisting—but she refused to let him loose. Instead, she held him tight, accelerating her lips' and tongue's gyrations. Raising her gaze, her wide unblinking eyes locked on mine, even as her head bobbed up and down, frantically, ferociously, her tongue tantalizing my member like a fluttering flock of hummingbirds. Simultaneously she rubbed his bottom half with her right hand, while her left hand secretly slipped under my legs, where it cupped and cuddled my avocados.

She would not let me free, and I had no choice.

She had mastered me physically; now she was dominating me sexually.

I had emancipated her all too well.

Against my will, I exploded, and I could not have been more ashamed. This beautiful young woman was now treating me with more affection than all the other women I'd known in my entire life put together, and in return all I could do was sully her with lust. All my years of pain and humiliation—to say nothing of enforced celibacy—detonated out of me in an obscenely powerful orgasm.

Desert Flower tried heroically to hold my emissions. Gagging, however, a considerable quantity of it flooded her cheeks and chin. Instead of stopping, however, she only redoubled her efforts, and at that point I lost all control. Racked with guilt, I lay back and submitted to her against my will, coming over and over and over.

The final orgasms were so fiercely numerous, the agony of my ecstasy forced me to shut my eyes. When I was finally able to open them, her mouth was still wrapped around my member, but now she slowly, gently stroked him, as if attempting to soothe and comfort our trembling friend. Her lips, cheeks, chin, even hair were awash in my milky semen, yet her wide obsidian eyes peered tremulously into mine, sad and sensual as an injured doe's—yet so inexpressibly beautiful they broke my heart.

Slowly, she eased herself up until she was on top of me. She opened her mouth, placed it over mine and speared me with her tongue. She laved my lips with her own, the fluid I'd so copiously bestowed on her leaking into my mouth.

When we finally paused for a breath, she asked, "Is it true that anything I do to you you will do to me?"

"Of course."

She guided my head down her throat, breasts, navel, crotch, and lissome loins. I was clumsy at first, but soon intuited that gentle was more arousing than rough. Circling the nub of her joy at first, I slowly, gradually crossed and crisscrossed it, inflaming her desire with tiny tender strokes, teasing out the cunning conundrums within, in the end ruthlessly grinding and ramming my tongue over her pleasure point in a mocking simulacrum of coition. Her hips levitated, pumped, and writhed hysterically against my brutal tongue and lips.

When her many orgasms at last subsided, she tried to push my head away, pleading that her button was too tired and sensitive for more abuse. I then did become a true monster, forcing her against her will to endure more prurient punishment, until her little bud reawoke and her hips again undulated in ecstasy.

After that my memories faded a little. I remember she attempted to slip under me for my first efforts at intercourse, but I stopped her, saying:

"Anything I do to you, you do to me, right?"

"Yes?" she said timorously.

Lying on my back, I hoisted her body up above my manhood and gently lowered her over him.

"You're in charge," I said.

"Yes," she said, her eyes shutting in ecstasy. "I'm not a slave. I'm not a slave."

"You have—?"

"The power!" she half sobbed, half groaned.

Eyes squeezed shut, lips locked in a half grin, half grimace, she began what would be the longest, hardest ride of her life.

Of mine too.

Desert Flower would never be a slave again.

Nor would I.

23

I'd barely fallen back asleep when Flower awoke me. She had a beautiful black obsidian blade, its ebony handle inlaid with turquoise and silver. She was holding it near my throat.

"You can tell them I died happy," I said.

"It's not for you. When I went down to get your breakfast, I heard Shield and Stargazer talking. They are sentencing Tenoch to the blade and the blaze—a thousand cuts, then hung by the feet over a scorching fire. They are serious."

"So?"

"Nobody deserves that, not even *him*."

"What am I supposed to do?"

"His cage is not far. You can get there before sunup. Slip the knife to him. Let him escape."

"I don't know . . ."

"Please, I will never ask you for anything again. You must do it. I hate the priests with their sacrifices, these vicious tortures, their infinite cruelty. No man should suffer the blade and the blaze, not even Tenoch."

"We can't stop evil everywhere," I replied.

"True, but we can stop this."

She handed me the obsidian blade, a new loincloth and sandals, and a small loincloth in which to conceal the blade.

"Go with Queztalcoatl," she said.

"And to the temple stone when they catch me," I muttered under my breath.

But she was the kindest, most compassionate creature I would ever know.

I could deny her nothing.

I stepped out of the astronomer's house into Tula's gray, predawn streets.

PART IX

24

Dr. Cardiff began her oral presentation:

"Four months ago a former student of mine—an archeologist named Rita Critchlow—stumbled across an eleven-hundred-year-old Toltec Codex on a dig in Chiapas, Mexico. She asked me for help interpreting part of it—some highly specific ninth-century astronomical sightings. An ancient Toltec astronomer had spotted an extraterrestrial object in the vicinity of what we call Sagittarius and their astronomers called *Chan*, or the Rattlesnake. He tracked the object until it abruptly vanished.

"A month later I spotted an interplanetary object in the same astronomical grid. My sighting squared exactly with the old astronomer's. Moreover, my object vanished just as his had."

"Any idea what happened to it?" Bradford asked.

"My preliminary readings indicated that the object was arcing toward our planet; the ancient Toltec had come to the same conclusion. He named his object Tezcatlipoca—the Toltec god of the endless night; of darkness, war, and death. He believed Tezcatlipoca was heading toward us to wreak hell on earth."

"And you believe the two objects are somehow related?" General Hagberg asked.

"They could be one and the same, and that Tezcatlipoca—which I call Sagittarius-X—*is* returning for a visit."

"Like Halley's comet?" Bradford asked.

"Precisely," Dr. Cardiff said. "Except the one I tracked was no comet, nor did the old astronomer describe his as one."

"And this object may represent a threat?" General Hagberg asked.

"Not long after this ancient astronomer spotted his object coming out of Sagittarius-Chan, his civilization abruptly and inexplicably went extinct."

"And you are suggesting this eleven-hundred-year-old man spotted something cataclysmic, which obliterated Tula and is now coming after us?" General Hagberg asked.

"An asteroid perhaps?" Bradford Chase offered.

"That would be bad indeed," President Raab said.

"In 1989," Dr. Cardiff said, "an asteroid capable of killing tens of millions of people came so close it passed through the exact position earth had been in only six hours before. In 2004 a hundred-foot-wide asteroid, which would have inflicted catastrophic damage, came within twenty-six thousand miles of the earth—one-tenth the distance of the earth to the moon."

"Isn't some monster-asteroid coming near us in 2029?" General Hagberg asked.

"Apophis 99942," Dr. Cardiff said. "On Friday, April 13, 2029, it will pass so close to the planet it will dip below our geosynchronous communications satellites."

"Apo-what?" General Hagberg asked.

"Apophis," Dr. Cardiff said. "An evil Egyptian deity. The enemy of Order, Light, and the Ancient Egyptian god, Ra, his name in Greek is Apep, the Uncreator. A serpent in the underworld, Duat, he dwells in perpetual darkness, attempting to devour Ra each night. Set, the Egyptian god of Chaos, holds him in check."

"He was also an evil alien on the TV series *Stargate SG-1*," General Hagberg said. "I did a little consulting on the show."

"We supposedly aren't at risk from it, however," Bradford Chase said.

"We actually don't know the risk," Dr. Cardiff said. "It's been so close to the sun, we've only been able to track it by radar. We haven't been able to view it through optical telescopes. We know relatively little about its density, composition, and rotation. We're especially ignorant as to how it reflects and absorbs sunlight, which it is receiving in high volume. Solar radiation can radically change its orbit—it's called the Yarkovsky Effect—if it is made of solar-absorbent materials. Passing asteroids can also affect its orbit."

"So we can't precisely predict the orbit," Bradford said, "because we don't know what it is."

"Exactly," Dr. Cardiff said. "We're trying to predict the content of a black box, when we can't see what's inside it."

"How big is this rock?" General Hagberg asked.

"It's one thousand feet across and an estimated twenty-five million tons, rocketing at us at twenty-eight thousand miles per hour," Dr. Cardiff said.

"That's almost as big as Devil's Tower in Wyoming," Bradford said.

"And it packs the punch of sixty-five thousand Hiroshima bombs," Dr. Cardiff said.

"Any idea where it would hit?" Bradford asked.

"Its most likely target would be several thousand miles off the California coast."

"Hope it takes out LA," General Hagberg muttered under his breath.

"I hear it gets a second shot at us," Bradford said.

"It returns in 2036—again on Friday the 13th. Regardless of what pseudo-experts tell you, the return is even more unpredictable. When Apophis passes by the first time, earth will represent its first close encounter with a major gravitational field. Depending on its composition, our gravity, and the tidal forces our gravity inflicts on Apophis, that passing could change not only its orbit but its physical shape. Earth's gravity could give it a major makeover and cause it to hit us on its return."

"I read in one of my reports that it has to pass through the right 'keyhole,'" President Raab said.

"We've extrapolated the existence of several gravitational keyholes. If it passes through one, that keyhole will change its orbit and send it crashing into earth seven years later."

"Why isn't NASA sending up a mission to deflect it?" General Hagberg asked.

"Deflect it to where? Regardless of what our pseudo-experts tell us, we don't know how close it will come to either earth or one of those catastrophic keyholes. We could deflect it straight into earth's orbital path."

"What should we be doing?" Bradford asked.

"We should have sent up a mission to pin a radio transponder on it," Dr. Cardiff said, "so we could accurately calculate its orbital trajectory. We never did that, so we won't know how close it's coming. We'll probably never know."

"But we do know which other asteroids pose a threat," the general said.

"Not really," Dr. Cardiff said, shaking her head. "The world has no effective scientific facilities dedicated solely to asteroid observation. A random assortment of amateurs with backyard telescopes spot them willy-nilly. Hopefully, they find the time to e-mail the findings to whatever observatories strike their fancy. We estimate there are one-thousand and one-hundred asteroids one kilometer across that will pass near the earth. At best we've detected only seventy-five percent of them."

"When will you confirm *your* sightings and finishing charting *your* object's flight path?" General Hagberg asked.

"I may not be able to," Dr. Cardiff said. "I've only been able to follow it by fits and starts. When an asteroid comes straight at you, you don't see it. So if this is a planet-killer, we may not see it until it touches and inflames the atmosphere. But then if we're close enough to see the flames, we still won't be able to report our findings. We'll be dead."

"You're full of all kinds of cheery news," President Raab said.

"If it is an asteroid and it's coming at us," General Hagberg said, "we're royally fucked."

"Like the dinosaurs who gazed at their interplanetary rock," Bradford said.

"Do you think your object *is* an asteroid?" Bradford asked Dr. Cardiff again.

"An asteroid, a flying saucer, an angel of God?" Dr. Cardiff said. "It could be Darth Vader's *Death Star* for all I know now."

"But you believe it wiped out Tula?" Bradford Chase asked.

"Something wiped out Tula," Dr. Cardiff said. "How else do you explain its almost instantaneous disappearance?"

"Tula could have been going through multiple crises," Bradford noted.

"Other crises were undermining Tula and no doubt helped to topple it, but none of them, even in combination, were sufficient to to eradicate it so quickly."

"Great powers are astonishingly resistant to catastrophe and astonishingly difficult to destroy," Bradford Chase said, nodding his agreement. "Germany and Japan were bombed and burned to the ground during World War II, yet they came back stronger than ever. After the Black Death Europe emerged from its Dark Ages even bigger and stronger."

"And Tula was the preeminent power of its age—arguably in Mexico's entire history," Dr. Cardiff said. "Yet something annihilated it overnight."

"But you do acknowledge Tula had other problems," President Raab said.

"Problems frighteningly similar to our own," Dr. Cardiff said. "Their own version of global warming had brought them continual drought and pervasive famine. Their hyperdependence on a single crop, maize, made them uniquely vulnerable to climate change."

"Famine's what finally defeated the American Plains Indians," General Hagberg said. "When Generals Sherman and Sheridan exterminated 99.99 percent of the bison, they had to surrender. They were that inescapably dependent on the buffalo."

"Same with us," Dr. Cardiff said. "If our food base was hammered as hard as Tula's, we'd each have to go a long way for a meal. Your typical meal travels on average fourteen hundred miles to your plate."

"What of Tula's other problems?" President Raab asked.

"A fascistic religious elite was tearing Tula apart," Dr. Cardiff said, "blaming the god Tezcatlipoca for their famine and assuring the masses that only en masse sacrifices to him would bring back the corn. Otherwise Tezcatlipoca would scourge the earth and extirpate the One-World root and branch."

"Tell them about the god-king, Quetzalcoatl," President Raab said.

"The god, Quetzalcoatl—which means 'the Feathered Serpent' in Nahuatl—was Tezcatlipoca's sworn enemy. Their last and greatest ruler was named after him. Known as 'the god-king,' Tula's Quetzalcoatl had been a legendary warlord. Establishing Tula as a land of unparalleled prosperity in which ears of corn grew big as watermelons, and honey and chocolate flowed like rivers, Quetzalcoatl then made Tula an unparalleled center of learning. Bringing the One-World's most gifted scientists, mathematicians, architects, and scholars to Tula, he commissioned the most spectacular architecture on earth—temple designs that the subsequent Mexican emperors could only clumsily and slavishly imitate. His mathematicians and astronomers conceived and completed the final edition and conclusion of their prodigious Long Count Calendar, which predicted that in a little over one thousand years the reign of homo sapiens on earth would come to an abrupt close.

"Around this time, however," Dr. Cardiff said, "Quetzalcoatl discovered compassion as well. If before he'd been a combination of

Alexander the Great and Pericles, he then became the Toltec Jesus Christ. Turning Tula into a peaceable kingdom, he abolished both human sacrifice and the wars they waged to capture and abduct those sacrificial victims."

"The priests must have loved him for that," General Hagberg said.

"They were an insurmountable problem. To bring back imperial wars and human sacrifice, they fomented insurgent uprisings, which exploded into all-out civil war. To stop the killing and save what remained of the kingdom, the god-king abandoned Tula and his people. Setting out in a reed boat, he headed east into the rising sun, promising to one day return."

"So religious fanaticism—along with drought-induced famine—was critical to Tula's collapse?" Bradford Chase said.

"Yes, but those two alone weren't enough to summarily expunge Tula. Also our old astronomer was adamant that Tezcatlipoca is coming out of Sagittarius to purge the earth."

"So what happens next?" the general asked.

"That's where Rita and her 'sister' in archeology, Cooper Jones, come in," Dr. Cardiff said. "Coop's a fellow archeologist and Rita's adopted sister. They believe they can find the second codex, which the first one refers to, and which they believe will describe Tezcatlipoca in specific detail."

"Any chance they might actually find it?" Bradford asked.

"That's why I asked for this meeting. Rita called me last night out of the blue. Cooper had just joined her in the small northern Chihuahua town, near where the first codex claimed the second would be hidden. They weren't there one week when they met a young goatherd who'd discovered it cached in a canyon wall. They found it through sheer serendipity. They've even photographed and translated it. Mr. President, the second round of astronomical observations are identical to my own second-round findings. Tezcatlipoca *is* coming at us."

25

President Raab briefly halted the meeting for a BlackBerry-and-coffee break. When they sat back down, General Hagberg had a question ready:

"What does the old astronomer tell us about whatcha-call-its visit? What should we expect?"

"Tezcatlipoca," Dr. Cardiff said. "He thinks Tezcatlipoca will smash the gate to the Underworld Road—which we see as Sagittarius—free the hounds of hell, then obliterate humankind. Ironically, we view Sagittarius as the gateway to the supermassive black hole at the heart of our galaxy."

"We call it a black hole, but the old astronomer called it hell?" Bradford asked.

"In a sense, yes," Dr. Cardiff said.

"Does the old astronomer say how Tezcatlipoca destroyed Tula?" General Hagberg asked.

"Rita says that story is in the third codex. The codices' author also expected to have the final draft of the Long Count Calendar fully transcribed and would direct the reader to that codex as well."

"Who's the author again?" Bradford asked. "You talk as if an as-

tronomer named Stargazer and King Quetzalcoatl were both con-
tributing to it."

"They both dictated large chunks of it to a scribe named Coyotl,"
Dr. Cardiff said. "He also gave a narrative of his own describing Tula."

"And he wrapped up a third codex and the Long Count Calendar," President Raab said.

Dr. Cardiff nodded. "Yes."

"In other words, we get two codices for the price of a single trip,"
Bradford said.

"If we can find them," the president said.

"You ask me, this Coyotl has a hell of a sense of humor," the general said.

"No, he feared the priests," Dr. Cardiff said, "and was trying to
protect both Quetzalcoatl's vision and calendar from them."

"Well, he was caching them a long, long way from Tula," the
president said. "He put a lot of effort into his work."

"How did Codex Three leave Tula?" General Hagberg asked.

"Rita said the city of Tula was ablaze, its people fleeing in full
panic. The codex, however, only tells us the consequences of Tezcatlipoca's actions. It doesn't describe the actions themselves."

"Not yet," Bradford said. "He was saving that story for part three."

Dr. Cardiff looked up and noticed the three men staring at her.

"What's wrong?" she asked.

"What's wrong with you?" General Hagberg said.

"It's the girls," Cardiff said, leaning back. "I'm putting them in
harm's way."

"This friend of yours—Rita," Bradford said. "She's the one who
got kidnapped in Chiapas. It was in the papers."

Dr. Cardiff nodded, noting that Bradford said it as a statement,
not a question.

"But you didn't tell her to go there either," the president said,
"anymore than you're telling them to go to Chihuahua."

Cardiff shook her head. "I suggested she and Coop go to northern Chihuahua and look around for the second codex. I thought it

was safe, and it would take her mind off the kidnapping. I even sent her some money for the trip."

"But you never told them to go into rebel country," the president said.

"No."

"Except those girls aren't just going into rebel country," General Hagberg said. "That's Apachurero country they're entering."

"That's what got Ms. Critchlow into trouble last time," Bradford said.

How does he know so much? Cardiff wondered, staring at him quizzically.

"Get her back on the phone," General Hagberg said. "Tell her to stay out of southern Chihuahua."

"Rita's got her blood up," Dr. Cardiff said, shaking her head. "You'd have better luck telling a buck wolf to drop a pork chop." She looked at Bradford Chase. "Any way we could have them forcibly abducted?"

"We can't even render terrorists anymore," Bradford said, grimacing.

"We could tell the Mexican government they were up to no good down there rather than see them killed," Cardiff said.

"They *are* up to no good," Bradford said. "Bring the federales into this, they'll jail them for illegal possession and transportation of black-market relics. They take pre-Columbian antiquities seriously down there."

"They're good for at least twenty years," General Hagberg said.

"And those Apachureros still remember how Critchlow got away," General Hagberg said. "A lot of Apachureros got killed."

Cardiff stared at him. How did the general know that? The papers hadn't reported it.

"A lot of officials down there are on the Apachurero payroll," Bradford said. "I'd be very careful about bringing the Mexican government into this."

"What if her sister threatened to go back alone?" the general said.

"Coop will never abandon Rita," Dr. Cardiff said. "Reets knows that."

General Hagberg studied Cardiff thoughtfully. "So it doesn't matter what you do, does it? Your friend 'Reets' is going for it."

Cardiff stared at him silently.

"And we do need the third codex and calendar, right?" the general asked.

"He's got a point, Dr. Cardiff," Bradford said. "Your friends might just pull this off."

By now Cardiff's stare was hard enough to hurt.

"To pull this off," Bradford continued, "you need civilians already in place with a solid cover story."

"Cover story?" Dr. Cardiff asked, incredulous.

"They're a couple of post-doc losers," General Hagberg said, "wandering the desert, looking for traces of lost civilizations. No one would ever take them for intelligence agents and tomb raiders, which is what they are."

"To make this work," Bradford said, "your team would also have to read glyphs, know the local languages, and want to do it really bad. That's critically important. Dr. Cardiff, you'd never get a team with all those skills and attributes on such short notice."

"So the question is what can *we* do," General Hagberg asked, "to help them?"

Again, Cardiff could only stare mutely.

"Brad, put Hargrave and Jamesy back into the game," General Hagberg said.

Cardiff continued her silence. Reets had mentioned those two men by name. They were the cold-blooded mercenaries who'd rescued Reets from the Apachureros—the most ruthless, violent, and politically powerful criminal organization in all of Mexico. Contrary to press reports, Reets had told her privately those two men saved her, not the federales, and that they'd seen far worse violence than anything the press reported. Beyond that, Reets would not comment.

So how had General Hagberg known their names?

" 'Graves and Jamesy," Bradford said contemplatively, using Hargrave's nickname. "That's a thought."

"How are you involved in this?" Cardiff asked Bradford.

"I've had some experience with Graves and Jamesy—also with the Apachureros," Bradford said. "When your friend was kidnapped, the general asked for my assistance."

"And I got to thinking since he and his guys saved Critchlow once before," the president said, "maybe we needed Brad and his boys on the team. That's one of the reasons I asked Brad to join us."

"You didn't run this through the CIA channels?" Cardiff asked.

"At the Agency today 50 percent of the personnel have been there less than five years," Bradford said, "and they're shackled by red titanium tape."

"I wouldn't trust them to carry a dozen eggs across the street," General Hagberg grumbled.

Cardiff stared at the three men in the room. Who were these people? They'd mounted an illegal rescue operation, putting themselves in legal and political jeopardy to save a stranger who'd happened to be her best friend.

Now they were offering to do it all over again . . .

What was going on? What kind of world had she walked into?

And she had judged them according to their clothes and diction.

"Dr. Cardiff," the president finally said, "I'm curious about Ms. Critchlow and Ms. Jones. Who are they?"

"I gave you their CVs, Mr. President."

"I mean as *people*. Brad and I couldn't find out a damn thing about them. No one would talk to the people we sent down there."

Cardiff leaned back in her swivel-recliner and took a deep breath. "They were the most mature, committed, and focused students I've ever known," she finally said. "Reets was the smarter and more garrulous of the two, Cooper the more gifted but withdrawn. A genuine eidetic, she's also a talented artist, born to decipher and replicate hieroglyphs. Her interpretative talent, Reets claimed, was almost clairvoyant, saying Coop read glyphs as if they were tarot cards, channeling their hidden meaning—the author's secret intent. Coop's late mom was Mexican—a full-blooded india actually; natural-born azteca pura. Even though Coop never knew her, Reets wondered if she was channeling her. Whatever the story, Reets said she saw more than lines and pictures and colors in her glyphs."

"What's that supposed to mean?" General Hagberg asked.

"Reets thought Coop was a bona-fide mystic," Dr. Cardiff said. "She once told me over a half bottle of Remy that Coop had 'stared death in its obsidian eye, divined the dark between the stars, and touched the face of God.' At the time I wrote if off to the cognac. When I got to know Coop better, I wasn't so sure."

"I want to know what *you* think of them," President Raab asked.

"I think Coop is . . . eerie."

"I now know less than I knew before," General Hagberg said.

"What about Critchlow?" the president asked.

"She was more cerebral, with an aptitude for astronomy, mathematics, and comparative religion. Since Mexico's pre-Columbian priests were obsessed with those disciplines, Reets's skills were crucially important. Together, they made a formidable team."

"That doesn't explain why they're willing to risk their lives down there," the president said.

"They are simply the most dedicated, disciplined, determined students I've ever known," Dr. Cardiff said. "Mesoamerican studies, particularly the Toltec Era of Quetzalcoatl, is their whole world. They have nothing else."

"They've never wanted husbands, kids, dogs, cars, parakeets, vine-covered cottages?" the president asked.

"Attractive and likable, they draw men, but their work always comes first, second, and third. When men pick up on that, they leave."

"There's no sibling rivalry?" Bradford asked.

"Reets is the only friend Coop's ever had."

"Sounds like there's a lot of *love* there," General Hagberg said.

Dr. Cardiff fixed him with a hard stare. "You're asking if there's anything sexual between them?"

General Hagberg nodded.

"No, but I've wondered about it from time to time. It's something else, though."

"You know *nothing* about their pasts?" the president asked, dubious.

"Not much," Dr. Cardiff said.

Which wasn't completely true. She'd had two brief glimpses of Coop's secret self. The experiences had unnerved her.

❧

Once over coffee, Rita had been holding forth on stellar creation—one of Cardiff's specialties—and Monica didn't like the young girl stealing her thunder. Treating Reets to her signature smirk, she leaned forward until they were nose to nose:

"Stick to what you know, ducks. You're way out of your depth."

"Ducks" was cockney street slang for "prostitute," and Coop had recognized it. Interposing herself between Cardiff and her friend, Coop leaned forward till she was right in Cardiff's face.

"Don't call her a whore, bitch," she hissed back.

At the time, Cardiff had been taken aback not only by the tone but by Coop's gall: To challenge a prof as notoriously ruthless as Cardiff was to court academic ruin. But more than her chutzpah, the glint in Coop's eyes had unsettled her.

Cardiff decided to settle with Reets another time, and within a week she had her chance. At a faculty cocktail party, Rita offhandedly remarked to Cardiff's adoring entourage:

"Science is not only the handmaiden to religion, it's well on its way to becoming the religion."

Cardiff decided to fire back.

"Where did you acquire your antiscientific bigotry? At your snake-

dancing, tongue-speaking childhood revivals? Where does an Appalachian hillbilly get off lecturing me on astrophysics? That is precisely the kind of thinking that incinerated the Mayan Codices and imprisoned Galileo."

Pressing her face close to Rita's, Cardiff gave her most patronizing sneer.

Cardiff read the mute hurt in Rita's eyes—in the tremor of her chin and the blinking of the wet eyes. Ordinarily Monica backed off at such a moment and gloated out her victory in private, but this time she wanted the public humiliation of the young grad student who, like all of them, viewed the scientist as a mortal god.

Pushing Rita aside, however, Coop immediately got in Cardiff's face.

Cardiff would always remember the eyes—eyes that said:

Hurt my friend, and you'll live it out with me.

A voice in the back of Monica's brain said: Don't rile that girl.

For reasons Cardiff never understood, she held no grudge. Continuing to see the two women daily, her respect and affection for them instead mounted.

By the semester's end, Rita and Coops had become the best friends she would ever have.

"Rita and Coop are the two best friends I've ever had," Cardiff said matter-of-factly. "That's what they're like."

"How did you become their adviser?" President Raab asked. "They aren't astrophysicists."

"I was never sure why they sought me out as their adviser, and in a sense you're right: I had no business advising them. I wouldn't have gotten involved except I found their insights into mesoamerican catastrophism—particularly Toltec catastrophism—irresistible. They made me the country's most prominent authority on global catastrophism. I was never exactly sure what I did for them, but I can state those years were prodigiously productive—for all of us. In attempting to determine the etiology of Tula's demise, we studied everything: the effects of global warming, drought, famine, plague, megavolcanism, and megameteor strikes. They educated me on the impact of religious fanaticism, economic oppression, and imperialistic aggression. Now, I fear, my efforts have put them into harm's way."

"Unfortunately," President Raab said, standing, "the National Security Council awaits. Some emergency meeting. Lord knows what."

"We'll do what we can for your girls," Bradford said, also getting up. "In the meantime you might want to take a look at this." He shoved the dossier stamped CLASSIFIED across the table to Cardiff. "The president has kept me inside the loop. As soon as he mentioned the name Cooper Jones, I began a work-up on her." The dossier had Coop's name on the cover. "I couldn't find that much on her, but her old man had an interesting life—most of it in prison. Here's his file jacket. He bootlegged the best 'shine in the entire south, to hear his customers tell it; and it got him killed. His rivals didn't like the competition. This girl grew up with a shotgun under her bed. She's hard trade." He fixed Cardiff with a tight stare. "I don't know about you, but I sure as shit wouldn't fuck with her."

PART X

TULA

26

ONE-WORLD, 1004 A.D.

Fire!

I snapped awake to the pounding of the alarm drum, warning of a fire. The immediate threat, however, was not some far-off fire but the dark shadow coming through my window. My sleeping mat was only two paces from the window, and the intruder flew through it like a big bat, its wings spread, flinging itself onto my supine body. An arm raised, and as I rolled to my right the intruder drove a dagger into the padded mad where I'd lain.

Reaching out as I rolled again away from the attack, my hand landed on something familiar—a star-cross, the X-shaped device carved from stone that Stargazer had just taught me to use. As the intruder pulled his blade from the mat and reared back to strike, I shot up from my prone position and hit him in the face with a jagged edge of the cross.

He screamed and stumbled backward. As I got to my feet the intruder went back out the window, slipping out and dropping from sight.

My room was on the second floor and the man would not have had a soft landing. I rushed to the window and saw that the intruder was quickly on his feet and on the run—but with a limp.

Thank the Feathered Serpent that Desert Flower always returns to her room in the main house, I thought.

Standing next to the window, I realized the drum was still beating. We had two types of drums: those that sounded the time and those that sounded alarm. This one was the fire alarm.

An alarm that had saved my life.

After catching my breath, I headed for the observation platform at the observatory adjacent to the house to find out why the drum was being beat.

There was nothing I could do about the fact someone had tried to kill me. When I reported it to Stargazer, he would assume that he was a thief even though there was little crime in the city.

I knew there was another explanation, one linked to the pattern of stars I wore on my flesh, but I knew no more about how—or why—the scars were placed there than I did when I first recognized them.

Most of all I dreaded telling Stargazer about the attack. Someone had previously tried to kill me with a bow and arrow, and already he knew my life was in jeopardy. He worried about my safety continually, but there was nothing he or I could do to prevent a recurrence.

When I eventually told him of the assault, he would worry himself sick, and he was sick enough already. I hoped to somehow postpone telling him.

Three years had passed since I was taken from the land of the Dog People and brought to the golden city of Tula. Like a caterpillar evolving into a butterfly—though perhaps not a very beautiful butterfly—the years with Stargazer had transformed me from a nomadic Aztec savage to the Royal Astronomer's trusted assistant, and a student and scholar of both the stars and the sacred Toltec glyphs. Our direct superior was King Quetzalcoatl himself, the mightiest god-king of all the One-World.

The reading and replicating of those arcane pictographs was an art I had slowly, painstakingly mastered. True, I had exceptional re-call, but still I'd had to memorize an incomprehensible number of glyphs, possessing not only thousands upon thousands of arcane de-tails but conveying the intricate sounds of thousands of words and their spoken inflections as well.

I then had to translate the Revelations of Quetzalcoatl—as the god-king was conveying them to Stargazer—into these multitudi-nous glyphs. I also had to record Stargazer's final draft of the Great Calendar.

My nights I spent at Stargazer's side. Observing and annotating the star-gods' movements and positions, I continually made notes for the End-Time Calendar. All day I spent poring over my notes and composing the codices.

We also spent considerable time monitoring the Dark Rift, look-ing for Tezcatlipoca arcing toward the earth. Stargazer believed he was coming after us. As Stargazer had said that night on the temple summit, the god of darkness and death was no longer content with human hearts and blood. Having subjugated the divine Feathered Serpent—the white god of learning and compassion, of divine wind and life-sustaining sea—once before in the heaven, Tezcatlipoca now sought to annihilate Quetzalcoatl's earthly emissary—and after that, all people everywhere.

Every night we searched the Dark Rift for another glimpse of Tezcatlipoca journeying toward the One-World. Stargazer had tracked him twice before, and each night we searched the sky for another sign of this earthbound fiend.

We were obsessed with the Last Day—how and when it would transpire. We felt that future generations deserved to know. With enough warning, maybe they could deflect the dark god or mitigate his violence or control its consequences. We did not assume that Tez-catlipoca would defeat Quetzalcoatl a second time and exterminate his followers nor did we concede that the dark god's hate was stronger than Quetzalcoatl's science and learning, his courage and love. With enough preparation and help from humankind, we believed the

Feathered Serpent could prevail. If there was some way to circumvent or deflect the wrath of Tezcatlipoca, future peoples might possess those means.

And we all wanted future peoples to know the story of Tula, the greatest city in history, and the magnificent works the god-king and his devoted followers struggled to achieve—her great advances in architecture, art, science, mathematics, and astronomy, culminating in the Long Count Calendar. We wanted future peoples to know of Quetzalcoatl's struggle against religious barbarism.

Tula's struggles added a personal poignancy to my labors on the Long Count Calendar and prophecy, and added insight to my writing. I felt Tula's story illuminated those other works. The story of her rise and fall was indeed a tragic epic of transcendent triumphs and what we increasingly feared would be devastating defeats. Recording and transmitting the story of Tula's Last Days became my driving passion, my reason for living.

As the years went by, the fruits of my labors piled up. I had completed enough codex sheets to fill many codices, and as Stargazer and I grew closer, and he and Shield became more and more excited about the project, we talked more and more about how best to preserve what was now clearly multiple codices.

First of all we needed a safe place to store them in Tula. Stargazer knew of a subterranean tunnel far beneath the city that could only be entered through a series of surreptitious entrances. That tunnel and its hidden antechamber became the storage site for our work and our most private meeting place.

More and more we also discussed where I should secrete the final codices. We were all at this point so fearful of the priests and their ability to coerce information from the populace, we concluded that the best way to preserve the codices would be in multiple hiding places. At the end of each codex we would tell the reader where he might find the next work. To store these volumes in a single place would make the concealment more difficult and the likelihood of priestly discoverery more probable.

We were desperate that the work be passed on to those who followed. We were informing them not only when humankind would face the Last Day, but *what* our brothers and sisters would face. That knowledge we felt was of crucial importance.

In any event, the codices were our record.

Working all night and all day, I barely slept. Still, I was exhilarated beyond words. I was doing work of transcendent importance.

I also no longer slept on the cold, hard dirt in a temporary maguey leaf and mud hut, or on the ground with the sky as my roof, but on a soft mat in the Temple of the Stars.

For most of my life I had squatted beside a cooking fire to eat, but now I sat at a table and enjoyed a rich array of meats and vegetables provided by servants who held a bowl for me to wash my hands before I touched food—and again after I had finished my meal.

I was an assistant skywatcher now, no longer an apprentice, and more important, Stargazer—who had lost his family years before to a virulent plague—had come to view me as a son. In return, he was giving me the family and home I'd never had.

The Temple of the Stars was the home, palace, and observatory of the Royal Astronomer and all those who assisted or served him. Most families in the compound shared two rooms—one for sleeping, the other for cooking and eating. Having no family of my own, I had only a single room and was privileged to take my meals at Stargazer's table.

The astronomy complex was in the Ceremonial Center, only steps from the main pyramid-temple where the high priest presided over the religious rituals of the government and people. On the opposite side of the pyramid-temple from the compound was the magnificent palace of the god-king Quetzalcoatl.

Every hour of the day and night an astronomy assistant kept watch of the heavens in order to advise the city of the passage of time. When the Sun God was in the sky, the assistant watched the shadow created against notches when the sun's rays were cast against a small wooden peg. At night, the assistant on duty observed

and measured the progress of the main star-gods* by using the same type of star-cross with its X-shape with which I had wounded the assassin.

Stargazer and I were responsible, among other things, for Tula's time announcements to the citizenry. Day and night the drum was lightly pounded once at the beginning of each hour. People measured their working day according to the beating of the Time Drum, and it also helped the watchmen on the city walls calculate when the guards should change shifts.

An hour after dawn, the drum was beat hard three times to let all the people know that it was the start of the workday. Twelve hours later, before the sun went down, the drums were again beaten three times to signal the close of the workday.

The only other time the drums were beaten was to alert the city in emergencies. The greatest emergency would have been barbarians at our gates, yet despite the constant pressure of the Dog People, that had not happened . . . yet.

The rapid beating of the drum signaled fire, and we'd had an extraordinary number of blazes for over a year—an epidemic of conflagrations that had raged across the land.

From the rhythm of the drumbeat I knew that the fire was not in the city itself, but somewhere beyond the city walls. Fire was a constant threat in our borderlands, where the barbaric Aztecs pushed against our civilized boundaries. The savages often set diversionary fires, designed to draw villagers and warriors away from nearby cities so they could raid and pillage them.

Not all fires were deliberate. Some started accidentally from campfires set by hunters and others were made by the Tlalco, the rain god who also sent down lightning. Tlalco was so much more generous with sky-fire than with rain, and the forests so desiccated

---

* Translator's Note: The main "star-gods" were the five planets visible to the naked eye: Mercury, Mars, Venus, Jupiter, and Saturn. Like the Greeks and Romans, the ancient mesoamericans knew that these five celestial objects were different than other "stars."

from the countless years of drought, I secretly wondered if Tlalco had changed and became a fire god.

Even our maize fields—particularly in the spring and early summer—were so chronically dried out they were little more than tinder-beds waiting for a spark. And with the maize fires came famine.

The priests blamed our god-king Quetzalcoatl. Their followers had, as my friends had predicted, become increasingly rebellious—especially when rumors leaked out that King Quetzalcoatl looked unfavorably on human sacrifice. The priests, who profited from the prolific sacrifices, were quick to encourage these criticisms of our king.

Feeding the resentment of the priests and their followers were the northern barbarians' hit-and-run fire raids. Drought and these arson raids had driven our people even closer to Tula, forsaking their farms for safety's sake and abandoning what little was left of our arable land to the Aztecs, all of which aggravated our food shortages.

The unending drought and these food shortages also played into the hands of the priests, who argued that Toltec sacrilege—particularly that of the king—was the cause of the gods-inflicted drought and the mounting food scarcity.

My former people did most of the raiding, but I felt no guilt. I no longer saw myself as an Aztec/Dog Person. In fact, I preferred to forget my primitive past. I was a privileged member of the household of one of the most powerful men in the empire. My present life was infinitely more preferable.

My life was not without its drawbacks, though. After two assassination attempts, I was obviously in some jeopardy. Also, my personal and professional lives were not particularly stable. I had not married because of my own fears and uncertainties about my past, as well as the massive commitment my work required. I knew from the way I was treated, both by Stargazer and the king, that my path in life was different. Where it would take me I did not know, but until I was assured of stability I did not want a home and family.

Instead of a marriage mat, I satisfied myself from time to time

with Desert Flower, whom I now saw as the most decent person I'd
ever known and an almost inconceivably gifted lover. Even in those
occasional dalliances, however, I had to be supremely careful. Premarriage coupling was forbidden by the priests, and I knew I was under their watchful eye. They hated everything Quetzalcoatl and
Stargazer stood for, and as Stargazer's trusted assistant I was a tempt-
ing target for them.

While Stargazer and Shield—with the help of their king—
might protect me from their attacks, I was not sure they could save
Flower if the priests came for her.

I did not want to see her forced into the life of a professional
courtesan, servicing warriors and public officials for her daily maize,
but if the priests condemned her, that would be her punishment.

I was heading toward the observatory, where I would join the astronomer. The Observation Point was at the top of a tower that was
the second highest place in Tula. Only the temple atop the sacred
pyramid was higher.

Stargazer and I made most of our star observations from the top
of the tower. Along the open walkway that went completely around
the top were tools that helped us measure movements in the sky.
Some devices, such as the pegs and marks used to measure the Sun
God's progress, were stationary; others like the star-cross were held
by hand.

The star-cross devices required using two of them many paces
apart or the use of objects on the horizon or even buildings: placed
on the tops of buildings were shapes that helped us keep track of
the Sun God, Moon God, and stars.

At the observation level we also had a small room with no other
openings to the outside except the door, with holes in the ceiling
that permitted rays of the sun to shine through. With the door
closed, we could block out daylight; through the rays entering the
small holes we could monitor and evaluate the Sun God's path.

The calculations were used for many purposes besides telling the time. Based upon the annual path of the Sun God, we determined when it was time for planting crops, even when the time was right to go to war—a very necessary calculation so the warriors could be home for when it was time to plant and time to harvest.

Stargazer's legs carried him slower and more painfully up the steep tower steps each year, so I found myself making most of the observations. I never revealed to him that I knew it was the weakness in his eyesight that caused him to use my sharper vision.

His lungs were also going. More and more over the years, he fought harder to conceal his gasps as he neared the top of the climb of step. He reminded me of my Aztec shaman father who, when he neared death, found it more difficult to find his breath after walking up a hill.

27

Dawn was breaking when I stepped out onto the Observation Point and waved to the Night Watcher, who would soon be getting off his shift. Throughout the day and night a Watcher was posted on the Observation Point to keep an eye out not just for fires, but approaching storms, invading armies, anything out of the ordinary.

He told me he had spotted the flames and smoke only minutes before and had immediately beat the alarm on a huehuetl drum.

The fire's smoke was visible, but it had broken out in the tree-lined hills to the south, not the north, which was Aztec country. Still it would eradicate game and raze crops. The drought-ravaged flora down there would fuel it for days. Game would be scarce for a long time to come, and when the conflagration ignited the nearby maize and bean fields the blaze would exacerbate Tula's food shortage.

At least the Dog People hadn't started the fire. Our priests would scream for blood, and the priests' hatred for my Clan knew no bounds. Had a Dog Person stood accused, anyone with Aztec blood in their veins would suffer. I might very well suffer.

Stargazer came onto the Observation Point. He was breathing heavily and I could see that his knees sagged as he walked. His knees no longer carried him well. But he also possessed vast pride—so much so that the two servants who had helped him up the steep stairway were waved away. He would have walked barefooted on hot coals rather than appear weak.

I wondered if there was any way I could conceal the attack from him. I could not see one.

"Another fire?" he asked.

"Yes."

"The Dog People?"

I shook my head. "Fire in the south."

He sighed and looked in that direction. "Better if it had been started by the Dog People than have gods cause it."

Man-made fires could be dismissed as accidents or the acts of enemies. Fires of unknown cause were acts of the gods and more problematic: if the gods were angry with us, their anger cast doubt on the king's competence.

We relied on him to mollify the gods and forestall their sacred fury.

Stargazer and the high priest might probe the motives and intentions of the gods, but they did not intercede on Tula's behalf. That was the king's role. If he failed, Tula was in trouble, and Tula had clearly fallen from grace.

Stargazer stared at me. I still felt the tension from the attack I had survived only a few hours ago. I had said nothing about it—hating to upset him—but he sensed something was wrong.

"I've been told that an intruder was seen leaving the palace compound," Stargazer said. "Tell me what you know about it."

I took a deep breath. He knew.

"Someone climbed up the vines outside my window and slipped into my room. He had a dagger." I shrugged. "I fought back, cutting his face, perhaps even his eyes, and he escaped out the window."

Stargazer nodded. "Escaped, but with more than an injury to his face. He was seen running with an injured foot. I will offer a reward for information about someone with an injured foot. This is the second time."

Yes, the second time. The first was on a hunting trip nearly a year ago when I was struck by an arrow that none on the hunting party claimed to have shot. The gods had decreed that I was not to die that day and be damned to the challenges and terrors of the Underworld—the arrow only grazed my shoulder.

"Once again the gods protected me," I murmured.

"Perhaps," he said. "Or perhaps the gods bide their time until our priests can flay you whole with your own razor-sharp knives and battle-axes."

I had to laugh at his jibe. After the first attempt on my life, Shield and Stargazer had added military training to my duties, and I now possessed a small arsenal of killing instruments. Shield himself had been training me in the use of cut-and-thrust weapons. Recently he'd added archery and javelin throwing to my studies. To my surprise I had a knack for combat. Shield said admiringly that I had an aptitude for killing.

But how could I defend myself against attackers I could not see—against assassins who sought my life for no discernable reason?

Stargazer interrupted my thoughts. "The king commands the presence of his astronomer and the Aztec known as Coyotl. Are you listening?"

Stargazer and I stared at each other. A command to appear at the palace was not unusual. But as fears and tensions were boiling over, and increased the risk that the king and his court would rise to a boiling point as conditions became worse, visits to the palace carried with it a threat that some kingly caprice would land a stargazer in hot water.

Since the star-gods determined our fates, it was all too easy to blame the star-readers—the star-gods' messengers—for the divine messages they conveyed.

"Tezcal will be at the palace," Stargazer said.

Tezcal was the high priest. From the first time we met he'd wanted my back on his altar and my blood on his blade. His attitude had not changed with the years.

"You know you are not to speak in the presence of the king unless he speaks to you. You also must not flinch or blink when Tezcal denounces you again to the king. Fix your eyes on your feet, and show no emotion. You must contain your rage. I've seen it slip out in the past."

An Aztec outcast, I was an easy target. Only the king's favor protected me from the high priest's temple-stone.

When or whether the king would withdraw his favor I could not say.

28

I walked with Stargazer to the royal palace, passing by the great Sun Pyramid as we went. I never made my way across the Ceremonial Center without remembering the day I first saw Tula. That day I was a half-naked savage with dirt between my toes. Now I wore the bright red mantle of an assistant to the Royal Astronomer, a triangular loincloth of soft white cotton and deerskin sandals. Best of all, when my stomach growled, it was well fed.

That same night I had slipped a dagger to Tenoch, he had slashed the ropes binding him, sawed his way out of the wooden cage, and gone over the city wall. But that was not the last that was heard of the Clan leader. He was a legend to every Aztec who hated Tula, who dreaded capture and feared the downward sweep of the high priest's obsidian knife.

Now Tenoch was the war leader of several Clans, and tales of his bravery and skill as a leader in battle grow.

Ayyo . . . if the high priest had even a hint that I had helped Tula's premier enemy escape, he would flay me whole, scorch what was left, then cut my still-conscious remains into a myriad of minute pieces . . . just as he and his colleagues had longed to flay and fry Tenoch. . . .

We met Tezcal, the high priest, as we approached the entrance to the palace of Quetzalcoatl. Clad in his traditional black robes, he still wore his black hair long. The dried blood streaking his hair was decorative rather than the result of a recent exsanguination. If he wanted the blood removed, he could have washed his hair.

He and Stargazer bowed and mumbled greetings to each other. Tezcal glared at me disdainfully, while I carefully kept my own features blank.

The king's palace was the largest structure in Tula, more than ten times the size of Stargazer's compound.

Entering, we passed between two great stone replicas of the god, Quetzalcoatl. The massive stone representations were of the entire feather-covered serpent's body, with a huge head, taller than a man, and serpent's two-foot fangs.

Standing with their backs to the stone god were dozens of the king's palace guard, Jaguar Knights colorfully arrayed in their jaguar uniforms, but armed with the finest obsidian-edged swords and spears.

Despite the ceremonial appearance of their uniforms, the king selected only hardened veterans who had proven their worth and loyalty to him in battle.

Serving in the royal guard was highly lucrative but came with a drawback: with common warriors Tula punished minor derelictions with minor punishments. For those same infractions, a Jaguar Knight was executed.

No weakness or errors were permitted when it came to guarding the life of the god-king.

No wonder the king was close to Smoking Shield.

Entering the palace was to leave the world of hot, crowded, noisy streets and walk in a paradise. Despite its appearance as a solid, massive building from the outside, half the interior space of the palace was a courtyard built around a small lake surrounded by a labyrinth of sweet-scented tropical flowers and shrubs.

In the center of the lake and scattered along the maze of paths through the junglelike vegetation were fountains spraying refreshing, cool water.

Walking through the exotic plants, we passed even more exotic animals: jaguars and ocelots pacing in jungle enclosures; predator eagles and hawks in stories-high aviaries, with brilliantly colorful quetzals and parrots and other tropical birds; golden pheasants and brown turkeys were plentiful, no doubt as suppliers of game for the king's table; a band of my namesake coyotes howled at us as we passed a fenced area where large crocodiles opened wide snouts to expose their teeth.

The most numerous animals were two-legged ones: people were everywhere, visiting nobles and wealthy merchants, awaiting the call for an audience with the king to beg for this, plead for that. Members of the court hurried along, carrying out their duties, while an army of servants kept the grounds clean and tables loaded with food.

Whenever I stood before Tula's god-king my knees and hands trembled. At age seven, he had been named Quetzalcoatl after the Toltec god of wind and storms, and his staunchest supporters saw him as the god-king—Quetzalcoatl's earthly incarnation.

Three years earlier, Stargazer had told me how Quetzalcoatl came to power. Before he could assume the throne, a high lord murdered his father, the king, and seized power. With a price on his head, Quetzalcoatl had fled to the mountains in the east. After a year in the wilderness, he returned. Tales abounded that he had communed with the gods, who had anointed him Tula's god-king. As a helmet he wore the head of a jaguar he was said to have killed with a single thrust of his spear.

Farmers left their fields, joining him as warriors, as he marched for the city. Seeing his warriors desert and a burgeoning army approach, the usurper fled.

Assuming the throne, Quetzalcoatl had shown the strength and mercy he would become noted for: he forgave all of the usurper's supporters except those who had actually participated in the murder of his father. The actual killers he had sacrificed. The usurper he had hunted down and brought back to the city. Rather than leaving it to the high priest to take the man's life, he'd engaged the man one-on-one and killed him in a fair fight.

"A fair fight," Stargazer said, when he had first told me the story three years earlier. "Any other king in the One-World would have had the man sacrificed by temple priests rather than risk personal combat."

I followed Stargazer and the high priest into the throne room, keeping humbly to the rear of the great ones. The king was seated on his throne. His sister, Zyanya, stood at his right side, slightly behind him.

The king wore a large headdress of brilliant feathers of the quetzal bird, shades of dark and light green, yellow, and bright red. The plumes were so rare and beautiful, many believed the bird was blessed by the gods and only royalty were permitted to wear its feathers. The gleaming gold headband was imbedded with jade and turquoise and festooned with the priceless plumes.

The headpiece was not just an elaborate piece of art—the dazzling feathers and jewels formed an image of the god Quetzalcoatl. The visage of the Feathered Serpent with its snarling fangs and violent countenance proclaimed that his namesake, the god-king, was not to be trifled with.

Rather than a simple cotton loincloth that most commoners wore, the king's clothing was of the finest cotton interwoven with strands of fine silver. His waistband was embellished with pearls, depicting a jaguar's visage. His sandals were soled in gold, their leather straps adorned with gems.

Royalty believed that jaguars were their own special protectors, and in Quetzalcoatl's case, his palace guard was composed entirely of Jaguar Knights, their leader Smoking Shield. Appropriately, the king's mantle was a great cape of jaguar fur.

We prostrated ourselves before the king, our foreheads touching the floor.

The king commanded us to stand, and we rose. Stargazer and the high priest stood before him while I remained two paces behind them.

Stargazer had told me repeatedly to keep my eyes on the floor unless the king addressed me, but my eyes could not help themselves—they slid up to Zyanya.

She was staring at me. I quickly dropped my eyes.

Suddenly the king was speaking directly to me:

"I am told you are ready to accompany me to the ballgames at Tajin, Coyotl. Are you prepared to stand at my side and tell me what the sky reveals about our duties?"

"Yes, majesty," I said reflexively, not understanding what he said.

I had no idea why the king was going to Tajin. I only knew the city on the Eastern Sea was where the championship ballgames were played each year. Teams from all the empires met there to determine which ball team was the best of all.

The event was important, because the ballgame was not just a sport: it mirrored the world. The game's action and outcome foretold one's own actions and destiny if the game was properly understood. As always in life, cosmic forces determined earthly fate and fortune. The pursuit of worldly power required a rigorous understanding of cosmic forces. The connection between the two was inviolable and he who flouted the gods' will did so at his peril.

The gods loved the game and smiled on its winners.

For the past two years Teotihuacán had been the victor. That we had lost a pair of matches to their players was viewed as divine disfavor. Teotihuacán had once dominated the One-World, and some saw the city's two victories as a sure sign that the gods were shifting their allegiance to that once dominant power.

Apparently, the king had decided Tula should defeat Teotihuacán on the ball court, and that the winner would receive not just a victory but the gods' blessing, which we all hoped would take the form of rain, sun, and a prolific harvest.

A more important question, however, as I stood before the king was why I—an astronomer's assistant—had been selected for the journey.

True, the journey of a week would be arduous. We would travel over mountains and down to the hot, wet region along the Eastern Sea. It would be hard on Stargazer because of his weak legs, but there was no need for him to walk. Nobles and dignitaries routinely made long journeys on litters carried by servants. He could have accompanied the king.

For reasons I did not understand the king wanted *me*.

My life was about to take another turn. I didn't know what direction the gods would spin me, but I intuitively understood that the markings on my body, the protection afforded by a king, the threat posed by his ravishing sister, and by armed assassins were all somehow part of my destiny.

I did not know, however, how long the gods would countenance my earthly existence.

"Good," the king said.

As abruptly as we'd entered, we were dismissed.

29

"You should have prepared me for his question," I said.

"He hadn't discussed it with me," Stargazer replied.

"Do you know why he wants me?"

"Shield and I have both spoken well of you, and I did recommend you for the trip. He seemed disinterested, though, so I never brought it up to you. I tell you I was as surprised as you when he asked you to come with him."

We were on our way back to the observatory, alone with our conversation, before Stargazer spoke in detail about the mission I was about to embark upon.

"You will be tested," Stargazer said.

"The king will not find me lacking—"

"Not the king. You will be tested by the Guardians."

The Guardians? I knew the word referred to a protector of a person or thing, but had never heard it used in regard to myself. Stargazer had spoken of it as if I should have known what he meant.

"It has been arranged," he said.

"I don't understand. Who are these Guardians? Why would they test me?"

We stopped and he stared at me, his eyes searching my face.

I had many questions and knew I would not get answers to them.

"My health is too frail for the trip," he said. "It works out well for both of us. That, I believe, was the king's reasoning."

"What about these Guardians?"

"They will know you are coming. They will find you in Tajin."

He was talking in circles and telling me nothing.

"What are they guardians of?"

"That you will learn when it is time for you to take your role."

He motioned for me to stop asking questions. I shut my mouth but could not eradicate the questions in my mind. I was confused. And frightened.

"You must not fail," he said.

"Fail at what?"

"Your duty is to tell the king what you see in the stars and to interpret your observations for him. He will rely on what you say to make his decisions."

"I understand."

"No, I don't think you do. Most of the time the sky does not change, but your interpretation of it will change based upon what the king tells you about the problem at hand." He grabbed my arm. "The king has many enemies. They're cowards who stand behind him with daggers ready to plunge into his back. They will get up the courage to strike when he makes a great mistake. You must not be the one who inadvertently helps his enemies by giving bad advice."

"I'm not capable—"

"He will rely on you because you carry the stars. You must also not fail when the Guardians test you." He gripped my arm tighter. "Be aware, my son. If you do not pass, they will cut out your heart. Not even the king can stop them."

Ayyo!

30

Late in the afternoon, I was returning from my stargazing duties. I'd been trying to confirm that we were accurately charting the time, and my brain was still lost someplace amid the stars. Out of the blue a servant surprised me, saying that Stargazer commanded my presence in the compound's temazcal, the House of Heat.

The House of Heat was a small, round hut shaped like a beehive. After heated rock from a fire mountain* was placed in the center, the door was closed to keep the heat in. Sitting naked inside, one's body sweated profusely while medicinal herbs were thrown on the stones to create healing vapors.

The sweat house was not used just for cleansing the body, but healing wounds and sickness and refreshing the soul.

Stargazer used his temazcal almost every evening as both his legs and his eyes grew weaker. He'd sometimes called me there to discuss our work or other matters of importance.

I paused at the entrance to the House of Heat and stripped off all my clothes and removed my sandals. Taking a maguey needle, I pricked my penis to draw blood so as to curry the favor of Temaz-

---

* Translator's Note: Volcanic rock.

calteci, the goddess of the sweat house. A statue of the goddess was at the entrance. I allowed the blood to drip into the stone bowl at her feet, mixing with the blood Stargazer had provided before he entered.

Entering the hot chamber, I got a quick glance at Stargazer before I pulled the door shut behind me and turned the interior back to complete darkness. He was seated, leaning back, his body wet with sweat. His eyes were closed and he appeared to be asleep.

I took a seat on a bench across from him and waited for him to address me, savoring the quiet time, the heat and curative herbs making my skin sweat tingle.

We sat quietly this way for a while and then I answered when I heard him utter my name in a whisper.

"You sent for me, Noble One," I said.

"Yes, yes, I sent for you, Coyotl of the Dog People. But that's not true now, is it? You are now Coyotl of the mighty Totlec, the caterpillar turned into a butterfly."

"Yes, Noble One."

"A butterfly now, but will someday you soar like an eagle? Will you fulfill the destiny that others expect? Or have the gods set out a different path for you to follow?"

I mumbled an incoherent response. Stargazer sometimes rambled on, a journey in his mind that he alone knew the point of.

Suddenly, however, he was silent, pinning me with a penetrating stare. This was serious.

"Listen, friend Coyotl, and listen well. Without your help and presence these last three years, I would not be in reach of completing the Long Count Calendar. More significant, you have been a son to me. I think you know I wish you well."

"I trust you with anything and everything," I said simply.

"I have some bad news. A close friend of ours has been murdered. You must do *nothing* to track the killer down or to avenge yourself on the killing. You must not even allow yourself the luxuries of anger, self-pity, revenge, or remorse. You must be made of stone. You must stay focused not only on our work but on your survival and hopefully your advancement. Both of those depend on your performance on this trip. If you allow yourself to be distracted by grief and rage, you will fail in your task, and I shall not be able to complete the Calendar, nor will you master the godly glyphs and record, then secrete the god-king's sacred vision.

"An intruder tied up Desert Flower early this morning. He then gagged and brutally raped her. When he was finished, he deliberately left this blade in her belly as a personal statement."

It was an obsidian knife, its ebony handle inlaid with silver and turquoise—the knife Desert Flower had stolen and, at her behest, I had slipped to Tenoch between his cage bars.

"I do not accuse you of its theft even though it disappeared from my room the very night you moved in, nor do I accuse you of smuggling it into Tenoch's cell even though he hacked his way out of his cage with such a knife and cut the throats of two sleeping guards. I did not accuse you then, and I do not accuse you now. If you did do it, I'm sure you did it for honorable reasons.

"Remember this, though, when you are tempted by anger, revenge, self-pity, or remorse: You have important things to do now— things that require your unswerving commitment. You have to stay focused. Your life, advance, and our work hang in the balance. Everything depends on your focus these next several months. Can you stay focused? Will you be made of stone?"

I had to answer yes. To speak otherwise would be to acknowledge my complicity in Tenoch's escape, and while Stargazer suspected my complicity, I knew he did not want confirmation. To have confessed my mistake would hurt the old man beyond all measure.

My face—a mask of blank impassivity—never betrayed my inner shame and rage.

"I shall be solid granite," I said.

"Swear."

"I swear. The work comes first," I said simply.

That statement also had the virtue of being both necessary and true.

Still I doubted I could honor that commitment. My initial shock was turning quickly to vindictive fury.

Tenoch had to pay.

Flower had meant too much to me.

"Go as a warrior," Stargazer said, leaning close, looking me in the eye, "and think as a warrior on the journey to Tajin. Be ready with your sword, spear, and shield. All your enemies will not be in the field.

"And take this."

He handed me the sheathed obsidian dagger that had taken Flower's life. Rising to his feet, he left the House of Heat, closing the door behind him.

Sitting alone in the black void, my fingers caressed the ebony handle while my mind spun.

31

We left the city for the journey to Tajin in a long procession of royalty, nobles, and warriors. Attired in a brilliant array of ceremonial clothes, Quetzalcoatl wore his headpiece fanned out, which made walking awkward. Sitting on a golden throne, twelve muscular warriors shouldered him instead on a palanquin. The throne was not only more comfortable, it made him appear more godlike, and many who watched him believed he was one.

Shouldering the palanquin was a great honor reserved for warriors who had proven themselves superior in battle. Walking in cadence, they steadied the king's throne and minimized its sway. Soldiers always, they nonetheless carried their weapons and shields as well as the king.

Light and strong, the palanquin was constructed out of timber logged on the hot, wet eastern coast. Inlaid with burnished gold, it was also striped with silver. The canopy over it was jaguar fur. At the top of the canopy's four corner posts were fierce eagles carved from large pieces of jade.

The eagle was the second great predator of the One-World, the denizen of the sky.

The royal palanquin was followed by a hundred nobles and five hundred warriors of the king's own palace guard commanded by Jaguar Knights.

I walked behind the personal bodyguards surrounding the palanquin. The Rememberer of History, the King's Steward, and the Royal Armorer were also in the small group, close enough to be called to the king's side at a moment's notice.

Stargazer told me that we would proceed with great fanfare out of the city, reinforcing the image of a glorious, godlike king. A three-day march would take us to the eastern mountain range and the end of the territory heavily patrolled by the king's army.

Before we proceeded up the mountain and down the other side to the hot, wet zone, the king would step off the palanquin and walk with the procession, wearing his battle dress and weapons.

"He will not again mount the palanquin until we are in sight of Tajin," the Royal Armorer told me. "Our neighbors all lust for the wealth of Tula. The king must be prepared in case we are attacked. He could hardly fight back while sitting on a throne five feet off the ground."

It was nice to know all his enemies weren't in Tula.

❧

Stargazer spent the five days leading up to the journey instructing me about duties I might be asked to perform for the king. Day and night, I had to keep track of the time. A timekeeper from the Temple of the Stars accompanied me to assist in this task. Keeping the time on the journey could prove critical. If an enemy force attacked, we would have to know how many hours we had before darkness or daylight. Such calculations were more difficult on the move, but using star-crosses and distant objects, we could usually calculate the time required.

The second duty was to keep track of where we were en route. No road existed over the mountains and down to the coast, though a narrow path worn onto the ground by merchants showed the way. But if the procession was attacked and driven off the known path, it was vital that we knew exactly where we were and the fastest way back to Tula, both for our warriors and for messengers sent for help.

Since the gods followed a set road across the sky, passing from one constellation to another, I could track them and gauge our relationship to them based upon their position. Knowing exactly where the star-god is supposed to be, I could determine our approximate position by ascertaining the angle of an object on the ground, like a mountain, with the god in the sky.*

As long as the sky stayed clear.

"Mistakes are not permitted," Stargazer had told me repeatedly.

I would be put to death if there were, but I was confident my calculations were correct. I was less confident of the terrain we had to traverse.

"Yes, yes, you know the paths of the gods, but it is even more important that you know the *will* of the gods."

Knowing the desires and intent of the gods was the duty of the king. The king in turn asked his astronomer to explain and interpret the signs in the sky. A king who failed to communicate with the gods and satisfy their whims was useless to the people.

Ayyo! As Stargazer pointed out so many times to me, an astronomer who could not guide the king into making the right decisions was useless to the king—and would soon find himself walking up the steps of the sacred temple to have his heart ripped out.

As our procession followed the road to the east gate to leave the city, we passed thousands of people lined up to watch. As the king's palanquin approached, people bent their heads and looked to the ground, careful not to meet the king's eye. The heads of children were pushed down to keep them from staring at the king. Only after the palanquin passed by did people raise their eyes to stare at it.

---

* Translator's Note: Ancient Aztecs/Mayas practiced celestial/astronavigation in a similar fashion to other ancient, medieval, and early modern societies around the world. The sun, moon, planets, and designated stars guided them across seas and, to a lesser extent, land.

Behind the king's palanquin and the group of bodyguards and aides following it, came a smaller palanquin carrying Zyanya.

The king's sister wanted to see the famous ballgames at Tajin, Stargazer told me. As usual, his words were underlined with a tone I interpreted as disapproval.

I knew from hearing others whisper that there was talk about the king and his sister. He permitted her to participate in royal audiences and even looked to her for advice on decisions to be made.

The closeness of their relationship puzzled some and titillated the imagination of others, some whispering she was more of a wife or concubine to him.

The fact that she was in her mid-twenties and had not married also stroked the rumors. Most young women married by the age of sixteen or seventeen, royal princesses even earlier because their marriages were matters of alliances with either powerful nobles or kings of other empires.

Offers to marry the only sister of the King of Tula came from every king of the One-World. It made no sense that the king would have her remain unwed, so the rumors spread . . .

Since defaming the king was punishable by death, no one suggested these things publicly. Still, rumors circulated.

And the rumors were hurtful. Incest carried with it both shame and the death penalty—in this case a long, slow, agonizing death. Regicide was not treated any more ruthlessly than such slander.

I was not concerned with the king and his sister. Still, my hackles lifted whenever Zyanya looked at me. When in the eastern mountains she ordered me to her tent, I was not pleased.

32

We halted the day's progress late in the afternoon when she summoned me. The king had left on a jaguar hunt and we would be alone.

After presenting myself to her guards, I was escorted in. Seated on a small throne, she held a jaguar-headed staff, a smaller version of the royal symbol of power the king carried.

I prostrated myself.

"Rise," she said.

Getting up, I kissed the dirt on my right fingers. My lips to dirt was the reverence due royalty when outside, where we were expected to kiss the ground they walked on.

She stared at me for a long moment.

"Do you know the reason the king journeys to Tajin?" she asked.

"The annual ballgames are—"

"That reason was given for purposes of state," she snapped.

I didn't offer another explanation. She obviously didn't care for the one I had provided—which was the only one I knew.

"Teotihuacán wishes me to marry their prince and heir to their king. My brother believes the union would not be beneficial to Tula."

I nodded, silent, understanding nothing of what she said.

"Our king will speak to the gods about the proposed union," she said, "but before speaking to the gods, he will ask his astronomers for signs of the gods' wishes."

What she said was true, but I had no idea what she wanted from me.

"True, true . . ." I murmured.

"Teotihuacán, like the Maya, is long past its glory. They wish to exploit such a union to their advantage, believing they can cut the heart out of Tula and feed it to their own worthless city." She paused. "Isn't that true?"

"Teotihuacán envies our city's riches," I said.

"They cannot be trusted," she said. "I don't trust our own traders and merchants. They complain bitterly about their taxes, even as they prosper beyond dreams of avarice, while our people starve and our crops dry, die, and blow away."

Again, I said nothing.

"But the nobles hope to profit from increased trade with Teotihuacán, even if it hurts Tula. If, however, the stars spurn that marriage union, my brother will also oppose it. Now do you understand?"

"I have no control over Stargazer's readings," I said.

"The decision will be made on this trip," she said, "and Stargazer is not here. For now, you are the Royal Astronomer. Do we understand each other?"

I nodded. "Yes, majesty."

"Then the stars will find the union unfavorable?"

"The stars are our wisest advisers," I said, "and I'm certain you will not be disappointed."

I could see from her face that the answer satisfied her. Leaning toward me, she smiled, then struck me across the face with all her might.

I was dismissed.

33

Staring up at the night sky, I wondered how many days were allotted to me on this earth. Whatever that number was, it seemed to be shrinking.

Because we were away from Tula, the king had chosen me to succeed as Royal Astronomer. My transition had been quicker and smoother than anyone could have predicted.

Somehow I saw Stargazer's hand in my rapid rise.

But what of the Guardians? I was to be tested in Tajin. I was ignorant of the questions they would pose, but Stargazer implied that if I gave wrong answers, they would kill me.

Ayyo . . . who said the gods did not have a sense of humor?

34

I had lived in the arid lands of the Dog People and the greener regions of the Toltec, but the hotlands between the Eastern Sea and the Eastern Mountains were completely different. For three days we had slogged through jungles alive with the chatter of monkeys, the cries of tropical birds, and the roar of jaguars; we avoided the bites of slithering snakes and crossed rivers where crocodiles ruled, all the while sweating as if we were in a House of Heat.

We had passed fruit forests that grew nowhere else but hot-wet places and thousands of trees called Weeping Women that were milked of a white liquid that soon formed into a rubber that could be molded many ways.

Ayyo . . . great jungle beasts and poisonous serpents were mere nuisances compared to the blood-sucking flying pests that swarmed us. Mosquitoes were truly created by sadistic gods to torment mankind.

Tajin was called the Place of Thunder because the Totonac people believed that their city was built by the Lords of Thunder, twelve old men named Tajin.

Perhaps to prove the legend, dark clouds, sudden downpours, and rolling thunder frequently rushed in from the sea as we approached and the city's walls and buildings of red, turquoise, and yellow rose from dark green foliage.

I was told by the Royal Armorer, who had been to the city before, that Tajin had about thirty thousand souls, about half the number of Tula.

"But no city of the One-World has more ball courts," he said.

Eighteen courts, by his count.

The reason for the great number of courts was that cities throughout the One-World sent teams to the Tajin to compete on the playing fields where life and death were wagered. The players used balls made from the rubber obtained from the Weeping Women and they played as if they were on a battlefield rather than a ball court.

We entered Tajin in the same manner that we left Tula, a brilliant, colorful procession with the king wearing his stunning headdress and carried on the palanquin.

The city was grand, but it was obvious that it was not built in the massive fashion of Tula. The palaces and other important buildings of Tula were of stone. But the Tajin buildings I saw as we progressed from the city gate to the ceremonial center were built with a mortar mixture of ground seashells over tropical hardwoods.

The king of Tajin awaited us in front of his palace, his headdress so heavy that when he greeted Quetzalcoatl, he had to be helped up.

The Tajin king pretended to be an equal to the Tula one, but in truth he paid tribune to Tula. And hated it, which was why another five hundred Toltec warriors were camped at the edge of the city when we arrived. Quetzalcoatl had sent them ahead to ensure that there would be no unpleasant surprises when we arrived.

We courtiers were invited to the banquet given to the king. As with Quetzalcoatl's palace, the Tajin royal palace was built around a courtyard, though the palace was neither as large nor as exquisite as Quetzalcoatl's.

Hundreds of guests, including most of the high nobles of the kingdom, gathered for the feast at tables under canopies that protected all from sudden downpours. As with our own royal dinners, dozens of different foods were laid out, some common like deer and rabbit; others such as wild boar and reed birds were rarer.

I had only experienced fresh fish from our Toltec rivers, and the variety of fish brought by the Tajins from the sea to the banquet was stunning.

Before the rest of us ate, lovely serving girls provided the two kings with water for their hands, holding bowls below the hands to catch the water falling off. After the royals dried off their hands, beautifully etched wood screens were placed in front of them so that they would not be seen eating.

After the royals finished eating, their hands were washed again, screens were removed, and we began our own meal.

While we ate, with nothing in front of us to hide the juices that dripped down our chins or the food that flew onto our clothes, the kings sipped spiced chocolate drinks served in golden cups and watched entertainment.

The grand show of the evening was Totonacs performing the ritualistic and dangerous Dance of the Flying Men.

Five men climbed a tall pole mounted in the ground and extending up sixty or seventy feet high. At the top of the pole was a small platform.

While one of the men danced and played a flute on the top, the other four men each tied a rope to one of their ankles and began a graceful descent, upside down, whirling around the pole as if they were flying, the ropes each unwrapping thirteen times, for a total of fifty-two times among the four of them.

The dangerous feat was a symbolic tribute to the spirits: The man atop playing the flute represented the celestial gods, the four flying men signified the four directions of the wind, while the fifty-two rotations around the pole symbolized the sacred fifty-two-year time period in the Calendar Round.

Since we arrived in the city, I anticipated contact from those whom Stargazer called the Guardians. I found myself wondering if the person contacting me would be the guest seated next to me at dinner or the servant putting food before me. But neither source offered to unravel the mystery for me.

That night my sleeping quarters were in the house of a nobleman across from the palace of a Tajin prince in which Quetzalcoatl had taken residence.

After dinner, I was invited to partake in the erotic pleasures provided to distinguished visitors.

The summons from the Guardians came in the shadow of the moon.

35

Standing in the banquet chamber of the Tajin nobleman who provided sleeping quarters for we Tula courtiers, his son explained the
exotic women in the room.

"The auianime are unmarried women who become consorts to
our soldiers and dignitaries."

"The same as in Tula," I said.

The nobleman moved away as I stared at the necklaces of tiny
skulls around the women's throats.

"You are fascinated with the skulls?"

The speaker was behind me.

I turned and found myself facing a woman who wore a black
mantle with a hood she let fall onto her shoulders. The mantle
covered her from neck to feet as a full cloak.

Unlike the other women in the room, she wore neither heavy fa-
cial colorings, tattoos, piercings, nor skull ornaments on her face.

"All of us have a fascination with death," she said. "We fear the
Lords of Death will take us, but honor those who kill the most. Our
warriors who capture prisoners to be sacrificed or who die themselves in battle are the most honored. Even the ballgame is a field of
death."

This wasn't the nature of conversation I heard from other women in the room, who focused on flattering comments about the man she was speaking to.

"Why do you think we have such a fascination with death?" I asked.

"Reward and punishment. That's what life is all about . . . and death. We end up in paradise . . . or hell."

"Who are you?" I asked.

Her words, dress, and manner were not those of a prostitute passed from man to man. Yet she did not have the mannerisms of a noble woman or even an ordinary woman. Rather, she had an aura of mystery and magic.

My first instinct was that she was a priestess, but those women spent their lives in a sacred temple and would not be found at a place of drink and sex.

"Yours," she said. "For the night."

36

"For the night?" I repeated.

Had any other woman in the room told me she was mine for the night, I would not have been surprised. They were there to pleasure men, but coming from her the statement surprised me. She was not a consort but a woman of elegance, beauty, and, I suspected, affluence.

Ordinarily, I would have been aroused and flattered. I was still shocked and mourning Desert Flower's death, however—so much so I was saddened by the woman's offer. After that night, Flower and I had not become full-blown lovers. Premarriage sex with women other than professional consorts was forbidden, and I was in no position to offer any woman marriage and children. As Bearer of the Word, I had given myself over completely to Stargazer and Smoking Shield, working often all day on my studies of the sacred glyph and all night assisting Stargazer. As his vision faded, I more and more acted as his eyes.

Flower and I also feared the priests. They clearly despised Stargazer, Shield, and myself, and the work we were doing. I had initially assumed the high priest was employing the assassin on my trail. Tenoch had clearly claimed credit for Flower's killing by leaving the knife she and I had provided him; yet even so, the priests

could have also hired him. They hated Quetzalcoatl and his advisers enough to ally themselves with Tula's most dangerous enemies—
if those enemies served their cause.

What man wouldn't eagerly want to lay with such a woman?

"What is it? Do you not want me?" she said softly.

"Yes, of course," I said.

She moved toward me, pressed herself close against my body,
then whispered, "Then we should go now, so I can show you."

"Show me what?"

"Something no other woman has ever done before." She smiled.

By the time we were in the room that was assigned to me in the
nobleman's place, I could not temper my urgency to have her. Still I
was reluctant. It was guilt, I'm sure. I'd had other women since that
first night with Desert Flower—consorts to be sure—and I'd made
no commitments to her except to protect her—a commitment I'd
clearly failed at. Still I had had no women since her murder, and was
uneasy about betraying her memory.

Unfortunately, my member had no such scruples. He was so hard
a cougar could have clawed him and not left a scratch.

Spotting my readiness beneath my loincloth, she laughed softly.

"What is so funny?"

"You should be a Jaguar Knight, for you have his predatory lust.
But, come, I will teach you to take your time and savor the banquet
to come—to enjoy all the dishes, not just the dessert."

I gazed in her dark pool of eyes and nodded like an obedient
child. This woman was not like the others who had come to my bed,
and I was not accustomed to taking my time.

Even though she still had her clothing on, I felt her nipples
against my chest. She made no effort to remove the long covering
over her body. Instead she undid the knot that secured my loincloth
and let it fall to the floor.

She took my bulging member in her hand, gripping it in a firm
and deliberate fashion, electrifying my body. Within seconds my
semen seeped between her tantalizing fingers.

"Ayyo," I said breathlessly when I had finished.

"Now we can take our time."

"How did you learn to please a man in such a manner?"

"I had a very good teacher," she said, smiling seductively, "and I have many more things to do to you."

She was not a woman of great beauty, not like Princess Zyanya, but there was an almost regal quality about her, the way she carried herself as if she *was* noble.

"First, I will clean you."

"Why?"

"You will find out."

I followed her to the layer of animal skins that had been prepared as my bed. After she had washed me, she stood up, then removed her covering. She wore nothing underneath. Her body had the firmness of youth, yet her mannerisms and spoken words told me she was older than my own age.

My first impression of a priestess still stayed in my mind—a priestess from a temple of love.

"Do you like what you see?" she asked.

"Yes."

She stood over me, legs spread apart, her hands moving up and down her own body in a slow motion. Her breasts were round and full, the nipples rosy and swollen. My manhood rose again as I watched her.

She looked down and smiled at me. She seemed to enjoy what she was doing to me. Her hands went between the bushy triangle of hair between her legs. She started playing with the black curly hair, exposing her parted folds of skin to me, then stroking that delicate little knob, writhing up and down, faster and faster, until she suddenly slowed down and then stopped. My own member was getting hard again.

"Come with me," she said, "and I will show you where the flowers of fire . . . grow."

I had fallen into a deep sleep in which I dreamt that Xochiquetzal, the goddess of love, had taken me to her cave filled with flowers and butterflies to make love to me. I awoke sensing that an intruder had entered my room.

A dark figure hovered by me, framed by the moonlight flowing in from the window. Duplicating my movement when I faced an assassin in Tula, I rolled away from the intruder, grabbing my dagger as I did.

"It is time," the woman said.

The mystery woman stood over me, her dark form framed by the moonlight coming through the window opening.

"Who are you?" I asked. I had asked her that question before and she had answered simply that she was mine for the night.

"Your guide. The Guardians command your presence."

37

We left the house of the nobleman, the guards at the front entrance treating us as if we were invisible as we passed. Perhaps they had received a gift large enough to make us invisible to them.

My guide refused to answer my questions and I made the choice to simply follow her blindly. My entire life had been wrapped in mystery—it was time the wrapping was torn open so I could see what was inside.

She led me to the most revered place in the city: the Pyramid of the Niches.

As with Tula and other cities, the tallest structure in Tajin was the sacred pyramid located in the center of the Ceremonial Center. Like other pyramids, the Tajin one had four equal sides, built in tiers, and a grand stairway of stone steps leading up the front to a temple on top.

A myriad of small openings covered the entire surface of the Temple of the Niches except for its 365 Niches, which resembled small open boxes. The niches' interiors were painted dark red and the exterior bright turquoise, creating a stunning contrast under the midday sun. That night, however, under the pale, bluish glow of the Moon God, the pyramid appeared haunted by the gods of the Underworld.

I followed my guide up the steep steps, expecting to go all the way to the top, and was surprised when at the level of the fourth tier she led me off the steps and through a secret door on the tier.

The door led inside a chamber lit by torches.

Three men in hooded black mantles awaited me. They were seated behind a small stone counter.

The torch light didn't reach them well enough to permit me to see their faces, but I sensed the terror they were capable of transmitting: priests were wielders of the sacred knife.

I shivered. I was a trespasser in a forbidden place.

"Show us the Mark."

The priest's voice was as dark and ominous as the hood he wore.

I opened my mantle to expose the scars. The woman who called herself a guide put light on the area with a torch.

A gasp came from one of the hooded men. "It's true, he's the one. The Keeper."

"The Keeper . . . *of what?*"

Without realizing it, I had spoken the question aloud.

"Where is the Dark Rift?" a Guardian asked.

"*In the House of the Magician!*" I shouted the answer. Deliberately. Rage was welling up inside of me. I felt the dagger I had tucked into my waist band. I had asked the question many times during my life and never got an answer. I no longer had patience for games. "Why am I here?"

"Where did you learn that phrase?"

The question came from the hooded man sitting in the middle. He had asked the other questions.

"I don't know. Perhaps from my mother. It flies from my mouth when I'm asked the question. Why is it important?"

I fought back my fury. I had my dagger and was now schooled in all or our cut-and-thrust weapons. During the last three years, Smoking Shield has schooled me in the martial arts, explaining that

I would no doubt need those skills, given the legions of enemies Quetzalcoatl, Stargazer, and he had acquired.

I needed answers to many questions, including the mystery of my birth, and the people in this room might well be able to help me with some answers.

"What do you remember about your mother?" a Guardian asked.

I had only one memory of her: her embrace before lowering me into the reed basket and pushing it off downstream. The memory evoked both love and loss and I fought to suppress it.

"I remember someone warm and comforting."

I also remembered her breasts, my head laying between them, her warmth against my cheek, a feeling of peace and comfort in my soul.

But I said none of that.

"Singing. I remember not words, but her voice, sweet and gentle, rocking me in her arms as she sang to me."

I also remembered a sweet scent and strong arms around me holding me tight, keeping me warm, nourishing me when I needed it.

But again I was silent.

"I don't have a name or a face to put with memories, only feelings."

The three masked figures held a whispered conference before the spokesman again addressed me.

"We have been told you have an infallible memory of the celestial heavens, that you can even remember the positions of the major gods during the changing seasons without doing sightings. Who taught you these things? The Azteca shaman who raised you?"

The question had never occurred to me. "No, I wasn't taught, it has always been there, in my head. The image of the sky is like that of my mother—it's a feeling that I can't define, it just comes to me."

"As any astronomer, you know the Dark Rift to be the Road to Xibalba, the Underworld. Do you know the Dark Rift to have any other meaning?"

"No. Only that it resides in the House of the Magician."

"Do you know what the House of the Magician is?"

I shook my head. "It is not one of the houses of the celestial heavens. At least, not one that I know of."

Frustration again swelled in my chest and pushed up my throat.

"Am I doomed to just answer your questions and never get answers to my own? What are you guardians of? Why have you brought me here?"

Another whispered discussion took place between the three Guardians before the one in the center spoke to me again.

"You know the story of the sky, but do you know the story of the land?"

"What do you mean?"

The Guardian didn't speak for a moment. When he did, his voice was grave. "Darkness is coming. The world of we Maya has collapsed and more will follow. For more lives back than anyone can remember, we were a proud civilization that had gathered the knowledge of an eon. Our civilization glowed, lighting up even the dark places in the One-World. But that our world ended was not because of the whim of the gods—it had been predestined.

"I know you understand, Coyotl, that the fate of each person is set at the time of birth. But did you know that the fate of civilizations and the world itself was also set at the time of creation?

"That the forces of destruction are already in motion when creation occurred, awaiting the moment when destiny is to be fulfilled?"

I realized what he meant. Four worlds had existed before the present one. They had, in turn, been destroyed by the loss of the sun, fierce storms, fire from the sky, and a flood. But I had never thought of empires and the world itself as having a predetermined fate, that the seeds of their destruction were set to sprout at a fixed time in the future.

"It is all written," the Guardian said, "and cannot be changed. Kings, slaves, empires, and worlds, all answer to the Book of Fates."

"What are you guardians of?" I asked.

"A treasure. Not the sort sought by men or kings."

"What kind of treasure?"

"The knowledge of the Ages. Too heavy a burden for three old men to carry."

"I don't understand."

"You will, my son, you will. In time you will understand even more than we who are called Guardians."

"When will I get this knowledge?"

"When you come to the House of the Magician."

"When am I to—"

"When it is time, your guide will find you."

"When will it be the right time?" I demanded.

"The time was set at your birth."

"What am I to do at the House of the Magician?"

"You have not been told?"

"Told what?"

"You will become the Keeper."

"The Keeper of what?"

A sound came from the Guardian. I took it to be a hoarse, humorless chuckle, but it sounded like a death rattle.

"The beating heart of the One-World."

I knew I would not get any further until they were ready to give me answers. But there was one question that burned in my mind, one question that I'd had ever since I could remember. A puzzle that sometimes felt as if it was going to strangle me.

"Who was my mother?"

That death rattle sound came again. Only this time I noticed it carried with it caution, perhaps even fear.

"Your mother was Ixloom."

It was my turn to gasp.

Ixloom. She Who Sees.

I knew her not as a woman, but as someone spoken of over cooking fires at night by the teller of tales—a legendary, perhaps even myth-ical astronomer-magician who was a mortal goddess.

That rattle again and then a question that stunned me because I had never asked it of myself:

"Should you not also be asking . . . *who is your father?*"

38

I was commanded to appear before the king early the next morning. I quickly shook off lack of sleep to appear alert before him, dressing quickly and hurrying to the palace he temporarily occupied.

The sky was clear, the day already warm and moist but a little cooler from a thunderstorm that had passed an hour earlier.

The star-god Quetzalcoatl* was in the morning sky on this day, though I knew few other people would realize it. The star-god was the brightest object in the night sky and was visible to everyone even in the daylight at certain times of the year.

What most people did not know was that the star-god was often faintly visible even in the daylight on some occasions, but it took knowledge of where to look in the sky . . . and exceptional eyesight. I had both.

I had been admitted into an inner chamber and was completely alone with him for the first time. I found it disconcerting. I started to prostrate myself but he motioned me to my feet.

"I will be playing the ballgame here in Tajin," he said.

I found nothing unusual about that. Tlachtli was a sport beloved

---

* Translator's Note: Venus.

by nobles and royalty. Not only did they play the game themselves, many had slaves that were true champions of it. Enormous bets were often placed on the outcome.

"Prince Tizoc, the heir to the throne of Teotihuacán, wants to form an alliance with Tula through a marriage with my sister. My nobles urge the union. I oppose it. Teotihuacáns are not to be trusted. They look hungrily at our riches and resent the tribute they must pay us."

He began to pace, talking more to himself than to me. He paused and stared at me. "I suspect that if Prince Tizoc could succeed me by marrying my sister, he would hasten my departure from this mortal place.

"I have challenged Prince Tizoc to a game of tlachtli. If he wins, he will have Princess Zyanya in marriage. If he loses, the marriage will not take place. He will be dead."

His statement left me shocked, stunned. The fate of empires—to be decided by a ballgame?

He looked past me, not waiting for a response from me. I was too surprised to give one. And I sensed he was reflecting upon something to himself, perhaps even struggling with conflicting thoughts.

"It will be in the hands of the gods. They will decide whether the marriage will take place," the king said. "However, my two most trusted advisers place great faith in you. I know you are helping Stargazer with crucial work, secret work—work we cannot speak of. So I am placing much trust in you as well."

I cannot stress enough the significance of the game—so highly esteemed was it that kings sometimes used the game to settle disputes with rival kingdoms. They conferred on the game oracular powers.

But now the king was wagering Tula's future and his life on this one contest.

Perhaps it ran in the family: When, as a young man, his father sought the throne, he challenged a rival to face him in a match— the victor would win a kingdom. His father had won.

I'd also heard that a Xochicalco king had waged his fortune on a game—and lost.

And now I was here with him—but for what? I couldn't control what happened on the ball court.

"It will be a skull game."

Ayyo! A skull game was how the annual final championship game was played each year in Tajin. The two teams with the best record of wins played a final game. The ball, however, was a human skull packed and covered with rubber. The captain of the team that lost the year before provided the skull. He donated his own head.

The Lords of Death could visit the game in two ways: when the loser's head was cut off by the victor . . . or during the play. A skull ball was much harder than an ordinary ball and often killed players in the course of the match.

I was speechless. The king was risking his kingdom and his life to avoid a marriage that his nobles desired and which seemed politically reasonable. It would bring the two most powerful empires in the One-World closer together.

A loss in a royal match would be interpreted by all that he was not favored by the gods—with crops thin from a lack of rain and our people growing hungrier, the loss would suggest again that King Quetzalcoatl had fallen from grace. The loss might embolden an ambitious Toltec nobleman or another king to attack him.

On the other hand, the Teotihuacán team had defeated Tula before. A victory by the king would also wipe away that disgrace.

"When will the match be held?" I asked.

"Today. I demanded an immediate game to keep Prince Tizoc from talking to counselors and refusing my challenge."

He told me why he had called me before him:

"I need to know what the gods feel about the game. Do they disfavor me so much they will permit Tizoc to win? Tell me what you saw in the sky last night."

My heart stopped. My breathing froze.

Last night I had failed to make my star sightings.

If I told him that I had been too busy making love and listening to tales of destiny from three old priests he would have me skinned alive—and *then* tortured.

"Are the signs that bad? You look faint. Do they hate me that much? Was there an Intruder god?"

"N-no," I stammered, "there was no Intruder god."

An Intruder was a god that streaked down from the sky with a trail of fire or across the sky with a tail.*

"My king, there were no significant signs in the—"

"Have you failed me? Did you—"

"No, my king, I have not failed you."

Interrupting the king was punishable by death. We both froze for a moment. I felt the earth opening under my feet. I saw myself being dragged up the steps of a temple and my heart being ripped out.

Then it came to me. There *had* been a sign.

"The gods have shown their desire," I told the king.

I was in a panic and the words flew out of my mouth.

"What are the gods' intentions? Tell me," the king said.

"Let me show you." I took the king to the window. "There. Can you see it? There." I pointed.

"See what? I see the sky, the Sun God. None of the other gods are visible."

I pointed again. "It's there, the star-god Quetzalcoatl, the god whose name you bear. It's not visible to everyone. I can see it."

"Yes, I've heard that there are times when some are able to see it in the daylight. Does its presence today have a meaning?"

"Yes."

"Tell me, what does it mean?"

"The star-god is rising at the very moment you have put forth the challenge to the prince. The rising sign is an indication from the god that he favors you in the match."

---

* Translator's Note: Meteors and comets.

I saw relief on the king's face. And I resisted the impulse to take a deep breath of relief.

"Just as the rise of Quetzalcoatl is a sign for war," I said, "it is a sign for the game of life and death."

He stared up at the sky, nodding. "It is good, it is good."

I had not lied to the king. The gods truly favored the king's match with the foreign prince. There was no other explanation for the star-god to permit me to see him this very morning.

39

The royal procession in Tajin's Ceremonial Center to the ball court was stunning.

Quetzalcoatl and Prince Tizoc paraded through the city to the ball court, carried on their palanquins with their nobles and warriors following. Both royals were dressed in ball-playing uniforms fit for a god, a magnificent array of feathers, gold and silver ornaments, and jewels.

The brilliant display was to impress the crowds. Before they entered the ball court, they both changed into the actual gear used in the game, though the front of their helmets carried the symbol of the order of knighthood that they belonged to. Quetzalcoatl's helmet bore the visage of a jaguar, Tizoc the countenance of a falcon.

Tlachtli is played in a long, narrow court. Courts varied in size and the ball court chosen for the match was sixty paces long and fifteen wide. The facing side walls were as high as three men.

I suspect the court was chosen more for the number of surrounding temples and other buildings that provided a view through the windows, steps, or roofs to observe the game. The interest in the city was intense—the mightiest king in the One-World was playing the future king of the second biggest empire in a game with both empires at stake.

High stakes were not just being played out on the ball court—the excitement among the nobility and wealthy merchants caused enormous wagers to be placed on the outcome.

Moving among the upper classes who crowded into the Ceremonial Center to place bets and watch the match, from the conversations I heard it was obvious that most believed Prince Tizoc would win the match because he was younger, bigger, and stronger than the king.

My armorer friend assured me that it was not size alone that would determine the winner.

"Our king survived alone the wilderness, fighting wild animals, wild savages, and killers sent by the usurper of his throne." The armorer pounded his chest. "He is more powerful in here than the Teotihuacán prince."

I didn't dare point out to the armorer that the king's feats of physical superiority had occurred over twenty years before the match to be played.

I also didn't mention that the death of either royal would probably lead to war between the two empires, but I heard that conclusion spoken many times by others.

My mind had been whirling in opposite directions as I tried to keep focused on the match that would decide the fate of empires while trying to untangle the cryptic web the Guardians had spun around me.

Ixloom . . . stories of She Who Sees had been told around the supper fire of my Aztec people as long as I could remember. She was said to be both priestess and astronomer of an esoteric Mayan temple cult with secret rites and knowledge of ancient wisdom. Because she never stayed long in one place, it was said she was capable of passing from the world of humans to the spirit world and back again at will.

212 · GARY JENNINGS

Despite all the tales I'd heard about Ixloom, I had never heard anyone claim they had actually seen her. My impression was that the less the storyteller actually knew about her, the tales of her mystical and demigod-like powers grew until she was portrayed as a magician empowered by the spirit world.

The revelation that she was my mother generated only more questions. Why had she abandoned me in the stream? Where was she now?

The question about the identity of my father had also stunned me. I'd always been curious about him, but my mother's identity had always seemed more important.

Our world was not just one in which many children were born from unmarried liaisons between auianimes and countless men, but many children were produced by female slaves and from rape during raids and wars. As with the children of prostitutes, none of these waifs were considered the children of the men who impregnated their mothers.

Nobles and wealthy merchants routinely had concubines, while kings and high nobles had dozens or even hundreds. The fathers also did not recognize their concubines' children.

There was one practical reason for this cruel indifference: recognition by the father would have meant the children were entitled to support and inheritance—and created murderous competition with the children produced during marriage.

But the fact the Guardian posed the question meant that the identity of my father held some importance to who and what I was.

The mystery of my parents' identities, the star cicatrices on my belly, and my secret knowledge of the Dark Rift and the House of the Magician were all part of the same enigma. Who in Mictlantecuhtli's hell was I?

As the anticipation over the match grew to a frenzy, I was busy assisting with the king's preparation and had to put aside the questions of my lineage. Because I had heard the tales of Ixloom while I lived with the Aztecs, one area of information I did pursue was to ask the armorer if Ixloom was known in Tula. He told me that some claimed that she had guided Quetzalcoatl from the wilderness.

"But then she vanished, like the spirit-woman she is," he said.

"Was she married?"

The armorer gave me a look of surprise. "Married? She was a priestess. They do not marry."

I asked more questions and soon realized that the armorer had also never actually seen Ixloom.

My mother was a ghost in my mind. I realized that she was a ghost to others, too.

40

The ballgame is the most significant sport and festive event in all the One-World. Not even the bravery of heroes of war were admired and sang about as much as champion ballplayers.

Wars were battles between armies, but the battle between ballplayers was personal, taking place on a small court and with either a few teammates or player-against-player. And just as death can reign on the battlefield, sometimes the Lords of the Dead visited the playing field.

The excited cheers of the people as the two players were paraded before them were not just because a sporting game was to be played—but that blood would be spilt. In a skull game, the Lords of Death were always present.

Private tents had been set up at opposing ends of the playing field to give the royals privacy in dressing for the game. They had their lavish uniforms adorned with brilliant feathers and gems removed and were dressed in the actual gear used by professional players.

They wore hip-cloths over their cotton loincloths. Tizoc's hip-cloth was of deer skin and the king's was a jaguar hide. The hip-cloths were parted on the sides to ensure they did not impede movement, but draped down in front and back to add a little protection against the sting and bruising of the ball.

Their helmets were made of layers of leather and they wore pads made of wood and leather on their ankles, knees, and elbows.

Around each player's waists was a yoke, a wooden support that protected their abdomens and hips. The yoke was wrapped in soft leather to make it softer against their skin.

Straps wound tight around their rumps pulled their buttocks together to lessen the sting from hits from the ball.

Red stripes were painted on the bodies of each of the players as a symbol of the blood that would flow during the game.

The playing field was an alley formed by a stone wall on each side. The walls and floor were made of cut stone. The floor of the court was leveled but left a little rough to permit running without constant slipping.

The walls were painted with colorful scenes of the story of the Hero Twins, two youths who played a ballgame against the Lords of the Underworld with the fate of mankind at stake. The boys, whose father had played and lost the game and his life, defeated the mighty lords.

The match between the Hero Twins, who had to play better than their opponents and overcome tricks and dark magic used by the Lords of the Underworld, symbolized war, death, and human sacrifice in the context of the cosmic struggle to survive in a hostile world.

To remind the players that their very lives were at stake, at the entrance to the court on the northern side was a tzompantli—a rack holding the skulls of the players who had been sacrificed after they lost a game.

The game could be played by two players competing against each other or in teams of two, three, or even four players. The king's counselors had suggested that the match be between teams of two or three on each side, but he insisted that it be combat between only him and the prince.

The king ordered that I take a place on top of the wall where the highest-ranking Tula nobles were placed. Across from us, atop the other wall, were the high nobles of Teotihuacán.

I had been questioned by our own nobles about the sign and repeated the fact that the king's namesake star-god was rising even if they could not see it. More than one looked dubiously up at the sky. Had the star-god been visible they would have had less doubt about the match.

The king and prince came out onto the court and the crowd cheered for the player their own fortunes rode upon.

Because the ballgame was considered a sacred ceremony, the players both made a sacrifice to the gods. They each made a small cut on their hand and let blood drip onto the ball and onto the playing field.

The sacrifices were made to the gods Xolotl and Quetzalcoatl, the patron gods of the ballgame. The two gods were twins, the sons of the virgin Coatlicue, the Mother of Gods, who also gave birth to the Sun, the Moon, and the other star-gods. Coatlicue gave birth to the gods after she had been impregnated by a ball of feathers that fell on her while she was sweeping a temple.

A stone image of her wearing her skirt of writhing snakes and a necklace made of human hearts and skulls was at a corner of the playing court. Her hands and feet were clawed—for digging the graves of those who offended her.

Xolotl was a god of both fire and darkness. He guided the Sun during its nightly journey through the Underworld. It is said that he is the source for ollin, the motion that made the wind blow . . . and that players needed during the game.

Xolotl and his brother Quetzalcoatl were engaged in an eternal struggle of night and day—Quetzalcóatl was the Morning Star, Xolotl was the Evening Star—and the ballgame itself was seen as a struggle between night and day.

A conch shell was blown to start the game and another great roar erupted from the crowd.

The king of Tajin rose from his throne and threw the skull ball into the court so that it bounced between the players. The game of life and death had begun.

Quetzalcoatl and Tizoc scrambled to hit the ball, Tizoc getting the first hit with his knee, sending the ball ricocheting off the wall. Quetzalcoatl hit it with his hip to send it toward the end of the court the other player defended. Tizoc hit it with his own hip, sending it back to give the king a stinging blow.

The objective was for a player to move the ball down to his opponent's end of the court. A point was scored if the player got the ball to the opponent's end. The first player to achieve three points won the match.

Strict rules applied as to how the ball was moved. Players could hit it with their feet, knees, hips, buttocks, and shoulders—the only prohibition was that the ball could not be touched by the hands.

Balls came in different sizes and weights. Some ball courts had stone rings mounted high up and the objective of the competition was to knock the ball through the ring. However, the small balls used for that type of game could be thrown by hand and were half the size of the skull ball used in the game the king would play. The skull ball chosen weighed about ten pounds, making it much heavier than balls used in ordinary games.

The heavy weight of the skull ball added danger to the game. Hitting the ball with the hip was not only a powerful stroke, but the hip was protected by the wood yoke worn around the waist. It was the safest and most effective means of striking, but that wasn't always possible. Hitting it with a foot, knee, or elbow could break the player's bones—and cost the player his head because he would be unable to compete.

The hip shot was second only to a much more powerful movement—getting under the ball and hitting it with a shoulder on the rise. The shoulder hit would rarely be used in a skull game because the ball rarely rose high enough to get under it with a shoulder.

The ball became as deadly as a blow from a club in battle when it was propelled at high speed and struck a player. Players had been knocked unconscious or killed by a blow to the head, or received broken bones and injuries that caused them so much damage inside their chests and abdomens that they died.

All that for an ordinary ball that usually weighed about a third of the weight of the skull ball. A skull ball was truly a club of war.

Ayyo . . . I worried for my king. Tlachtli was called the game of war because the ball court became a battlefield in which life and death were decided.

The struggle to control and direct the ball grew fierce—and painful, as each player worked not only to drive the ball downcourt but to slam it into the opponent. It was obvious that each of the players had devised the same strategy: ensure a quick victory by crippling or killing the other player.

Ayyo . . . it was true that a skull match ended up in the death of the loser, but the game was supposed to be played as an ordinary one. What was happening on the court was a confrontation between warriors on a battlefield, not competitors in a sport.

It wasn't long until I could see that the king was breathing a little faster than the younger prince, though the king's features were always kept frozen in a neutral countenance no matter how the exertion was affecting him or how hard the ball slammed into him like a blow from a club.

The oppressive heat made both men sweat profusely.

Brutal . . . That was the word that came to my mind to describe the blows from a ball almost as heavy as a stone.

Quetzalcoatl made the first point, but the prince made the next two, taking a clear advantage. And no matter how the king tried to keep the strain on him a secret, I could see that the heat and exertion were taking a toll on him.

I glanced at Princess Zyanya. She was not hiding her stress at seeing her brother slowly being whittled down.

Prince Tozin suddenly crashed into the king, sending the king down. The tactic was a violation of the rules that required players not to batter each other with anything but the ball.

The prince looked up where the princess was seated and shot her a look of triumph. In return he got a glare of sizzling hate.

Quetzalcoatl got slowly to his feet and limped to get into position for play to resume. His knee pad dangled and blood flowed down his leg. I knew what had happened. The prince hadn't just deliberately run into him—when he got close, he had hit the king's knee with an upward motion that wasn't obvious to the spectators, almost all of whom were elevated above the level of play.

A dirty trick . . . a dishonorable act.

The king had a right to ask the Tajin king to forfeit the game in his favor and I prayed that he would. But instead he resumed play: he wanted a clean victory, not one that others would hawk as a defeat turned into victory by the king's plea to a subordinate king who would not dare refuse to grant the request.

The play restarted and Quetzalcoatl hit the ball off the ball, and then he slammed into the prince as the ball came back.

Tizoc appeared to be confused. He stood almost in place, taking only a step forward as Quetzalcoatl maneuvered the ball until he had it high enough to get under it and rise up, slamming the ball with his shoulder.

The shoulder hit, in which the player put the full force of his entire body into propelling the ball, was the most powerful in the game.

The king could have sent the ball down the court to make a point. Instead, he sent the ball into the prince's face.

Ayyo! Tizoc got a blow to his face as brutal as if he had been struck by a club. His nose exploded with a burst of blood and he staggered back and fell, falling on his side to the playing surface. Clutching his abdomen, he bent upward, then tried to turn and roll over to get to his feet.

Quetzalcoatl directed the ball close to the prince's face and kicked the ball, sending it against the prince's head.

Tizoc collapsed back down and lay on the ground, bleeding from his head and abdomen, his eyes open but glazed, his body writhing on the ground like a snake whose head had been chopped off.

The king quickly made points to win the game and came back to stand over Tizoc and raise his fists in triumph.

The crowd roared and began to chant over and over:

Feed the gods . . . Feed the gods.

The king of Tajin brought out a bejeweled obsidian sword and gave it to Quetzalcoatl.

The king walked around Tizoc, raising the sword in the air to the show it to the crowd.

Blood, they screamed. *Feed the gods.*

Prince Tizoc, still dazed, managed to get onto his hands and knees, but he was unable to gain his feet.

Quetzalcoatl stepped up to the fallen royal, his sword in hand. He paused and looked up.

I looked to the princess. The expression on her face shocked me.

She was in a heat of passion.

The expression on her face was akin to the sexual ecstasy a woman explodes with when her lust has been fulfilled.

Quetzalcoatl turned to the fallen prince.

Still unable to get upright, Tizoc was on his hands and knees before him like a dog.

Quetzalcoatl raised the sword.

41

Quetzalcoatl was dressing into his magnificent parade uniform when I entered the tent that had been erected for him next to the ball court. His palanquin was outside and his personal guard was forming to escort their king in triumph to the people of Tajin.

"You were right, young stargazer, my personal star-god was behind me in the court. Not just his brother Xolotl, but I felt Quetzalcoatl himself possessing me. He took over my body and directed every move I made. When my own strength was expended, he entered my body and his strength was my strength, his ollin was my own motion."

"The stars do not lie, my king."

"Stargazer has told me that often. He also told me back in Tula that his legs no longer carried him far and his eyesight was blurring. He suggested I take you with me to Tajin as my seer and that I make you my Royal Astronomer. He said he would support and assist you and continue to mentor you for as long as he should live. He said that you were unusually gifted and that you would serve me well. As usual, I am pleased I followed my old friend's advice. He has been my mentor too."

I bowed. "I am overwhelmed, my king."

He dismissed me. As I turned to leave, I noticed in the pile of clothes and gear he had used during the match a small, bloodied obsidian dagger that stuck out from the wristband.

I stared at the dagger. Obviously, a supersharp blade was not part of a ballplayer's uniform. What was it doing attached to his wrist?

The answer literally smacked me in the face: the prince had blood pouring from his abdomen.

I sucked in a gasp to keep from expressing what I realized: The king had used the blade to gut the prince.

Ayyo . . . he had not relied solely upon the will of the gods, but had given fate a hand.

The king saw me staring at the blade and I froze, fearful that I had exposed the fact that I had stumbled onto his deceit.

"The death of Prince Tizoc," I said, "was predestined by the gods at the time he left his mother's womb. The path a person takes from birth to death is not always apparent. Sometimes the gods use mortals to bring about the fate they have decreed."

Instead of a command to have me killed on the spot, the king treated me to a small smile.

"The gods act in mysterious ways," he said.

PART XI

42

Cooper Jones needed almost a half hour to scale the forty-foot canyon wall. She did not trust her San Miguel GPS this deep in the desert and had brought a pocket sextant to double-check it. Now that both GPS and her satellite-phone were missing, Coop felt lucky to have that old-fashioned instrument.

Fearing they were in the wrong canyon, Coop needed to verify their position. Using a chronometer and her electronic pocket, which measured the angle between the pole star and the rising sun, Coop could calculate their latitude/longitude and then locate their position on their grid map.

The sun would rise in a half hour, its predawn gray already illuminating the eastern rimrock—but the pole star was still visible. She also had a full moon, which—in combination with the broad swath of the Milky Way—lit the surrounding terrain with surprising clarity.

Instead of the pole star, however, Coop found herself staring at Sagittarius—the gateway to the Underworld Road, the Toltec highway to . . . hell. Through that gateway, some legends had it, the Night God, Tezcatlipoca, and his infernal horde would pour out on

December 21, 2012—the End Date of the so-called "Long Count Calendar."

Cooper's eyes drifted over her harsh surroundings—a lunarscape of labyrinthine canyons, grotesque rock sculptures, and desiccated gullies.

As the predawn grew lighter, the camp below came to life. Their mule-packer, Martinez, was already up. Overloaded with grain, water, rations, and gear, their three pack mules were hard-used and needed looking after. Martinez continually rubbed the stock down with an old grain sack, periodically treating their saddle-galled flanks and withers with neat's-foot oil and canteen tequila, which he said he'd brought along only for that purpose.

From the canyon rim, Cooper could see the two private contractors, Jamesy and Hargrave, rising from their bedrolls and stretching. Broad-shouldered and hard-looking, private contractors, they each sported a strange assortment of tattoos, some of which were military; others looked like they might have been jailhouse needlework.

Jamesy was now bent over the small portable double-burner cook stove, brewing coffee . . .

Shortly before the team entered the canyonlands, they'd camped by a stream and Cooper had stumbled on Jamesy finishing his bath. His pants were on but he was bare-chested. An ancient knife or bayonet slash transversed his chest; a mean red bitch of a bullet scar that entered and exited his right shoulder still looked tender and raw. He bore the broad white stripes of some hellish torture chamber on his back.

That night she walked Rita Critchlow away from the fire and described his scars. Her old friend was not surprised.

"Don't worry about it. I've been with them before," was all Reets would say.

"But the scars?"

"There are some very bad people in this imperfect world," Reets said, looking away.

"The bullet hole in Jamesy's shoulder was still fresh."

"He's recovering."

"I don't like it."

Critchlow shrugged. "You weren't in Chiapas."

"I read the papers. The federales rescued you."

"Jamesy and Hargrave did it."

Cooper touched her friend's arm. "Why did the papers lie about it?"

"We lied to them to get out of there."

"It was that bad?"

"You saw the hole in Jamesy's shoulder. He took that bullet for me."

The next day they entered that endless slickrock maze known as the canyonlands . . .

Again, Cooper turned her sextant heavenward and fixed it on the pole star. Calculating their latitude and longitude, she shoved a small Maglite between her teeth, and located their position on the grid map. They were in the right canyon at the right place.

So where was the urn and the third codex?

Then she caught a glimpse of a campfire up-canyon—a straight-line distance of maybe one-thousand feet. The way the canyon twisted and zigzagged, however, it could be as much as a mile on foot.

She took Jamesy's Tasco Spyglass out from the cushioned carrying case looped to her belt. Five inches in length, the brass telescope opened to a full fifteen inches and weighed only a pound and a half. With its 25X magnification, the campfire appeared less than forty feet away.

The distant campfire's glow reflected off the canyon walls, lighting up a group of campers—hard-looking men, rising from their bedrolls and stretching.

A woman—naked, bleeding, her face swollen—was also visible. She was staked out, spread-eagle, on the canyon floor. A man who had lain on top of her was leaping off her, his pants down around his knees. While he clutched a hemorrhaging ear, the woman spit something out of her mouth and gagged.

She'd bitten off half his ear in midrape.

Kicking her repeatedly, the man pulled out a pistol from his holster and shot her in the face. Even from a thousand yards Coop heard the pistol-crack. The other eight men were pointing at his bloody ear and laughing. Three of them were drinking bottled liquor.

They each took turns kicking the dead woman.

Coop counted nine bandits, a dozen horses, and three pack mules. She had to get back down the canyon wall.

Just then a man raised a pair of binoculars in her direction, and suddenly the bandits were pointing at *her*.

The small but powerful Maglite between her teeth had given her away. Nine murdering rapists in filthy fatigues, camouflage T-shirts, and a bizarre assortment of headgear—triple-creased Smokey the Bear hats, sombreros, baseball caps, and fedoras—were strapping on side-arms, machetes, and canteens, and slinging crisscrossed bandoleers across their chests.

Breaking camp, they weren't even bothering to bury the poor woman they'd raped, tortured, and murdered.

43

"They saw your Maglite?" Jamesy stared at Cooper in blank disbelief.

"They pointed and stared," Coop said. "Yes, they saw it."

Unholstering their pistols, he and Hargrave checked their loads. Old-fashioned government-issue .45s instead of nines, Jamesy had explained earlier they had more stopping-power. More resistant to sand and water, they'd been the marines' weapon of choice in Baghdad. Ejecting their magazines, they slammed them back in and racked the slides. After chambering rounds, they thumbed off the safeties. Martinez was already unlimbering a third .45 from a pannier. Inserting a clip, he also chambered a round, then handed it to Rita Critchlow.

"We could run for it," Coop said.

"We have mules," Hargrave said, shaking his head. "They have horses."

"You saw them rape and murder that woman," James said.

Martinez was unpacking a duffel bag containing three burlap-wrapped, well-oiled twelve-gauge pump shotguns, which Coop had not even known were packed. Racking the slides, the two men fed shells into the loading slots underneath the breech.

"The M1897 Winchester twelve-gauge pump—best combat shotgun ever made," Jamesy announced pleasantly. "Who wants the extra?"

"Give it to Coop," Rita said. "Her hillybilly father used to take her deer hunting."

"When he wasn't running 'shine," Coop said.

"I'm going to do the talking," Rita explained. "I need to appear unarmed." She shoved the .45 between her pants and the back of her shirt.

"You know the language," Jamesy said.

"She knows fucking Nahuatl," Hargrave said.

Jamesy handed Coop the shotgun.

"Loaded, chambered, locked, and cocked," Jamesy said, "with a big shot-pattern. Aim, squeeze the trigger and keep it pressed—right against the trigger guard. When you rack the slide, the pump-action will release the hammer. It's like a semiauto but more reliable in all this sand."

"Each shell has nine .33 caliber pellets," Hargrave said. "You can get off fifty-four pellets in eight seconds. A thirty-six-round machine-gun clip won't throw that much lead."

"Don't let him get too close to you, Rita," Jamesy warned. "Our shotguns throw a lot of lead."

"I won't let him kiss me," Rita said.

Hargrave studied their surroundings. "The boulder cluster here'll provide defilade; so will that one a hundred feet up-canyon. You take the first one, Jamesy. I'll get the second."

Hargrave handed James Martinez the mules' lead mecate. "Hobble these mules out of eyeshot," he said. Swinging onto his own jack, Jamesy took them both back down-canyon.

The mule-packer with the rheumy sightless eye said: "I was a soldado in my youth. I can fire a pistola, señor."

"You can't even see your pack saddles," Hargrave said, refusing to hand him a weapon.

Racking the fourth .45, he handed it to Cooper.

"I don't need two guns," Coop said.

"If this thing goes south, turn it on yourself."

They all turned to stare up-canyon.

"As soon as you see them round that far bend," Hargrave said, "swing your mules sideways. Coop, stay behind Rita, but off to the right. Loop the shotgun's sling over the saddle pommel, but keep it on your side of the mule, where they can't see it." He looked closely at the two women.

Jamesy jogged back up to them, and the two men then jogged up-canyon to their boulders. Within minutes, the bandits rounded the far bend, halted, and conferred. The two mounted women and the old packer halted. Dismounting, they swung their mules between themselves and the bandits.

A single horseman rode up. Mounted on a deep-chested bay, his dirty work pants, collarless brown shirt, and worn brown fedora were covered with dust and sweat. His broad nose, flaring cheekbones, and face were nut-brown under the dirt. A single cartridge belt was strapped across his chest, two-thirds of the loops empty. He kept his nickel-plated revolver with a worn walnut grip in a cross-draw holster on his left hip.

"What are you three doin' in our canyon," he asked in bad Spanish-English. Coop could tell that neither was his native tongue.

"Looking for buried treasure," Rita said.

"What you find?"

"Nada. We've given up."

"Muy malo," he said. Too bad. "Mucho banditos in these canyons tambien. Luckily, we federales. We take you back up-canyon—to safety."

"We're not going your way."

"Ah but you are." Then he said to Martinez, "After, of course, we look in your packs first—make sure you ain't stealin' treasure from our country."

"But I told you we have nothing," Rita said.

"Oh, you got something. Them mules is something. Them sad-dles is something."

So that's that, Coop thought.

"But we can't give them to you," Rita said with a cheerful smile. "We'd have to walk."

As if to answer her question, he laughed hackingly, took a brown liquor bottle out of a saddle bag and upended it. The tequila glugged, and he did not stop till he was sucking air.

"Since we federales, you do what we say."

"Where are your badges?" Rita asked.

He treated them to the most obscene grin Coop had ever seen.

"Come on," he said. "Don't make me say it."

"You've seen the movie too?" Rita asked.

He shouted back at his compadres, telling them she wanted to know if they had seen "the Sierra Madre movie." His words were more Nahuatl than Spanish but Coop could make them out.

They all shouted in English: *"We don't need no stinking badges!"*

Christ, Coop thought, *has everyone seen that fucking film?*

"But if we give you the mules," Rita said, smiling again, "then we would have nothing."

"Naw, you still got something: You still got your puta pussies." He turned his head and half-shouted the last sentence, using the Eng-lish word *pussies,* again eliciting raucous guffaws from his men.

Wheeling in his saddle, he flung and shattered the empty bottle against the canyon wall. Before Coop could take her eyes off the smashed glass, he had his nickel-plated revolver aimed at her friend's chest. It was a .44 Colt Peacemaker with a seven and half inch bar-rel. Using the mule in front of her for defilade, she tore at the pistol behind her back.

Its hammer was snagged in her belt's leather webbing.

Out of the corner of her eye, Coop could see the eight bandits behind the man in front of them drawing their weapons. Coming out from behind their boulders, Jamesy and Hargrave hammered double-aught buck into the bunched-up men, racking the shells so rapidly their blasts merged in her ears into a single composite thunder-crack. Reverberating off the arroyo walls, the roar echoed up and down the canyons in endless replication like rolling thunder in hell.

The bandit before them turned to look.

At which point Cooper saw it:

The back of the man's ear—livid, raw, ripped off, blood encrusted.

The man she'd watched rape and kill the woman.

Even as both of the women's mules bucked and bolted down-canyon, Coop's Winchester pump was levitating into her hands, as if it had a will of its own. Leveled on the bandit's chest, her first load of double-aught was hitting him square, its nine .33-caliber pellets lifting him a foot above the saddle. Trigger still down, she continued racking the slide, the second load of .33-caliber pellets catching his cranium in midair at full apogee, barely a second after the first round had hit.

Even as his horse bolted and raced up the canyon, his left rowel hooked under its latigo and his mount dragged him up-canyon at a hard gallop. Meanwhile, two bloodied bandits charged up the horse's trail, their weapons cocked, bearing down on Rita, who was directly in their path. Coop stepped in front of her friend, the trigger still down, still working the slide. She pumped her last four rounds into the charging men as fast as she could rack the slide. The two riders were hammered out of their saddles.

As the two mounts thundered past, Coop thought of them as the Riderless Horses of the Apocalypse.

PART XII

44

ONE-WORLD, 1004 A.D.

We left Tajin in triumph, with the king and princess in a far better mood than when we arrived. While we marched back across the flatlands, Xolotl, the god of black clouds and lightning, hurled thunderbolts at us while Tlaloc, the god of the rains, opened the sky and dropped deluges on us from Tlalocan, the warm, wet paradise where the souls of those who have died from drowning rest.

The king privately cursed the rains, which shunned his parched farmlands but satiated these humid hotlands.

We were less than a day out of Tajin when Xolotl threw fire to the ground that struck and killed a member of the king's honor guard. Standing over the man's body, I spoke to the king loud enough for others to hear.

"Xolotl has shown his disfavor because he was once again defeated by his twin brother Quetzalcoatl. The lightning strike was meant for you, my king, but your patron god protected you."

The pronouncement brought general relief from the thought that the king was disfavored by the gods.

From the flatlands we entered thick jungle foliage that followed us until we were beyond the foothills of the mountains. We were halfway up the mountain before the air lost its hot-wet flavor.

When we left Tajin, I left behind my old identity and assumed a significant new role. As the Royal Astronomer I ranked with the high priest and highest nobles of the empire. I dressed differently and had I demanded it, I would have been carried in a palanquin, though one not as grand as th e king's.

What I did not leave behind in Tajin were thoughts boiling in my head. I mourned Flower, as another man might mourn a wife; and I missed Stargazer as another might miss a father. I realized then that Tula was my true home—the only one I recognized as such.

I didn't know who my true parents were, but the cryptic remarks made by the Guardian who had questioned me raced like a wild boar through my head. I was to be the Keeper of something found in a place called the House of the Magician. Keeper of what? The bleeding heart of the One-World?

Ayyo . . . it made as much sense to me as the star pattern carved onto my stomach and my mother abandoning me to be a coyote's dinner.

That an assassin might be waiting for me in Tula was also never far from my mind. Where did spilling my blood fit in with the mystery of my birth and the Guardians?

We were over the mountains when word came that the Hill of Knives was under attack, was a day's march from us.

The "hill" was a mountainous mound of the black rock spit out by a fire mountain.* The obsidian mined at the hill was the main source of the valuable material in the One-World. Weapons-makers could split the jet-black rock into thin, sharp cutting blades that were prized throughout the One-Word not only for their beauty but for their military value. These craftsmen fabricated the finest battle-axes, knives, spear-points, and arrowheads out of the basaltic rock.

To lose control of the Hill of Knives was tantamount to a defeat in war.

---

* Translator's Note: A fire mountain is a volcano. Obsidian is formed by a type of lava flow.

The king who controlled the Hill of Knives and that precious resource had an overwhelming advantage in battle over those who relied on far less lethal weaponry. As long as Tula had commanded that mountain, Tula enjoyed that advantage. To maintain that control, Quetzalcoatl kept a high lord bivouacked there. Commanding a force totaling over one thousand warriors, the base was less than a two-day march from Tula; hence, our king could quickly reinforce it if the need arose.

The need had arisen. We would face an army of Dog People, whose charismatic leader was uniting the Clans and threatening the obsidian hill. The leader was Tenoch.

Ayyo . . . I was beginning to understand that life was a circle.

PART XIII

THE HILL OF KNIVES

45

As we approached the Hill of Knives, our scouts reported that the enemy was nowhere to be seen, which caused a great deal of consternation among our officers. We were merely the king's personal guard, not Tula's expeditionary force—which would not arrive until the next day. We were here, however, and they weren't.

Only the king seemed unperturbed.

The king had already ordered Princess Zyanya home under heavy guard. The princess had wanted to stay. She had argued that he could not afford to use part of his personal guard to see her back to Tula. Whatever her vices, cowardice was not one of them.

I had heard much about the Hill of Knives, the martial wonder of the One-World. I had imagined a mound the shape of a sacred temple from which skilled workers would split off the obsidian sheets. I saw now, however, that the Hill of Knives occupied the sides of multiple hills in the midst of a pine forest.

The hills were not solid obsidian. The black rock had instead seeped into them when the gods were angry and the fire mountains unleashed their molten rivers. Some of the molten material became rock, some of it infused these hills.

When the Hill of Knives was born, no one knew. It happened at a time so far back not even a Rememberer of History knew the date.

Hundreds of mines were scattered over the mounds. The mines were small, similar to shallow water wells. Chunks of obsidian were broken off inside the wall and brought to a flat area where larger pieces were further broken up to make them easier to be packed off to Tula by porters.

Obsidian had natural fractures that permitted pieces to be sliced off by chipping at it with hard rock chisels. The worker chipped along the fracture lines, often using wood or even bone to soften the blow and prevent the piece from breaking into pieces too small to be worked.

A small amount of the obsidian was worked into usable pieces such as knife blades and arrowheads at the site, but most of it was carried to Tula on the backs of porters.

The king had a monopoly on obsidian mining and allocated only enough of it to cover the cost that the High Lord incurred while guarding it.

In Tula the obsidian chunks were sold to craftsmen who turned the rough materials into the weapons of war—arrowheads, dagger blades, and the sharp edges of swords and battle-axes; into razors for shaving faces, mirrors, jewelry, and other household items.

While the sale of obsidian jewelry and mirrors was unrestricted, agents of the king prohibited the export of military obsidian except to Tula's allies—and even then only in small quantities.

The Hill of Knives was the largest source of obsidian in the One-World. The king who controlled it possessed a prodigious arsenal. When Teotihuacán controlled it, every king in the One-World paid tribute to it.

Now Tula commanded it.

The Royal Armorer came up beside me as I studied the miners at work. He was dark of skin for a Toltec, his white cotton uniform and quilted tunic contrasting brightly with his complexion. Like all of the soldiers, his hide sandals were laced up to his knee.

"The Hill of Knives is a disappointment, is it not? Because of its importance, people expect the Hill to resemble something sacred, like the ceremonial center of a city. Never have the gods created something so ugly yet so significant.

"Some people believe that a worker at the hill merely walks around, picking up pieces shaped like dagger blades, arrowheads, and all the other objects made of obsidian. But as you can see, the obsidian comes in chunks that have not been worked into useable shapes. We create those blades, not the god of fire."

En route to the Hill, I ordered the Royal Armorer to provide me with a warrior's uniform and weapons.

When the king questioned my intent, I lied to him about my motives:

"I want to be at your side during the battle. But I cannot serve you if you surround me with warriors. I don't need a personal army. I can defend myself."

The armorer provided me with the warrior battle gear. He tried to dress me as a high-ranking courtier, but I told him I wanted the simple uniform of a common soldier, though I accepted the better protection provided by the body armor composed of thick quilted cotton, stuffed with ground shells found on the shores of the Eastern Sea.

I chose a macquahuitl, a wood sword with obsidian edges, for my primary weapon and a short battle-axe that could be thrown. Both the sword and the axe had the thicker obsidian blades reserved for nobles and knights.

I requested a modification to my battle gear that made the armorer's jaw drop. "I want an obsidian blade placed at the tip of each of my sandals."

Smoking Shield had trained me well in hand-to-hand conflict and taught me to turn my feet as well as my hands into weapons.

"That's dishonorable!" the armorer told me.

I insisted it be done. I was tempted to tell him that what he considered to be "honorable" as a citizen of a rich Toltec kingdom was different from what I had learned as a Dog People warrior and under the tutelage of Smoking Shield.

The knights and nobles who commanded units of warriors wore elaborate uniforms into battle. While not as colorful and awkward to move around in as those worn in parades and festivals, the uniforms all had tall headdresses of feathers. The higher the rank of the commander, the higher the headdress, until it came to the king, whose brilliant feathers soared three feet over his head.

Each headdress was distinctive so that warriors would instantly recognize it as belonging to their commander. The purpose of the headdresses was to keep warriors grouped around their commander, no matter what direction he took.

Even more useful at keeping a unit grouped and moving together were the banners called pamitls. A military commander's insignia, a pamitl was made by mounting a spear shaft to a brace on a warrior's back and placing a representation of the commander's patron god on top. Mounted in this manner, the staff stood straight up behind the warrior, with the god-image several feet above the warrior's head.

A military standard served two purposes: it elevated the unit's symbol high enough so common soldiers could follow their commander in the direction he moved, and by being mounted on the back it left both hands free to fight. It also, however, made the commander a target for the opposing forces. The enemy sought high-ranking captives, and by announcing the commander's rank the standard increased the risk that its wearer would be taken prisoner. Moreover, when a commander was captured or killed pandemonium ensued.

Except for the king, the commanders carried the pamitls. And his tall jaguar image was carried by a standard bearer whose duty it was to stay close to his side.

I had no intention of commanding warriors, nor did I want to flaunt my authority as a highly ranked courtier. Unlike the king and commanders, I was not concerned with the course of the overall battle. I chose to dress as a common soldier because my intention was to move during the battle like a jungle cat and pounce on a single prey when I had the opportunity:

I would seek out Tenoch on the battlefield and kill him.

Ayyo . . . I had made a terrible mistake in helping him escape years ago. That he was now powerful enough—and bold enough—to attack the most prized asset of the greatest empire in the One-World was for me beyond bearing. I was responsible for unleashing a monster capable of devouring the land and lord I served.

I'd considered none of these possibilities when I passed Tenoch the dagger. He not only returned to the Clan as a hero for having escaped from the heart of Tula itself, but he had seen the city . . . knew now that the tales of its beauty and riches were not lies.

His escape over a city wall had burnished his reputation as well. To Dog People who got close enough to Tula to see its mighty walls, the indomitable barriers appeared as imposing as mountains. But Tenoch knew from personal experience that the ramparts were not unassailable, that he himself had climbed them to leave the city and that an invading army could do the same. And he also knew how the city was defended from the inside. My instincts screamed that Tenoch had come to the hill to obtain obsidian for an attack on Tula.

If there was to be a battle at the Hill, I knew how the Aztecs would fight it—and the easiest way to defeat them. As with Toltec warriors, they would leave the battle if their leader was slain. But killing Tenoch would serve another purpose than the winning of a single battle—not only would the Aztec warriors turn from an attack if their leader went down, but the Clans would return to bickering and infighting, with an occasional raid into Toltec territory rather than massing for a concentrated attack on Tula.

Over and over, I regretted that I had done as Desert Flower asked. Had I refused her, she would be alive now and Tula would not be battling the Dog People for this indispensable prize. Hopefully, I would strike him down in the upcoming battle and the secret would die with him.

My thoughts and plots were interrupted by the armorer commanding me to report to the king.

"Beg the gods that he doesn't have your head cut off just for appearing before him. He is not in a good mood."

"Have the Dog People been sighted?"

He sneered at me. "I am his armorer, not his seer. You should consult the stars yourself, astronomer."

46

As I hurried toward the king's tent, I thought about the Hill.

Where was the enemy?

We had now learned that the Aztec attacks that had brought us here were little more than skirmishes. Moreover, the High Lord stationed at the Hill to defend it had then left on a hunting trip, taking half the Hill guards with him. He had left the obsidian mines largely unprotected and had not returned until our small band had arrived.

We were told the Aztec army was a formidable force, much greater than those units defending the Hill. With the High Lord gone and the guard force depleted, why had the Aztecs not attacked the Hill with their full might and occupied it? Why indeed? When the Dog People were dominant, they attacked.

Though the king did not indicate that he was concerned after his briefing, the royal commanders quietly voiced concern among themselves.

Nor did an Aztec attack on the Hill of Knives make any sense. Deep in Tula territory, they could not supply and reinforce their forces and would ultimately be overwhelmed. Tula was capable of fielding an army that was much larger, better trained, and better equipped than the Dog People.

The only sensible tactic was to attack, grab as much obsidian as they could get, and run. But they had not taken any of the valuable fire rock.

When I voiced my concerns to the king at the time, he seemed oblivious.

What was Tenoch up to? I wondered. What was the king up to?

※

Before I reached the king's tent, the conch-trumpeters blew assembly and our men lined up for the march. I wondered if we were leaving the Hill and returning as fast as possible to Tula.

When I entered the king's tent, he was dressing for battle.

"What is your feeling about meeting your own people in battle?" he asked. "You may find yourself in a fight to the death with a warrior you were raised with."

I kept my face blank, but he'd shocked me. I kept my intention to kill Tenoch a secret. Given my value as his astronomer, he would never let me do it. The mere fact that I wanted to would cast doubt on my loyalty.

"The Aztec Dogs enslaved me, then offered me up as a human sacrifice. I am only alive today because Stargazer intervened. I am not Aztec anymore nor am I loyal to them."

Smoking Shield—the commander of his Jaguar Knights— interrupted us with the Hill's High Lord as his prisoner. He wanted to know why he was under arrest.

"For treason!" the king shouted.

When the king approached him, the nobleman dropped to his knees.

"Treason. The Hill was never seriously under attack. You deliberately left for a hunting trip so the Dog People could pretend to make an attack without concern that they would be pursued."

"I am your—"

"Traitor! One who accepted a Dog People bribe and agreed to give them obsidian. You pointed them toward an obsidian caravan heading toward Tula, which was an easier and more productive target. Thanks to you, the Dog People walked off with enough obsidian to make thousands of weapons."

The guards dragged the sobbing High Lord out of the tent. I followed the king and other courtiers. His commander announced to the assembled warriors:

"The High Lord had plotted with the enemies of Tula."

The penalty was death.

I looked away as the commander's sword was raised.

47

I found myself alone with the king in the tent. The army waited outside for the order to march. Both the king and I were dressed in our battle uniforms, except for the tall headdress of feathers he would put on just before the battle began. If we engaged the enemy in battle. We had to catch the Aztecs in order to fight them, and that was not likely to happen, I thought. The Dog People were nomads . . . they could march for days without food or rest while Toltec warriors needed to stop and sleep each night.

The king paced back and forth in his tent.

I stood perfectly still, daring not to utter a word.

He finally paused and faced me.

"You know this Clan leader, Tenoch. He was once your leader and our prisoner. I also know what you're thinking. Something is wrong about this attack. Tell me what it is."

I took a deep breath. "My king . . . I believe everything I heard . . . except when it comes to the Dog People bribing the High Lord of the Hill of Knives. That is not the way of my people."

"Your leaders take bribes, but do not give them."

"Yes. Furthermore the Aztecs' strategy makes no sense. The

deception is too complicated. They are too far from their supply lines and cannot win in the long run. Tenoch avoids such risks."

The king nodded repeatedly. "Do you think Teotihuacán is behind this?"

"Teotihuacán didn't have the time to set up this scheme after you won the match."

"Then who is behind this ruse?"

"Some of your nobles in Tula."

A small bitter smile spread on the king's face. "Along with the priests—the high priest in particular."

He had known the answer but wanted me to confirm it.

"They believe the gods have abandoned me," the king said. "I have not commandeered enough blood for them to offer Tezcatlipoca. Some believe that he will wreak revenge on Tula and that Tlaloc will not bring rain . . . not as long as I am king."

I shook my head. "Tlaloc has his own reasons for not bringing rain. And the nobles that oppose you do it for the wealth and power they will reap if they claim your throne."

"If I lose the people, their motives may not matter."

"The people love you, sire. I have heard and seen their love."

"They love to eat as well, and fear starvation. Those with empty bellies will listen to the death priests."

"If you traded more obsidian to other kings for maize—"

"They would use it to make their armies stronger and attack us. Tell me of Tenoch—how he thinks, how he fights."

"Like a wild beast. Not mindless, not like a crocodile who goes after anything that moves or a snake that strikes anything that gets too close. He's a jungle cat . . . a jaguar who lies patiently in the darkness for its prey and then suddenly attacks. That is how Tenoch thinks and acts."

I thought about how he acted in captivity, never giving quarter or asking for mercy. Never thinking about his actions but acting with animal instincts to fight back.

"He only knows to keep pushing forward," I said, "never retreating, never surrendering. He favors surprise attacks most of all."

"How does he attack? How will he position his army?"

"Attack?"

Then it came to me—I knew exactly how Tenoch would fight. I had seen him make attacks on other Clans and Toltec villages. He would use the same maneuvers in an attack on us.

"He attacks from behind cover. Ambush. That is how he thinks. He will not openly face a stronger enemy."

"Why?"

"Tenoch may have an army, but he knows only small-unit fighting. He can't command a large force."

I paused and met the eye of the king.

"He's planning an ambush."

48

I had finally contrived a plan to kill Tenoch. Had I told the king, he would have forbidden it on the grounds that it was suicidally bold . . . and he would have been right.

I'd cursed myself a thousand times for slipping Tenoch the knife, and now I had to atone for that act and kill him. If he was taken prisoner—and we did strive to capture soldiers alive—he would expose my role in his escape.

For the king's part, he decided to pursue the Aztec force but left a third of his warriors behind to defend the Hill in the event that the Aztecs returned.

"The High Lord's warriors cannot be trusted," the king said. "Members of my guard will stay not only to defend against the Dog People but to ensure that our precious obsidian isn't stolen by traitors among our own people."

As we marched, he deployed scouts to warn of potential ambushes.

On that march, I was not part of the king's entourage, so I could slip away from the main force. I quickly did so, becoming a deserter.

Out of sight of the warriors, I opened a shoulder sack that was supposed to contain tortillas. Instead, it had clothes and other items

I had purchased from porters. I changed out of my Toltec battle dress and fashioned a crude facsimile of an Aztec foot-soldier's uniform, daubing bands of green paint on my bare face, arms, and legs.

I was now indistinguishable from the Dog People warriors.

I could not openly possess the obsidian sword but had no way to hide it. Regretfully, I hid it in bushes so it wouldn't be found. The battle-axe was short-handled, and I hid it in the tortilla sack that I carried slung from my shoulder.

I carried my dagger sheathed in my waist cloth.

Needing a display weapon, I hewed a thick tree limb into a serviceable club.

I could only hope and pray I would not run into my former Aztec brothers. I'd grown several inches over the years, and my martial arts training under Shield had pumped up my muscles. I did not think I was instantly recognizable as the old slave, Coyotl. Still, one never knew.

If I was captured by the king's men, he would no doubt see me as an Aztec traitor.

Ayyo . . . A man without a country, I had to kill Tenoch. Only his death could justify my seeming betrayal of the god-king.

49

I picked my way through the high rocks and the stands of mountain pine, staying well above the king's small force while they crossed the valley floor. I knew Tenoch would wait above them somewhere along the way, also cleaving to the high ground. His warriors would then sweep down on the royal forces. If Tenoch's troops were too far upslope and too far from the Toltec army, they would lose the element of surprise. They would require too much time to engage their foe.

So I was well above them.

Staying ahead of the king's forces wasn't difficult, despite the rough rocky terrain. The king's exhausted army moved even slower than we had on the way to Tajin. The king not only wanted to spare his warriors, he too would be watching for Tenoch. Looking down, however, I would spot him first.

While the Dog People would not be as high up as I was, Tenoch would deploy scouts up here, and moving stealthily slowed me down. I would be hard-pressed to reach Tenoch before he launched his ambush.

I moved through brush and around trees and rocks for three hours before I spotted the lookouts. Five Aztecs were hidden in a cluster of rocks that formed a ridge near the top of a hill overlooking the valley.

Keeping out of sight, I sat for a while and looked around, spotting another group across the valley floor. I had to make sure when I made my move that I wasn't seen by either set of lookouts.

I went to the top of the hill and moved slowly and quietly until I was well past the lookouts. When I thought it was safe, I moved farther down the side of the mountain. My objective was to find the main camp of Tenoch's forces.

When I spotted the encampment, it was where I thought it would be—Tenoch had placed his army in a heavily wooded area not far above the valley floor. Concealed by trees and close to passing soldiers, Tenoch would strike the king with an overwhelming force and surprise.

I settled in the brush and waited. I tried to spot Quetzalcoatl in the sky, but the day was too bright and the star-god too elusive, even though I knew which part of the sky to study.

Ayyo . . . Why didn't the god show himself to me? Had I fallen from favor with him? I pledged that any blood I spilled today I would tithe to him.

When I saw lookouts running toward the main forces, I came out of hiding and went after them, staying back far enough so they wouldn't see me. My plan was to be mistaken as a lookout when I reached the main force.

As I hurried through the brush and around trees I suddenly realized someone was behind me—and coming fast. I took a deep breath and prepared myself to meet his eye as he passed. I, too, was of the Dog People.

As he came trotting alongside he asked, "What Clan are you, friend?"

I turned to reply and my blood froze.

He was of my own Clan, a man my age with whom I had played as a child.

Ayyo! The gods truly had damned me. He was one of the warriors who fled the day that Smoking Shield and his men attacked us and Stargazer, spotting the star markings on my body, had spared my life.

Recognizing me instantly, he gaped, then raised his spear.

Smoking Shield had taught me well. I did not stand on ceremony but kicked him in the knee with the razor-sharp front of my scandals. He cried out and I followed with a body-slam. He hit the rocky ground hard.

Still he came at me again, this time with his spear. Deflecting it with my club, I kicked him again, catching him under the chin with my spiked sandal toe. The blow smothered an outcry.

He was mortally wounded but still thrashing. The blood flooding his mouth and windpipe stifled his cry.

I dropped down on him with both knees, pinning him with his back to the ground. Raising my dagger high, I drove it into his chest.

Gasping for breath myself, I worked my dagger back and forth to enlarge the hole in his chest, then shoved my hand into the opening and clutched his heart. It beat in the palm of my hand. Wrenching it out, I raised it to the sky where I knew the star-god would be flying.

"Nourishment for you, Quetzalcoatl!" I shouted to my personal deity and savior, who had guided and protected me during my river voyage in the reed basket. "Drink and make me strong from your strength."

50

Rubbing the dead warrior's blood on my face, I hoped to further conceal my identity. Taking his spear, I discarded my crude club.

I melted into the Dog People's main force just as they were organizing behind their leaders' pamitls. Even among the Aztecs, pamitls included many different representations of gods and animals. I was looking for an iridescent male hummingbird radiating reds, blues, and greens. When I saw it, I knew I had found Tenoch.

High on the hillside, I was surrounded by warriors. As I moved toward the hummingbird pamitl and the warriors amassing behind it, none of them recognized me. Tenoch had his back to me and was still a considerable distance away, but I knew it was him. He'd stained his bare skin blue, the symbolic color of Huitzilopochtli, "Hummingbird of the South," the war god of our Clan.

Other Clans found the choice of a hummingbird as a god of war unacceptable, preferring a god associated with the eagle or the hawk, the jaguar or the ocelot. Tenoch, however, insisted our Clan pay homage to the hummingbird god because no other creature had the ability to fly both backward and forward, upward and downward, and even hover in midair. He viewed the Dog People in the same light, blown by the winds of fate and forced by the gods into eternal peregrination, never knowing which direction they would wander.

That the gods now drove them south seemed a propitious sign. The south boasted a warm, green, wet climate in which the Dog People could conceivably prosper.

He had placed himself in the front lines, which increased the risk that he might be killed. The enemy almost always attacked the leader, hoping that his death would throw his warriors into doubt and confusion by taking down his pamitl.

But it also earned the loyalty and respect of his men.

Somehow I had to work my way through those men and drive my battle-axe into Tenoch's skull.

More and more, I viewed my assault as a suicide mission.

Now that I was in the thick of the Aztec army, I would not escape after I killed him. I would be swarmed and hacked to pieces within seconds of my killing blow.

Also the closer I got, the more difficult it became to move through the mass of warriors grouping for the attack. I was fifty paces from Tenoch's position with the spear in one hand and my other hand gripping the battle-axe still hidden in my sack when the attack conch was blown and the entire mass of Aztec warriors surged forward.

The royal army was within range, and Tenoch's army was beginning its assault. Breaking into a downhill run, I had to fight just to keep from being trampled. As the troop density around Tenoch tightened, reaching him seemed more and more a fool's errand.

Moreover, Tenoch's horde was not racing toward the king in a disorderly mass, but in the shape of a spear—a sharp point at the front tapering back to a broad formation at the rear. Tenoch had turned into a brilliant tactician and commander.

From my viewpoint at a position elevated behind and above the front of the formation, I could see where the point of the spearhead was aimed. Unlike Tenoch's frontline troop position, the king—easily identified by his raised jaguar pamitl—was in the center of his forces. Tenoch was going for the jugular of the Toltec army—*the king himself*.

Tenoch the barbarian, Tenoch the Clan leader of the Dog People, was now *Tenoch, the master of war*.

This was no Flower War—a battle fought for sacrificial prisoners rather than land and booty. In our world, Tenoch's strategy was intrinsically dishonorable. It was not the way one *civilized* empire battled another.

No, avoiding warrior-to-warrior battles and instead thrusting a phalanx into the opposing army to assassinate the opposing ruler was a dishonorable act, a tactic of barbarians who didn't know the rules of civilized war. Individuals might work their way through the fray, seeking to engage a king, but generals did not throw an entire force at a single ruler. Military honor was vested in one-on-one conflicts, and that strategy nullified the possibility of such honor.

The king's army had formed into a standard Toltec formation of knights and common warriors. When the pointed end of the phalanx hit, it split the army in two and began a drive directly at the king's position. I could see from the confusion around the king that the maneuver had surprised them.

Tenoch's standard was in the middle of the Aztec phalanx and the attack's momentum carried it forward. He was going to make the kill himself.

Had I not been in a state of fear and panic I would have admired Tenoch's audacious daring. If it succeeded and he killed the king of the greatest empire in the One-World, his name would be repeated by Rememberers of History for eternity. History is the polemic of the victor, and Tenoch's Rememberers of History would forget the disgracefulness of his tactics.

Tula's fate would also be sealed. Believing they were blessed by the gods, Tenoch's horde would become an unstoppable juggernaut.

I pushed forward in a furious panic.

51

Tenoch's forward push, while bold and deadly, left his flanks ex-posed, permitting the Toltec force to attack him on both sides. As Aztec warriors turned to face those attacks, I found an opening and quickly closed the distance between me and Tenoch.

The battle became a confused mass of warriors engaging in sin-gle combat. During these encounters, I saw foolish Toltec warriors attempting to take Aztecs as prisoners; such feats were in pursuit of glory rather than victory.

If they continued in their folly, they would achieve neither.

The king's men were better protected in their densely woven cotton and maguey-fiber body armor than the Aztecs, who fought almost naked except for their loincloths and the officers' mantles. Still the Toltecs' tactical ineptitude became painfully clear as their enemy swarmed over them.

As I came up close enough to hurtle my battle-axe at Tenoch, a Toltec warrior broke through the Aztec range and came at me. I had the spear in my left hand and my hand on the battle-axe. I couldn't bring up the spear in time to use it. I pulled the battle-axe out of the sack.

The warrior came at me, rearing back to throw his spear. If I didn't stop him immediately, I was dead. My only chance at preventing the spear launch was a head shot. Hurling the axe at him, it flipped two full turns and glanced off his head. He went down, but I'd lost my axe.

I continued charging forward. Keeping the spear in my left hand, I pulled out the dagger. Avoiding another Toltec who wanted to engage me, I got up behind Tenoch. Other Aztec warriors were crowding around him and I used the mass confusion to slip through an opening. He was directly in front of me, his back to me, the standard wobbling back and forth as he moved. We were both being pushed and bumped by warriors fighting in every direction.

Dropping my spear, I surged forward. Closing in on him, I slipped the dagger into his side. He gasped as I twisted the blade and pulled it sideways. I kept my face turned away from him and hoped that my surreptitious stab was not glaringly apparent.

I glanced at him as he pitched forward to fall, taking the standard with him.

Ayyo! It wasn't the face of Tenoch I saw. I recognized the standard-bearer as another member of the Clan.

I realized what Tenoch had done—he used another warrior to carry his emblem into the battle. As the Toltec focused on the standard and fought to get to it, Tenoch was free to move ahead to accomplish his goal of killing the king.

The warriors of my Clan wore the blue markings symbolizing the hummingbird god. They were directly in front of me. Certain they were clearing the way of Tenoch to the king, I picked up a fallen Toltec sword. Joining the phalanx, I moved forward with it.

Not far from me I spotted a warrior's headdress and knew for sure it was Tenoch's. Only he was permitted to wear the headdress of the war god.

Beyond Tenoch was a tall standard of striking beauty, replete with iridescent colors: the battle standard of the king.

Tenoch was closing in for the kill.

52

Pushing forward, I continually defended myself against Toltec warriors while squeezing in between the Aztec fighters. Fighting my way through a break in the formation I was finally two paces from Tenoch's back. Raising my blade, I caught a movement out of the corner of my eye. I ducked, falling sideways, as the blade of a sword slid by my head.

For a startled moment filled with wonder I stared into the eyes of the Royal Armorer. He recognized me, too—and stopped the second sweep of his sword a split second before it would have decapitated me. The pause was little more than an eyeblink, after which two warriors locked in bloody combat crashed into him, pushing us apart.

As I hacked my way toward Tenoch again I knew that at any moment the armorer might be coming up behind me, ready to cut me down.

The tide of battle pushed and pulled the mass of warriors back and forth like waves bouncing off walls. For every two steps forward I went, I was pushed back another as I hacked at anyone who got near me. Toltec, Aztec—it didn't matter. Whoever was between me and Tenoch was my foe.

With my breath coming in gasps and my strength fading, I drew deep within myself, calling on the mightiest of the gods, Quetzalcoatl, to give strength to save the king.

I avoided a spear thrust into my gut, but the Toltec warrior using the spear brought the butt end up and connected with a blow that caught me across the head. I went down, seeing a burst of stars as if darkness had fallen—and for a moment it had for me.

I lay on the ground with my head buzzing, blindly slapping at the ground around me for my sword.

Staring up, my blood chilled—the king was down, only feet from me. Tenoch hovered over him, raising his spear.

In the distance, a conch horn sounded.

I leaped up as if I were on fire. My right hand grasped Tenoch's left hand, throwing his aim off balance and sending the spear tip into the ground.

For a moment the Clan leader's eyes met mine, but unlike the armorer who had paused for a second in surprise, Tenoch never hesitated. He let go of his spear and pulled his dagger out.

I heard the sound of the conch again just as I kneed him in the groin. He grunted and stumbled. I hurled myself on top of him, ramming him in the stomach with my knee. But snake-quick, he still managed to drive his dagger into my back.

Suddenly my left hand closed around the handle of my lost sword, lying on the ground. Raising it, I drove the blade into Tenoch's throat—so hard it impaled the earth under his neck. Releasing the handle, I left it thrumming in his throat.

My enemy was dead.

Instantly the frenzied Aztec attack had stopped—the Dog People were retreating.

I heard a shout of "No!" as a blow struck me in the back between my shoulder blades. I flew forward, hitting the ground, my breath taken away.

Half twisting on the ground, I looked up at the Royal Armorer as the king pushed him away from me.

The armorer had struck me with a broken spear.

The gods had protected me—three times. The heavy quilted vest beneath my mantle had blocked all but the tip of Tenoch's blade when he stabbed me in the back. My hand had found my lost sword a moment before Tenoch sent me to Mictlantecuhtli's hell. The Royal Armorer had only a shattered weapon to strike me with in that final moment of battle.

"Why did they run?" I asked the king.

"Your Dog People leader isn't the only one who understands deception. I ordered the unit I had left back at the Hill of Knives to sneak up behind us and attack once we were engaged in battle. When the Aztecs heard the conch horn, and saw the reinforcements sweeping down on them, they thought the whole Toltec army had arrived and fled. And, of course, you killed their leader."

53

The king defeated the Dog People . . . but the fact that an Aztec Dog Man had saved the king's life and slain his mortal foe had tarnished his victory.

Still he had survived.

But then another event sullied his success as well. Back at the palace, he informed me that an entire shipment of obsidian had vanished from the Hill.

"The Dog People took it," the king said. "Rumor has it that a deputy of Tenoch's has taken command and is crafting weapons with which to arm the various Clans."

"The Clans have never trusted each other enough to band together for war," I said. "They spend more time fighting each other than fighting us."

The king gave me an intense stare. "Times have changed—and not for the better. They are armed and united."

"Are you planning an attack on these barbarians?" I asked.

Even though I said it, I knew that it was not possible to gain a victory with an expedition to the north.

The king shook his head. "You know how the Dog People live,

constantly on the move. They will scatter like a handful of dirt blown by the wind if we come after them."

"You would never catch them, let alone kill them," I concurred.

"I'm certain Teotihuacán played a role in the attack on the Hill of Knives," the king said. "The assault on the Hill was planned long before my victory over their prince at Tajín. It would have been planned for months. And the High Lord whose duty it was to defend the Hill would have been part of the plot for a long time." He locked eyes with me. "But the High Lord did not act alone. He would not have betrayed me unless treason was rampant in Tula."

"Do you still suspect the priests?" I asked.

"The high priest himself, though I have no evidence." He paced some more before turning back to me. "Do you understand the consequences of what I have told you?"

I understood. Highly placed nobles and Tula's religious rulers were plotting with Teotihuacán to the south. Teotihuacán was plotting with the Aztecs to the north. When the attack came, it would come from both directions.

While treason and revolt fermented within.

The king would battle enemies on three fronts.

"I am going to attack Teotihuacán," he said.

A good plan. Our king would not only confront a foreign foe, he would force the nobles to march with him rather than hide in their Tula palaces and plot his downfall.

"In any battle, the aggressor is the victor," the king said.

"Yes, that is the way of war," I said, "You will want a reading of the celestial—"

The king empathically shook his head.

"You have a greater duty to perform for me."

I dropped to my knees. I would have thrown myself in a fire mountain to make up for the night I passed a dagger to Tenoch.

"Anything, my lord. You will need to know when the star-god Quetzalcoatl is—"

"Bring me back the Dark Rift."

He could have cut off one of my arms and I would not have been more surprised.

"What do you want me to do? I know nothing about the Dark Rift except as it appears in the sky."

"And on your belly," Quetzalcoatl said. "You will go to the land of the Maya. It is there."

"The land of the Maya?" I asked in disbelief.

A journey to that land would be both long and dangerous.

"Your destiny is in the Dark Rift," the king said, "as is mine. You, Stargazer, and I, we are the fate of Tula—and perhaps that of future generations to come."

PART XIV

54

I left Tula on a palanquin bound for the land of the Maya, with twenty soldiers guarding me. I wore the headdress of a high noble of Tula and carried with me a glyph that told all I was an ambassador of the great king of Tula. Any who opposed me would answer to the greatest empire in the One-World.

I was a treasure of the king.

I didn't know why.

As an ambassador of the greatest ruler in the One-World, I would be welcomed by a reception of high nobles in every city I came to on my journey. After that, I would be entertained by the kings themselves.

Not long ago, the armorer said as he was once again outfitting me, a Toltec noble or even a commoner could have traveled the One-World end to end and no king or headman would have demanded a toll nor steal his purse. But as the problems with the Aztecs and Teotihuacán increased and the land grew thirsty from a lack of rain, the empires in the One-World that had once quaked before Tula had grown bolder.

Most would still hesitate to molest a high-ranking ambassador carrying the king's authority, he assured me.

"Most" did not mean all. . . .

With the enemies of Tula growing, I had my own plans on how to travel. Beneath my fine clothes I wore the dress of a warrior. Beside me I carried a sword, battle-axe, dagger, spear, and shield.

I also took care in selecting my route. The quickest route was to go south past Teotihuacán and over the mountains to the coast . . . but that would be dangerous considering that war was coming very soon.

The next best route was over the mountains to the east that we took to Tajin. On the other side of the mountains, we would follow the coast down to an area where there were boats big enough to take me farther down the coast to the land of the Maya.

To Tajin and the sea was the route I chose.

The first night out of Tula I stopped at a rest house adjoining a camping area. The armies of porters and merchants—who carried goods from not just the length and breadth of the Toltec Empire but the entire One-World—stopped there at night. Because of my rank, the entire guesthouse was turned over to me.

However, someone was already there, preparing it for my arrival. The woman who guided me to the Guardians in Tajin waited in a black hooded robe of exquisite cotton to guide me to the land of the Maya.

She greeted me with a fine meal, acting nonchalant, as if it were nothing unusual, as if I should have known she would be there. And I should have, she told me, as we ate.

"I am here to warn you that you are taking a dangerous path. The king's enemies know he has sent you on a mission of great importance even if they don't know exactly what it is you seek. Given the opportunity, they will roast your feet over a fire to obtain that information."

She was right, of course, and I had been too busy and excited about the journey to prepare for the dangers I would face on the road. I had not been watching my back.

We made love and I fell into a deep sleep, lulled by a good meal, nectar of the gods, and the libidinous ministrations of a goddess.

I awoke sometime in the night and asked a question that had nagged at me since I first saw her in Tajin.

"What is your name?"

She was silent for a moment and I wondered if she would answer me.

"Ixchaal."

Ahh . . . she was Maya, not Toltec. "Ix" was a common beginning to Maya female names.

Ixchaal was a name I also knew. As with my mother, Ixloom, it was a name identified with mystery and magic. The goddess Ixchaal had one face that was a goddess of love and another of a fierce jaguar—she had the fiery passion to love or to kill.

The name fit her. I had experienced her exotic side . . . and suspected that someday I'd see the wild animal in her.

I had gone back to sleep when she woke me.

"Men are outside the window," she whispered. "Others are in front."

As was the custom in the mild climate, the windows were open.

I snapped awake. "My guards—"

"Gone. Shhh . . . keep your voice down."

"How do you know?"

"I have looked."

I grabbed my long sword and took a position at the side of the window. With a sword also in hand, she went to the door.

A man leaned in, a bow and arrow in hand.

I swung the sword with all my might, giving an Aztec war cry as I did.

The sharp black blade caught the man across the arms and chest, severing his left arm. The arm fell into the room as he recoiled backward, bumping into someone behind him.

The door flew open. As a man rushed in ready to launch a spear,

Ixchaal dropped low and swung her sword, cutting off a knee. Others were behind him and with another Aztec war cry I flew by her and hacked at them wildly, swinging the sword at anything that moved.

I followed them outside, bursting out the door without realizing I had passed one of the assassins. He was now at my back with a sharp-edged club.

As I whipped around to face the threat, Ixchaal leaped on his back and pulled a dagger across his throat.

The body had hardly hit the ground before she said, "We have to get out of here. They'll be back and there'll be more of them."

We were safe for the moment. The encampment of porters had been aroused by my yells. In the moonlight I could see that dozens of the travelers were milling about with weapons in hand. We had to get away from the guesthouse before daylight made it easy for the assassins to find us.

My old training of being a nomad got us away from the guesthouse quickly with sacks we carried on our backs to keep our hands free for weapons. My most prized possessions—jade and cacao beans to pay our way and weapons to clear the way, along with tortillas—were already packed.

My guards and servants were gone.

"Some were paid to betray you, others were frightened away. The king's enemies sent them. The assassins would have disabled you first, then tortured your mission out of you."

Dawn was breaking as we left. Instead of going on the road I took her into the wilderness, in the direction opposite to the one the assassins had fled in.

She had been right—I needed her.

She moved fast. She was strong. And she was deadly with weapons.

I had finally seen the jaguar face of Ixchaal.

"They were Aztecs," I said. "Strange . . ."

"Not strange. Had you been killed by Toltec servants of a noble-man, even more noble heads would have fallen, adding to the tzom-pantli skull rack the king is already filling with those who betrayed him. This way the Toltec nobles can attack you with impunity. They can use the Aztecs to do their murderous bidding, then blame the assaults on the Aztecs."

For the first time I saw her smile.

I could understand why those plotting against the king would want to kill me now that I sought something that the king hoped would help him against them. But it puzzled me that they hired Aztec assassins to kill me at a time when I was not a threat.

"But I'm not a threat to them."

She didn't answer my comment, but I could tell she knew some-thing.

"What are you hiding from me?"

She ignored the question. As we walked, another thought tum-bled out of my head:

"The nobles plotting against the king didn't hire the assassin who attacked me in Tula, did they?" I asked.

A guess on my part, but in a way I couldn't define I knew that the attempt on my life had been personal, not political. Stargazer would have been the obvious target for a political assassination.

"You killed the assassin."

She didn't look at me.

"Are you going to deny that you killed him?"

"We have a long way to go and a short time to get there. Save your breath for the journey."

I growled under my breath. I was not accustomed to being alter-nately bodyguarded, then bedded down by a goddess.

She veered south.

"Tajin is that way," I said, pointing at the easterly direction I had been leading us.

"We're going to Teotihuacán."

I sucked in a sharp breath. "Are you insane? They hate us and have to know that we're preparing a war against them. If they captured the king's astronomer—"

I stopped. She paid no attention to my concerns. She kept on walking in the direction she had chosen—toward our enemy.

I caught up with her. "Answer me. Have you gone completely mad? We would walk into the beast's mouth in Teotihuacán."

"We can't take the Tajin path. It's the direction they will expect you to take. Now they know we will fight back, they'll be more cautious next time. We won't be able to stop them. Continue on the road to Tajin and you will die on it."

She was right. But there was another route.

"We can go west and avoid Teo—"

"No, it would add weeks to our journey. We need to take the shortest route to the south—Teotihuacán to Cholula, then to a fishing village where we can arrange a boat to take us down the coast. Besides, when they can't find us on the Tajin road, they will assume we went west to avoid Teotihuacán. The one place they will not look for us is heading for Teotihuacán itself."

I had to agree that there was logic in the route she chose. But it was also insane for us to walk into Mictlantecuhtli's maw. What they would do to the king's astronomer if they caught me in Teotihuacán would make even the lords of hell quake.

Ayyo. Ixchaal was not insane to make this journey—I was.

Well, I thought glumly, at least she knew why I was chosen.

55

We kept going, resting seldom and only briefly. Having slept almost half the night, neither of us felt compelled to stop—not with Aztec killers hunting us.

When we approached a sizable village with a marketplace, she told me we would purchase new clothes, that we could not travel as wealthy Toltecs. We replaced all our possessions and clothes—from sandals on up—with peasant garb.

"You must forget you were a high-ranking Toltec official," she warned me. "You are now a humble porter who carries the goods of others on his back."

"I was born to the role," I said.

"Discard everything you have," she said. "*Everything*. Even your soft cotton loincloth will give you away."

I hid the pieces of precious jade that we would use for trade. My dagger and short-handled battle-axe and Ixchaal's short sword went in our shoulder sacks. Ixchaal secreted more jade on her person.

We buried our old clothes and possessions in the forest. When we came back out onto the road we were porters. Porters conveyed almost everything in the One-World, and the roads swarmed with them. We would be indistinguishable from these itinerant laborers.

We chose to transport turkey feathers as our trade goods, because they were light and inexpensive, making our loads less burdensome and ourselves less attractive to thieves than if, for instance, we'd carried valuable parrot plumes.

Ixchaal took the lead.

I trudged behind her.

In three days we reached the pass bordering Teotihuacán. Coming down the mountain, I saw the city for the first time. High and distant, it took my breath away.

"The first abode of the gods," Ixchaal said.

When I first saw Tula, I was dazed and awestruck by its wealth and wonder. If Tula, however, was a gorgeously glittering gem, Teotihuacán seemed to me as an entire crown—grand, sacred, spiritual, dignified.

If Tula was meant to be envied, Teotihuacán was to be revered.

Looming above the city's center were two towering temples—the Pyramid of the Sun and slightly smaller Pyramid of the Moon—each higher than the sacred pyramid at Tula.*

"This is not a dream," Ixchaal said, as if reading my thoughts. "They are real."

"The city is infinitely larger than I imagined."

"More people live here than in Tula."

"What was it like during its golden age?" I asked.

"Twice as many people resided here then—over 250,000, I am told."

To see it from this godlike vantage point—stretching out in all directions, a universe unto itself—moved my heart and snared my soul. I felt we were approaching hallowed ground.

"Who built this great city?" I asked softly. "The Toltec? The Maya?"

---

* Translator's Note: The Pyramid of the Sun is the third largest pyramid in the world, only slightly smaller than the second largest, Egypt's Great Pyramid of Giza. The largest pyramid is at Cholula, not far from Teotihuacán. Mexican pyramids were shorter than Egyptian ones because they had flat tops.

"No one knows. The Teotihuacáns speak a language similar to the Nahuatl of the Toltec and Aztec, but that was not their original tongue. No one knows what language the first people here spoke. They reputedly walked and dwelt among gods."

I shook my head. "No one knows what civilization built the greatest city that ever existed in the One-World? Or by what name they called themselves? Or what language they spoke? Ayyo . . . the gods mystify us for fun."*

We stopped at a rest house at the foot of the mountain. When a group of porters left for the city, we fell in with them.

"The roads are not as safe for travelers here as they are in Toltec territory," she said. "From here on you will find that merchants and their porters only travel in large groups and stay ready to defend themselves. The farther south we go, the worse conditions will become."

Like Tula and Tajín, fields of maize, beans, chili peppers, and agave surrounded the city. Only when we were close enough to see the city walls did we glimpse the empire's fallen state.

"The paintings on the city walls have faded," I said.

"Everything in Teotihuacán has faded," she said.

The guards at the gate were rude and crude. They extorted bribes from travelers—particularly the merchants and traders—openly holding their hands out. At times they even pulled people aside, ripping apart their goods and roughing them up if they thought them vulnerable to coercion.

We clearly had no bribes to proffer, however, and we flowed easily through the gate, appearing to be part of a group of porters whose leader readily paid off the guards.

The difference between Tula and the City of the Gods became even more apparent after we entered. As with the city walls, the

---

* Translator's Note: Not even modern science has been able to discover the identity of the civilization that built this city that would have coexisted during the greatest days of Rome and would have rivaled that city in size and grandeur.

artwork on the residential compounds was no longer bright, colorful, and fresh. Trash and human waste accumulated on the streets. The water in the fountains was fetid.

Shouts went up and people fled the street, pressing against the surrounding buildings. We joined them.

A high lord or royal on a palanquin was being carried down the street, surrounded by angry, arrogant warriors who clubbed anyone who got in their way. Unable to break through the mob and find a safe haven, we were trapped out in the street. When the club-wielding warriors came our way, I had no choice but to absorb their blows—and hopefully those aimed at Ixchaal. When I was sure one was coming, I put my arms around Ixchaal and turned so my back was exposed. When the blow fell, I treated the guard to a gargan-tuan groan, hoping to convince him that he'd painstakingly dis-charged his duty . . . that all the demons in Mictlantecuhtli's hell could not inflict more agony.

After the palanquin and guards passed, Ixchaal and I returned to walking.

"Thank you," she said.

I smiled. "You've saved my life—more than once."

"That is my duty."

"You've also taught and shown me much. I will never see any-thing like Teotihuacán for the rest of my days."

"For the simple reason that there is nothing under the sun like Teotihuacán. Not only the greatest city ever in all the One-World, even today the pyramids, temples, and palaces serve as the fount from which most of our art sprang—so much so that most of what you see throughout our land are slavish imitations of this city's won-drous works. Quetzalcoatl and the other gods called this city home and strode its streets, sanctifying the very ground; you can feel their presence to this day."

"Perhaps the gods' early presence inspired Tula's artists and sci-entists," I suggested.

"Teotihuacán was certainly the envy of the One-World," she

said. "Even the Maya mimicked this city's temples, buildings, and streets. Your Dog People long to conquer a kingdom and carve out an empire like Tula, not knowing that Tula is a failing reflection of what you see here."

We traveled the city's dark and narrow backstreets rather than its broad, bright thoroughfares, knowing that we'd be less visible.

Entering the Ceremonial Center undetected, we stood before the mountainous pyramids dedicated to the Sun and Moon gods.

"Stairways to the gods," Ixchaal said.

Her eyes watered with tears.

I felt an immense power radiating from the sacred temples. How could they have been built by the hand of man? It was unimaginable to me. Only gods could have created a city so vast and various— both divine and yet proudly profane.

"How could Teotihuacán have fallen from grace with the gods?" I asked.

"The merchants and nobles grew rich and fat and weak," she said. "They no longer built temples, created art, and defended their kingdom. They became more interested in hoarding wealth and indulging their most brazen lusts. They dishonored the gods and themselves."

She locked eyes with me, as if she was challenging me to dispute what she was about to say.

"They had forgotten that the gods reward only dedication and discipline, that they despise irresolution and weakness. The gods will destroy Tula, too, if she continues to squander her inner strength."

She told me that a brutal king and a cruel cadre of nobles ran the city, that they oppressed the people and disdained mathematics and astronomy, learning and science, architecture and art, the wind, the sea, the stars—the ways of the Feathered Serpent.

"Like Tula, Teotihuacán has not been favored by the rain gods," she said. "The people have languished as the food supplies have shrunk. This evil elite of merchants and aristocrats even aggravate famine's flames. Blocking the sale of grain, they force their starving people to hand over everything they own for shriveled ears of maize."

We started to go around a group of four Teotihuacán city guardsmen talking and laughing on the street in front of their barracks. They had obviously dipped deep into a gigantic jug of octli. Demon drink had stolen their wits, assuming they had any to begin with, leaving behind only their rude, obnoxious, mindless behavior.

As we went by one of them grabbed Ixchaal, dragging her toward their barracks.

Disguised as impoverished porters, we were helpless.

"Come woman, we will fertilize your garden until you grow fine warriors like us."

I started to react and she shot me a warning glance.

They were all armed with obsidian-bladed axes and swords. My weapons were stowed in my bag, and the guards outnumbered me.

She twisted out of the grip of the warrior. The warriors crowded around her, laughing and pawing at her. They pulled her toward their barracks and I started for them.

"*Run!*" she shouted.

I froze.

"*Complete your mission!*"

Her final words where shouted as they pulled her through the doors of the barracks.

I forced my feet to keep moving, down the street, one foot after the other.

Ixchaal. *They have Ixchaal.*

They would use her unto death, then throw her out onto the street—or kill her to stop her screams.

I hesitated, looking back, fighting with the logic of obeying her command. If I intervened, I would die in the attempt. And the mission would fail.

I had to continue forward. She was right. That was why she was sent to guide me. Like my mother, she was a Woman Who Sees.

I suddenly spun around and looked back to the barracks. Something exploded in me—*rage*. Even more important to me at that moment than the fate of empires and generations yet unborn was the woman I loved.

I dropped my load of feathers on the street. I pulled my long sword as I ran for the barracks.

I burst into the building, startling three guards who were laughing and talking.

My thoughts were a blur—everything around me blurred. I hacked and kicked and jabbed, killing with the rage of a jungle cat whose mate had been threatened.

Suddenly there were no more warriors standing. Blood was splattered on the walls and ceiling and on me.

The barracks had only three rooms and I ran through them, looking for her.

She wasn't there.

I spun in a circle, sword at the ready, confused.

She was gone. Vanished. In the name of Quetzalcoatl . . .

Where did she go?

PART XV

56

In one of the interbranching arroyos, Hargrave found soft ground strewn with rocky deadfall. He and Jamesy took turns digging—a mass pit for the bandits, a smaller grave up the gorge for the bandits' rape-and-murder victim. They dug them beside the canyon wall so that when they piled rocks on them, passersby might mistake the stones for a rockfall rather than a burial cairn.

Their entrenching tool had a three-foot handle and a collapsible shovel head. Awkward to operate, it blistered hands and cracked backs. Every hour or two Martinez, Coop, and Rita would spell Jamesy and Hargrave as best they could. Afterward, they hitched the corpses to the mules and dragged them to the big pit. Jamesy brought the girl back belly-down over a pack mule.

By the time they'd interred the bodies and piled on the rocks, the sun was at its zenith.

Throughout the work, they said almost nothing.

"Up to me, I'd have buried the poor girl and let those hideputas rot," Rita said.

"This many bodies, the buzzards would've staged a convention over them," Hargrave said as he dropped a last jagged rock onto the mass grave.

"Tornado clouds of vultures," Hargrave said.

"Which would bring federale planes searching these canyons," James said.

"Someone, somewhere will know we were here," Hargrave said.

"The illegal guns alone would get us life sentences," said Jamesy, dropping a last rock on the girl's grave.

"They might even reopen Chiapas," Hargrave said.

"I'll never believe we're shut of that one," Jamesy said.

"You left out concealing and transporting priceless artifacts," Rita said.

"That'll also get you life down here," Hargrave said.

Jamesy gave Rita a hard stare. "Working for you has a lot of downward mobility."

Martinez headed down-canyon to get three of the mules, which he had cross-hobbled there. When the packer came back, he was smiling. Coop stared at him in stunned surprise. No one had ever seen him smile.

"What's so funny?" Hargrave said.

"You no guess what I find down-canyon," the mule-packer said.

"Montezuma's ghost," Jamesy said.

"A mule is tearing up some creosote."

"He's just being ornery," Hargrave offered. "Jacks are like that."

"I'll say," Rita said, glaring at the two men.

Coop started up-canyon. "Come on," she said, "he wants us to look at his damn creosote."

The old man led them to the uprooted creosote. It had been growing between the canyon wall and a cluster of five large boulders.

Looking behind the boulder they could see the surface of a cache, including the dim outlines of its bricks. The cache's pale coloration matched that of the canyon wall perfectly: a square-shaped, sealed-off hole in the canyon wall two feet above the ground, three feet on edge.

Concealed by five, not three, boulders, the directions had been

inaccurate. Eleven hundred years had placed two additional boulders and a dried-up creosote bush in front of the cache.

Getting out her small handpick, Coop went to work, chipping
away at the ancient mortared-up bricks. After two hours, she ex-
tracted from the open hole a large black ceramic urn over two feet
high, with a thick bulging circumference. A big stopper nearly ten
inches across tightly sealed off its top, and the Feathered Serpent's
vermilion likeness blazed across the vessel's front.

57

Pushing hard for the rest of the day, they stopped only once to round up the nine riderless horses, strip them of their gear, and send them down-canyon toward water and graze.

At night, they traveled afoot by star- and moonlight, leading their mules by their mecates. When they could no longer walk, they cooked their beans, dried beef, tortillas, and coffee on a concealed burner. Despite the evening desert chill, they refused to risk an open fire.

In the early predawn before the two women were up, Hargrave and Jamesy shook Martinez awake. Hargrave walked him up-canyon, while Jamesy went through his gear with a pocket Maglite. The beam woke Coop, who sleepily watched Jamesy rummage through the mule packs and panniers. Holding two objects in his palm for a few moments, he studied them. Coop had never seen eyes so empty of emotion.

Placing them on the canyon floor, he crushed both objects with a boot heel.

What was that all about? Coop wondered.

Jamesy picked up the flattened objects and their entrenching tool and returned up-canyon.

When she woke, the sun was spilling over the canyon rim. Hargrave and Jamesy were packing the mules, not Martinez.

"Where's Martinez?" Coop asked.

"He didn't make it," Jamesy said.

"What happened?" Coop asked.

Jamesy tossed Coop her GPS and satellite phone, both of which he'd smashed.

Martinez had had her missing GPS and satellite phone.

The mule-packer had stolen them from her.

"Martinez was working for the Apachureros," Hargrave said, "telling them about the codices, how valuable they were and where we were headed."

Coop stared speechless.

"He confessed up-canyon," Jamesy said. "He said they had his son and that he was trying to buy the kid free of the gang."

Rita put down the coffeepot and walked up beside Coop. "You didn't believe him?"

"No one gets out of the Apachureros," Hargrave said.

"What's the difference?" Jamesy said. "He'd tell them about your third codex as soon as he had the chance. We never would have got shut of the 'Pach if he did that."

"You didn't—?" Coop started to ask.

"You saw what they did to that girl," Hargrave said. "The 'Pach would have sent more men just like them."

"He set us up," Jamesy said. "He admitted it."

"We saw the text messages on his cell phone," Hargrave said, "and they weren't all from the Apachureros."

58

They rode three straight days, sunup to sundown, pushing on even at night, leading the mules afoot. On the fourth day, they left the canyons and reached a farming village. Hargrave made a single encrypted phone call to their control.

Two days later, a contact met them at the Rio Noches under a stand of cottonwoods. An American with dark wavy dyed hair and a thick mustache, he wore a light tan summer-weight suit, a black shirt, and a gray tie. There were no name exchanges or introductions. Rita later referred to him as "Mr. Tan."

Swapping their stock for a dirty nondescript gray Ford van and new IDs, they loaded the gear they were keeping into the van. When they finished, Hargrave turned to their contact.

"You got the other stuff?" Hargrave asked the man.

"In the van under the false bottom."

Coop didn't have to ask what that was. Hargrave had meant additional weapons.

"We added some other stuff you might need—three five-gallon cans of gas, extra rations, a first-aid kit, even a liter canteen of brandy. We figured you guys deserved a drink."

Hargrave nodded, then held out his hand. Coop thought Hargrave wanted to shake.

Mr. Tan handed him two black silk money belts.

"Pesos and dollars—small, medium, large denominations, used untraceable bills," he said. "Enough here to retire on."

"And thanks," Jamesy said. "Especially for the brandy."

"My idea," the agent said. "Don't tell anyone."

59

Coop wondered what new firearms lay under the false bottom. The men were keeping the .45s—the guns Hargrave and Jamesy loved so much yet managed not to fire. When she asked why they didn't get rid of the shotguns, Jamesy said that buckshot didn't leave ballistics evidence.

The lunatic asylum had clearly opened its gate. She had to get Reets and herself away from these people and back to the States.

Fast.

She had to make her poor deluded friend understand this was insane.

Even though they now had a van, they still drove hard—all night and most of the day, going through their full tank and two rectangular gas-filled jerry cans before finally stopping at a remote country filling station. They wanted to put as much distance as possible between themselves and the Chihuahua canyonlands. They fled not only the federales, but now feared Las Apachureros were dogging their trail. They did not know how much Martinez had told them.

And they had yet to open the ceramic urn, examine the codex—if it was inside—photograph, and translate it.

The man in the tan suit had left a bag of paperback novels in the car. In her previous life, Coop had enjoyed reading an occasional thriller. Compared to her recent experiences, she now found them silly.

After two straight days and nights on the road—driving in shifts, sleeping in the car—they took the four-wheel-drive van off the main road, driving until they found a secluded spot concealed behind a thick stand of trees where they could sleep out, risk an open fire, and cook a hot meal. Too tired for anything elaborate, they lay back on their bedrolls and ate canned chili with jalapeños on heated tortillas. They drank cold beer that Jamesy had bought at their last gas station stop.

The stress of the past week had gotten to all of them. Hargrave uncapped Mr. Tan's liter brandy canteen and openly drank from it. Tossing the canteen to Jamesy, he said:

"I think we all need a drink."

Placing the ceramic urn between his legs, Hargrave sat there by the fire and in its light struggled to loosen the urn's plug. Periodically applying lit embers to the urn's neck, he twisted the urn's top and simultaneously pressed petroleum jelly between the neck and stuck stopper.

"Hargrave's good at this sort of thing," Jamesy explained.

"He's done this before?" Coop asked.

"He got the codex out of the first urn," Rita said, "before I attempted to translate it."

Jamesy upended the canteen and handed it to Rita, who upended it in turn . . . without even bothering to wipe it off.

This is not the Rita I grew up with, Coop was thinking. The girl who was the epitome of manners. The Rita who befriended Coop, the rough hillbilly kid with no friend; who took her under her wing and sanded the rough edges off her; who had encouraged Coop's gift for languages, then dragged her into Mayan studies classes.

What happened to you Reets?

What's happening to you, Coop?

Nor was Coop the only one questioning Cooper Jones. Ever since the shoot-out, she had caught all three of them sneaking puzzled looks at her.

Finally, Jamesy pried.

"Who's your friend?" Jamesy asked Reets, nodding at the silent Cooper.

"My sister, my friend," Reets said.

"Back in that canyon," Hargrave said to Rita, "your sister and friend killed three men in less than eight seconds."

"Like she was kicking tin cans," Jamesy added.

"And also saving our asses," Hargrave said. "Otherwise those three would have gotten away. Them 'Pach'd be all over us by now, if they had."

Silence.

"Reets, we asked you a question," Hargrave said.

"Coop?" Rita asked.

"Whatever," Coop said tonelessly.

Rita lay back on her bedroll and stared at the stars.

"In grade schools kids called her Red," Rita said to no one in particular. "Not for her hair, which is jet-jet-black, being that her mother was Mexican and from Chihuahua."

"So why did they call her Red?" Jamesy asked.

"For redneck. Redneck Trash, to be precise."

"Did you call her that?" Jamesy interrupted.

"No, Jimmy Cameron was the last guy to use that expression. She knocked out four of his teeth."

"They were baby teeth," Coop said.

"He bawled like you knocked off his left testicle," Rita said.

"I'll take Cooper Jones backing my hand any day," Hargrave said, still working on the plugged urn.

"She saved me from a charging grizzly when we were twelve," Rita said matter-of-factly.

"This I gotta hear," Jamesy said.

"No shit," Rita said. "Coop and her father hunted for the cook pot. By twelve she'd shot and skinned countless squirrels, rabbits, deer, and coyotes."

"We didn't skin and eat coyotes," Coop said, still staring at the stars.

"I want to hear about charging grizz," Hargrave said. "Coop killed one in West Virginia?"

"Aren't any grizzlies there," Coop said, sitting up. "It was just a Brownie."

"A brown bear big as a grizz—bigger when she charged," Rita said.

Coop shut her eyes and lay back down.

"She took you hunting bear?" Jamesy asked.

"No, I just wanted to hike through the woods with her, and learn to fire a gun," Rita said. "I was carrying her father's .30-.30 lever-action Winchester and pretending I was John Wayne. Coop had a twelve-gauge pump. Out in the woods, she spotted bear tracks, and while she bent over them, I wandered off to look at some wild flowers. Seeing a bear cub, I put down my rifle and picked it up. Its mama materialized out of nowhere, growling like a hell gate flung wide.

"Coop reached me just before the bear. Her double-aught buck scattered too much to stop the bear cold. Hitting the mama in her lowered, charging head, the buckshot only seemed to make her mad.

"The bear was a dozen feet from us when Coop's next load hit her in her right shoulder, but this time in a closer pattern—tight enough to smash the joint. The bear stumbled but kept on going. Six, maybe seven feet from us, Coop's next shot struck the other shoulder in an even tighter group, shattering most of the joint. The bear skidded to a halt not three feet from our shoes."

"Twelve years old and you broke down a charging grizz," Jamesy said, curious.

"A brown bear defending her cub," Coop repeated, correcting him.

"Bigger than a grizz," Rita said. "It wouldn't go down. Two broken shoulders, three feet away, and she got back up. Rising on her haunches, she staggered toward us on two legs."

"What did you expect?" Coop said to her friend. "You wouldn't let go of the cub."

"The cub was shaking. I was shaking. I didn't know what to do."

Hargrave stopped working on the urn. "So what happened?"

"Coop put the fourth load into the heart," Rita said, "and the fifth in her gaping mouth . . . in midroar."

"At . . . point . . . blank . . . range," Jamesy said, carefully enunciating each word.

"Just as fast as she could rack that slide," Rita said.

"Like back there," Jamesy said.

"You got it," Rita said.

"What did your mother say afterward?" Hargrave asked Coop, his forehead furrowed quizzically. "About shooting bears at point-blank range?"

Coop sat up and stared at them. "Mom died when I was born. Dad said he admired my poise."

"Her father was shot and killed a month after the bear incident," Rita added.

"Hunting accident?" Jamesy asked.

"Coop and I figured it was moonshiners who didn't like the competition."

"My dad made really good 'shine," Coop said.

"And then?" Jamesy asked.

"We had nothing," Coop said. "Little more than Salvation Army hand-me-downs—and I was headed for the state orphanage," Coop said. "Reets forced her family to take me in."

"How'd you feel about making the cub an orphan," Jamesy asked, "like yourself?"

"Not good," Coop said with a sad shrug.

"And so you gave up hunting?" Jamesy pressed.

"There was more to it than that."

"*I got it*," Hargrave said.

Warming the urn's neck with an ember and working petroleum jelly into the neck and stopper, Hargrave had successfully loosened it without chipping or cracking it. Easing out the stopper, they all heard the sucking hiss of incoming air.

"I got to say, Coyotl had his shit together," Hargrave said. "The motherfucker vacuum-sealed the urns. No wonder the codices are so well-preserved. Know how he did it?"

"Applied heat to them," Coop said, "before he stoppered up the tops—just like you preserve fruits and vegetables."

"I never made preserves," Jamesy said.

"My God," Coop said, as Hargrave handed it to her, "this one's in incredible condition."

Eighteen inches square, it had a jaguar-skin cover, the pages pale with age but the glyphs still luminously lucid . . . as if defying chance, nature, time itself.

"We'll wait till tomorrow to photograph them," Hargrave said. "We'll do it right here in the sunlight. The light's too bad right now."

"But we can read them now," Coop said. "Rita, get our photos for one and two. Let's read and review them in sequential order."

"They're on my thumb drive," Hargrave said. "I'll boot up the computer."

Grabbing the Maglite, Coop and Rita opened the codex, slowly deciphering the complex glyphs.

60

After reviewing the computerized photos of codices one and two, Coop and Rita moved on to the newly discovered three.

"Can you really read that shit?" Jamesy asked Cooper, as she pored over the codex's amatl-paper pages, the pocket Maglite in one hand.

"It's harder than it looks," Rita said, "and Coop here's the best."

"What's it say so far?" Jamesy asked.

"Most of these writings are allusive, allegorical, perhaps encrypted," Coop said. "Some of what I'm doing is extrapolation. I think I get the writer, though."

"Good," Rita said. "There's a lot there I don't get."

"For the most part these codices have been the astronomer's and the god-king's narrative, dictated to the slave-scientist-scholar who identifies himself by the glyph, Coyotl," Coop said. "However, in codex three, we have passages written by Coyotl himself. He's chronicling the decline and fall of Tula."

"Queztalcoatl couldn't have written his sections himself?" Jamesy asked.

"He dictated some of it for sure," Coop said, "but I doubt King Queztalcoatl could read glyphs, let alone compose them. The astronomer probably wouldn't have been much better at them either. They're impossibly difficult to master, and essentially all of the Toltec glyph scholars were priests—people trained in the art of hieroglyphics since their childhood."

"Glyphs not only convey words through visual imagery," Rita explained, "each glyph has encrypted into it the sound the word makes. The linguistic synergy of sound and image requires a genuine gift for glyph reading and composing. Most of us lack the talent to read and write Nahuatl glyphs."

"How did Coyotl learn them?" Hargrave asked.

"The king and his astronomer recognized that Coyotl had a gift for glyphs, then found someone somewhere to teach him," Coop guessed.

"They obviously wanted someone to record this work," Rita said. "Not trusting the priests, they hand-trained their own Boswell."

"Who?" Jamesy asked.

"An eighteenth-century doctor," Rita said, "who recorded in longhand the comments and conversations of his friend, Samuel Johnson, eventually organizing them into his biography."

"Never heard of him," Jamesy said.

"You wouldn't understand even if you read the book," Reets said.

"Why not?" Jamesy asked.

"It's literature," Coop explained.

Jamesy's scowl was painful to observe.

"You sure Coyotl wasn't a priest?" Hargrave asked.

"Priestly codices," Coop said, "are religious in character. This Coyotl, however, is into secular science. If anything, he despises the priests. He's says up front he's afraid they'll find and burn his magnum opus here."

"He essentially says in his commentaries that Quetzalcoatl was at war with the priests," Rita said.

"Quetzalcoatl didn't believe in human sacrifice," Coop said, "and they did, blood being their stock-in-trade. It caused a schism between them."

"What else do the codices say?" Hargrave asked.

"That we have one more river to cross," Coop said, scanning the last page. "This isn't our last codex."

"Says right here: 'To Be Continued,'" Rita said.

"I'd hoped to get the hell out of Dodge," Jamesy said.

"Tell it to Coyotl," Rita said.

"I have an announcement to make," Coop said. "Tonight is the end of it—at least for me. I can't work under these conditions. I don't have the proper research materials to translate these glyphs accurately, and the whole thing is too goddamn dangerous. Soon as we return to civilization, I'm catching the next plane home. I'm not Lara Croft, Tomb Raider. You guys need a battalion of commandos, not me. Reets, you're coming with me."

"Never happen," Rita Critchlow said.

"A battalion won't cut it, Coop," Hargrave said. "We have exactly what's needed. It's got to be a small-unit operation, run by two people who know the languages and what we're looking for."

"A full-scale intelligence operation would attract too much attention," Jamesy said. "It has to be small, mobile, completely clandestine."

"Also, Coop, if we don't translate these here and now," Rita said, "we'll never do it. We can't smuggle them out. Sure, I'll borrow these codices while we're down here—which is against the law—but I won't steal them outright."

"I'm fucking out of here," Coop said.

"You don't understand," Hargrave said. "This thing is so big and bad, we have to do it. We have no choice."

"Want to bet?"

"We need you, Coop," Rita said. "I can't read the glyphs like you do. No one can."

"You want to take on the Apachureros and the federales, fine," Coop said. "I'm no mad-dog killer."

"You were back there in the canyon," Jamesy said, laughing.

"Fuck you."

"You can do what it takes," Rita said. "You always could."

"I'm not dying in some godforsaken desert or spending the rest of my life in some Mexican prison."

"I can't do this without you."

"I'm on the next thing smokin'."

Silence.

"You can do what's necessary," Rita finally said.

"I've changed. You and your family changed me."

"Tell that to those three men you cut in two," Jamesy said.

"Coop, you blew them clean out of their saddles," Hargrave said. He said it awestruck, clearly meaning it as a compliment.

"Fuck you."

"'Fuck you.'" Jamesy repeated, slowly pronouncing each word. "That's real smart. I thought you said you'd changed. Rita, you didn't change this girl enough."

Rita ignored his sarcasm. Instead she was moving closer to her friend.

"I need you," Rita said. "Like you were before—back there in the canyon."

"The past is dead."

"Coop, you saved all our asses back in that canyon," Hargrave said. "That counts for something with me."

"If they'd gotten away," Jamesy said, "we'd have all been friolles."

"Someone else can keep the world safe for democracy," Coop said.

"No time for someone else," Jamesy said.

"I talked to Monica," Rita said. "You didn't. We have to find that fourth codex. Everything depends on it."

"You have no choice," Hargrave said. "We have no choice."

"You think any of us would be here if we did?" Jamesy said.

"Unfortunately, Coop," Rita said, "you're all we've got."

"And we're all you got," Hargrave said.

Coop stared at them, silent.

"Why do you think we dumped our cell phones and GPSs a few days ago?" Rita asked.

"You also smashed mine back in the canyon," Coop said.

"We smashed them because we'd been bugged and double-crossed," Hargrave said.

"How do you think those 'Pach found us in the canyon?" Rita asked.

"The mule-packer set us up," Coop said. "Martinez had my sat-phone and GPS."

"Which hadn't worked in those canyons for over a week," Rita said. "None of ours had."

"That's why you brought your sextant," Hargrave said.

"Someone in Washington is on the 'Pach payroll. His son told him."

"Bullshit."

"His son told him by text message," Hargrave said. "He showed us the message on his own cell phone."

"Coop," Rita said, "we can't trust anyone now except ourselves."

"Hey, good news," Jamesy suddenly shouted, after rooting around in their provisions. "I just located a second tequila canteen—you know, Martinez's medicinal tequila." Taking a healthy swig, he handed it to Rita. "Not bad for rotgut."

"Beggars can't be choosers," Reets said.

After taking a healthy swig, she passed it off to Jamesy. After his libation, he turned to Cooper.

"Come on, Coops," Jamesy said, handing her the tequila canteen. "A little alcohol cleans the blood and clears the mind. Pretend it's your old daddy's 'shine. Seal the deal with some hooch."

Coop turned to Rita to shoot her an angry look when . . .

Reets's jaw was trembling in and out, mute tears covering her cheeks. Struggling to smile, Rita fought the tears back. "You have to do it, Coops. I need you—the old Red who broke down the bear."

"Be a hero," Jamesy said, throwing a comforting arm around Rita.

Then holding up the tequila canteen, he offered up a mock toast. "Come on, Coop, do it for Planet Earth!"

"Do it for our country," said Hargrave, taking the canteen from Jamesy and helping himself to a slug.

"Do it for *me*," Rita whispered.

"Goddamn you all," Coop said.

"Our good swords carve the casques of me, because our hearts are pure," Jamesy sang out drunkenly.

"Goddamn you all to hell!" Cooper shouted.

"I'll keep it hot for you," Jamesy said with an ingratiating smile.

"Come on, Coops," Hargrave said. "Join the brigade."

She gave them all a long, angry, all-embracing stare. "I'm out of here tomorrow."

Turning her back on them, she rolled over into her bedroll and shut her eyes.

61

Later that night, her comrades were well into the second half of tequila canteen. Cooper knew this because they woke her with their drunken, ear-cracking singing. Hargrave was a booming basso profundo, Jamesy a hoarse whiskey tenor, while Rita Critchlow rang the rafters with her searing, soaring, surprisingly melodic soprano. Together, they wolfishly wailed and hilariously harmonized an ancient, bloody, brutally barbaric war ballad, the chorus of which went:

> *When your back's against the wall,*
> *When your towns and cities fall.*
> *Black powder and alcohol.*
> *Black powder and alcohol.*

What's happened? Coop wondered. *Your best friend has gone muy mucho loco? Have you both stumbled into a lunatic asylum? What have you gotten into?*

Ah hell, she thought mordantly. *Why not? In the destructive element immerse. Come on, Coop, join the fucking brigade.*

Raising a hand, Coop shouted, "Hey, Jamesy, throw me that canteen."

PART XVI

LAND OF THE MAYA

62

ONE-WORLD, 1004 A.D.

Ixchaal was gone.

When a guard barrack's search turned up nothing, I had no choice but to race out the rear, leaving the four dead soldiers in my wake. Had I not caught them weaponless and by surprise, I would have journeyed to the Dead Land in their place. To conceal my blood-splattered clothes, I pulled my mantle tight around my body.

I escaped through a labyrinth of narrow twisting streets—where I believed I'd be more inconspicuous—before risking the main thoroughfare that led out through the city's south gate. Fearful of attention, I tried not to hurry. Still I had to reach the gate before the drum-alarm sounded and the gates closed.

The open gateway was in sight when I heard the drums thunder, instructing the city's gatekeepers to close the gates. I had dropped the large backpack of turkey feathers before entering the guards' barrack. Still—fastened to a waist rope—I carried a small bag of cacao beans, which were much sought after throughout the One-World. Digging into the bag, I grabbed a handful and scattered them at the feet of the gate guards.

Pointing to the highly prized delicacy on the ground, I sang out: "Someone dropped their cacao beans!"

As the guards and travelers dropped to their knees, scrambling after them, I slipped through the swinging gate a second before it slammed shut.

🌀

Two hours from the city I slowed my pace. There were no signs of pursuit. The winds of war were blowing, and Teotihuacán's rulers had graver concerns than drunken soldiers murdering each other. They had hostile armies to worry about.

I had hoped to catch up with Ixchaal, certain that she had gone in the same direction. Several times I described her to food vendors along the road and asked if they had seen her. None had. Her disappearance worried me. She might still be following behind me, delayed by the closing city gates. I might even have passed her in my haste to leave the city, but I wasn't optimistic.

Finish the mission, she told me, and I didn't see that I had any choice. Moreover, the mission was an increasingly daunting task. I had vast distances to travel, and I knew nothing about the terrain and the people. Worse, I was entering lands where the people would no longer speak Nahuatl and, being a foreign traveler, people would view me with distrust.

I'd concealed Quetzalcoatl's royal glyph beneath my clothes. Under ordinary circumstances, as the armorer pointed out, it would have mandated safe passage almost anywhere in the One-World.

With Tula at war on two fronts and its nobles plotting against the king, Quetzalcoatl's enemies would now be less intimidated by his imprimatur, bolder in their opposition, and more suspicious of a royal emissary passing through their realms.

I fell back on the disguise Ixchaal had concocted for us: porters hauling plumes. Purchasing a pack of turkey and duck feathers, I joined a caravan heading in the direction I needed to take. My load was not only light again, the feathers in these regions were not so precious as to provoke the greed of thieves and of bribe-hungry toll and tax collectors.

I continued my trek, keeping a weather eye out for Ixchaal,

asking people continually whether they had seen a lone woman. My heart was heavy because I missed Ixchaal.

Nonetheless, I felt she was safe. A woman of mystery and magic . . . she would not abandon the mission. We were destined to meet again.

She had taught me many things, the most important of which was that a mere mortal should never love a goddess.

63

CHOLULA

A steady three-day trek took me out of Teotihuacán's territory and into that of the Olmeca–Xicalanca peoples. Having conquered the coast along the Eastern Sea, they had extended their empire over the mountains to the great plateau region of Anahuac.

I passed the Great Pyramid of Tlachihualtepetl at Cholula, seeing it only in the distance. Appearing more like a flat-topped mountain than a man-made temple, it was even larger at the base than the immense Pyramid of the Sun at Teotihuacán and almost as tall.*

That night at a campfire of porters, I drank octli and listened to a storyteller explain how the colossal pyramid rose from the plains outside Cholula.

"In the Time of the Fourth Sun—before the One-World that existed—the four corners of the sky were held up by great mountains," the storyteller said.

Before the Time of the Fourth Sun, there had been three other

---

* Translator's Note: The Great Pyramid at Cholula still stands today, as do the pyramids of the Sun and Moon at Teotihuacán. The Cholula pyramid is not just the largest pyramid in the world, about one-third larger than the Great Pyramid at Giza, but is the largest single monument ever built.

Suns. The gods had destroyed each previous Sun Age by ripping that world apart with darkness, hurricanes, and fire. Chalchiuhtlicue ruled the Fourth Sun Age. A water goddess, Chalciuhtlicue became the wife of Tlaloc, the god of rain and master of all the seas, rivers, and lakes. Insulted by another god who accused her of overweening vanity, Chalchiuhtlicue cried for fifty-two years, causing a flood that drowned the world.

At the time of the Fourth Sun, giants, rather than people, populated our world. When the great Flood destroyed them and their world, seven giants escaped the waters by climbing to the top of one of the mountains and hiding in a cavern. By the time the giants left the cavern, Quetzalcoatl had fashioned human beings out of bones from the Underworld dipped in blood.

Thus, life was reborn.

Later, on solid ground, Xelhua, one of the seven giants who survived, gave thanks to the gods by building the great pyramid at Cholula. Lining up tens of thousands of men, Xelhua commanded them to pass bricks hand to hand to hand until millions of bricks were laid in all and the colossal temple was completed. When the pyramid threatened to reach the heavens, the gods hurled fire onto the workers, forcing them to stop.

"People are doomed whenever they invade the abode of the gods," the storyteller said, finishing up his tale.

I followed a well-worn mountain trail favored by porters and soldiers that ran all the way to the shores of the Eastern Sea. Far to the south of Tajin, the region was hot and wet; during that particular season, it was more so. The skies rained incessantly, and the warm air stayed habitually humid.

I heard that farther south the weather was even warmer. The storm gods lashed that land so ferociously they knocked down towns, devastated croplands, and even leveled forests.

I had reached the seacoast but was still two dangerous weeks from the Maya lands. The rainforest between the Olmeca–Xicalanca and the Maya to the south was overrun with clans wild and predatory as rampant panthers.

Ixchaal had intended to find a merchant boat that would drop us off at Jaina on the Maya coast. Following her plan, I booked passage on a vessel hewn out of one of the towering trees that lined the banks of the larger jungle rivers. The trees were cut down upriver and floated down to the beach along the sea. There, workers hollowed them out with stone axes. I had never seen trees as large as these slender giants taken from the lush forests of the region.

Ten oarsmen rowed the boat down the deep coastal waters. We often oared far out beyond sight of land to avoid the currents and winds that could drive us ashore and batter us on rocks and reefs. As soon as we lost sight of land, however, sea demons entered my body, bringing with them convulsive nausea and stomach-churning delirium.

I had never been on a large body of water nor viewed such vast unobstructed expanses before. The Eastern Sea seemed to go on forever—even though I knew that it terminated in the cave of the Sun God.

Each dawn the Sun God departed his cave, brilliantly illuminating the horizon, then lighting up the entire sky as his journey progressed. At sundown he entered his evening abode—the cave's western entrance.

The merchant and I discussed these matters . . . when I was not disgorging my bilious stomach into the foaming sea.

Ayyo . . . I would have surrendered my firstborn to Tlaloc to be relieved of that vile sickness.

The merchant was of medium height, had a broad square face, and wore his black hair in a ponytail. Dressed in white casual traveling clothes, he was an inveterate journeyer, an easy companion, and an expansive teller of tales.

A seller of rubber goods, he had craftsmen construct them out of the milk of the Weeping Women trees that produced rubber up the coast near Tajin. The priests and their wealthier worshipers burned

some of these small rubber offerings at the temples in hopes of pro-
pitiating the gods.

Perhaps I should have asked him to immolate one of his god-
dolls for me on that boat.

A feather peddler never would have attempted such an ambitious trip, so I told the merchant that my master sent me south to
evaluate the market for obsidian mirrors.

The merchant gave me insights and warnings into what I would
encounter when I arrived in the land of the Maya.

"Their language differs from yours, but you should be able to communicate with traders. In the cities most of them speak Nahuatl because it is the language of commerce throughout the One-World."

"When you travel through the land of the Maya you will witness
everywhere their failure to appease the gods. We hear stories that
Tula people starve because King Quetzalcoatl has lost favor with
our deities."

"Are the gods still punishing the Maya?" I asked. I had already
heard many stories, but this merchant had been trading with the
Mayas for most of his life.

"Yes, and the Maya are in their death throes."

"How are they punished?" I asked.

"The Sun God has scorched the land while the Rain God with-
held his bounty—even as the storm god blew down cities, wiped out
forests, and inundated the land with floods and mountainous waves.
Then the rains stopped and the Sun God dried the land again until
the ground beneath their feet cracked.

"While the other gods battered the land itself, the Lords of Death
visited the people. Whole cities were wiped out by disease, starvation, and endless war."

"Why did the Maya fight wars when everything else in the land
was so bad?"

"*Because* things were so bad. Wars distract the populace from
their rulers' oppression, exploitation, and from catastrophes such as
famine."

He told me that bandits, village headmen, and local warlords controlled many of the roads. He did not see much difference between these officials and the outright outlaws.

"They extort illegal tariffs from travelers, while their failure to repair roads has made trade from the coastal towns inland to the bigger cities difficult. Where there were once wide, smooth roads for porters and caravans, now they must transport their maize and pottery in mud or over parched terrain in choking thirst."

He shook a finger at me. "You will see," he said, "you will see. The gods punish them. They will punish you, too, if you traffic with these brigands."

64

Jaina was a town on the Maya coast. A tidal marsh divided the city into two parts. At high tide the marsh flooded, cutting off the outermost portion of the city from the mainland. Many long-dead Mayan nobles were entombed on that tidal island.

"They were buried there," the merchant said, "because they believed the sea was more likely to transport them to the Sun God's cave than to the darkness of Xibalba."

Xibalba was to the southern region what Mictlantecuhtli's underworld was to our northern land.

Jaina's position on the sea placed it on a main trade route to the large cities inland. During normal times Jaina was a two-day walk to Uxmal.

"The trip can now take you into eternity if you run into murderous brigands or bloodthirsty priests abducting people to be sacrificed," the merchant told me.

Several Nahuatl-speaking merchants suggested I join a caravan large enough to employ bodyguards and to cover unavoidable bribes. The weekly caravan would not depart for five days, however, and I couldn't wait. I had to risk the trip without protection. Again, I disguised myself as a porter and carried merchandise that would not incite the thieves' greed. Ayyo . . . I learned that in this region turkey and duck feathers were highly valued, so I could not carry them on this leg of the journey.

The value of one's cargo also determined the toll payments paid on leaving and entering a city. Bribes were also commensurate with the cargo's value. Those who could not cover these extortionate tariffs were driven off with clubs or whips.

A beggar suddenly appeared at my side and I jerked back, startled. Most of his face was covered with a mask of Ahpuch, the skeletal Maya God of Death; his exposed flesh had hideous red lesions. Dangling from around his neck was a dead owl.

I had watched the guards shun disease-ravaged beggars, fearful that demons might invade their own bodies. I had also noticed that they would not touch anything they handled. Throughout the One-World we also believed that to disturb the seriously diseased was to provoke the gods, who in their own inscrutable way accommodated the severely afflicted. After all, if the gods had not sanctioned their illness, they would have been dead.

The beggar gave me a twisted smile from his disease-eaten lips.

"I'll show you the way."

His voice was a low, rasping guttural whisper.

"What are you talking about?"

"The way to the Magician."

I followed the man as he meandered through the marketplace, purloining fruit at a stand. The merchant yelled at him but did not interfere.

He never turned to see that I was following.

Growing impatient, I couldn't play whatever game he had in mind. I hurried and caught up with him.

"Did Ixchaal send you?" I asked.

Ignoring me, he took a tortilla from a baking woman and wrapped it around a pepper he took from another vendor. Again, the merchants weren't happy, but no one tried to stop him.

"Did Ixchaal send you?" I asked again.

Turning his back on me, he walked away.

I followed him out of the marketplace to the outskirts of the town. The farther we got from the main road to the trade route out of town, the emptier and more decayed the buildings appeared.

I found vacant buildings strange. Teotihuacán may have fallen from grace with the gods, but it was not an abandoned ruin. I feared what I saw in Teotihuacán was a civilization that had lost the will to live.

The beggar led me to a hovel on a street that appeared to be totally abandoned. He disappeared inside the small building, leaving the door open behind him. I stood outside and stared at the open door and hesitated. Removing my short-handled battle-axe from its hiding place, I walked slowly toward the open door, then dashed through it. Inside, I spun around, ready to chop at anything that moved.

Nothing was there—nothing human, at least.

On the floor at my feet were the ragged clothes the beggar had been wearing. Alongside the clothes was a clay pot of berry juice.

The owl was there, too, staring up at me with dead eyes.

I raised the clothes and took a whiff of them. Instead of the filth of a beggar, I was sure that they had the erotic scent of the flower oil Ixchaal wore.

65

I left Jaina on the road that would take me to Uxmal. I wore the beggar's clothes and the grotesque mask of the god of death. Berry juice had given me the disease marks of the soon-to-be-dead. I hung a dead owl from a sisal cord around my neck.

"I'll show you the way," she had croaked in her beggar's voice. "The way to the Magician."

I'd gone over every movement the beggar had made, the few words spoken to me, the scent on the clothes. I was sure it had been Ixchaal and cursed myself at my stupidity.

The guards collecting tolls from those leaving and entering the city backed away as soon as I approached them. They gave me venomous stares but none was brave enough to demand bribes or wield the clubs they swung so freely at others.

As I walked, others moved aside to give me plenty of room on the road.

The disguise was masterful because it incited in everyone universal dread: the dread of death.

The owl's screech portended death; when people heard the owl's cry behind them and turned to look, they found the hideous skeletal Ahpuch standing behind them. He grabbed them with his clawed hands and dragged them down into the Underworld, where his own special domain was the bitterly frigid ninth level of hell.

Ayyo . . . I feared offending this pitiless god myself, but I told myself I honored the god by reminding people to be fearful of him. Hopefully, the God of Death was busy with too many others to worry about an insignificant cur of the Dog People.

The land outside the city was as bleak and depressing as the mood in Jaina. Fields that died of thirst were left fallow. Farm houses and villages were turning to dust. The people looked defeated; as I approached they fled into their houses.

The dark and gloomy atmosphere made me wish I were back in golden Tula. With Ixchaal in my arms.

66

A day out of Jaina—saddened and angered by the world I saw around me—I gave up my guise as the Death King. Pulling out my battle-axe, I swung it at my side in plain sight, all the while glaring at would-be robbers. I must have still looked like Death, because thieves backed away and honest people ran.

No longer a golden glittering land and the fount of all civilization, the Maya world was going straight to hell—Mictlantecuhtli's *and* Xibalba's Underworlds. While all knew the King Quetzalcoatl had collected in Tula the knowledge of the ages, along with the One-World's most talented artists, its greatest craftsmen, and astronomy's, medicine's, and architecture's most brilliant luminaries . . . most of that intellectual treasure trove he had purloined from the Maya. Ravaged by religious zealotry, political tyranny, and economic oppression, that world was destroying itself before my eyes.

A civilization that had recorded the history of the present world and the four worlds that came before in books made of fine paper was now relegating its history to memories of village storytellers—the so-called Rememberers of History. Where enlightened doctors had once prescribed medicine and treated the sick, now ignorant shamen fed their patients festering rats' eyes and putrid snake poison as alleged curatives, killing more people than they healed. Disease ravaged a population that was once healthy and hardworking.

Cities were abandoned because the surrounding farmlands no longer produced food and commerce had stopped.

Roads and even cities were swallowed by jungle. Palaces were unkempt, the bright paint on city walls faded and flaking off; great statuary, pieces that took years or even lifetimes to create, were crumbling.

The people were crumbling.

The civilization was broken.*

Worse of all, I saw in the Maya's decline and fall a tragic foreshadowing of Tula's future.

If the priests and the Dog People had their way.

In a strange twist of the divine fate, the high civilization of the Maya was fading while the lowly Dog People in the south were rising.

The difference between the Toltec, Maya, and Aztec was that my Aztec brothers were hungry—ravenous for the luxuries they saw others enjoy while they slept on dirt and ate what vultures left behind. Now those hungry wolves eyed the choicest loin in the One-World: Tula.

Ayyo . . . The world around me was becoming more fragile and dangerous.

And then I saw Ixchaal.

---

* Translator's Note: Europe fell into a Dark Age after the fall of the Roman Empire that lasted from the sixth to eleventh century, much the same time period that high Maya civilization flourished. As Europe was coming out of a Dark Age, the Maya were falling into one.

67

Late in the afternoon, an hour before Uxmal—in a jungle-shrouded waste that would have once produced maize and beans for the city— I spotted Ixchaal. She waited beneath a sapodilla tree. Even from a distance, I could see that she was rested and relaxed.

I refrained from racing toward her and carefully wiped a relieved smile off my face. I had agonized over her fate for many a night when I should have been sleeping; I looked for her amid the countless passersby when I should have been watching my back.

That I would never truly possess Ixchaal, I already knew—it would be easier to possess Quetzalcoatl's wind and water. But I was more comfortable with Ixchaal nearby. I liked her.

Joining her under the shade tree, I set down the sacks that held my food and weapons and sat down. She handed me a clay cup of cool fruit juice, and I stared at her over the rim as I sipped it.

Finally, unable to hold my tongue, I said, "Was that you in Jaina wearing those beggar's clothes?"

"When I saw you stumbling moronically around the market-place, I thought I had better get you out of there. The Jaina king's soldiers or constables would have spotted you before long, then tortured our plans out of you."

"Was there a reason you didn't tell me it was you? A reason we couldn't have traveled together?"

"After we were separated in Teotihuacán, I decided that it was safer for you to travel alone. Almost all travelers are men. A man and a woman on other than a short journey would have immediately aroused suspicion."

"What happened in Teotihuacán?"

"Inside the barrack, the commander insisted on having his pleasure with me first. He took me into a room. After he closed the door, I knocked him out and went out a window."

"And left the city without me."

"I hurried to catch up with you. I assumed you had obeyed my instructions and had gone on without me."

She acted as if we had not parted amid catastrophic violence; as if we were two travelers who had simply bumped into each other.

"We will be going after darkness," she said.

"What happens after dark?"

"The Guardians will tell you."

"You know, I'm getting tried of—"

"It's your duty, your birthright."

"Tell me about my mother."

"You must earn your answers."

"Earn them? I traveled almost from one end of the One-World to the other, fighting and eluding killers who wanted to cut out my liver and feed it to their dogs. What am I supposed to do to earn your trust? Will my death convince you and the Guardians that I'm trustworthy?"

She appeared to be deep in thought for a moment, and then nodded her head.

"That would be a start."

After dark, Ixchaal led me along a jungle path.

I was not happy about being surrounded by heavy foliage in the darkness. Night belonged to the fiercest creature in the One-World—the jaguar, he who kills with one bite. Weighing as much as three men put together, the beasts could roar like the hell-crack of doom when attracting a mate or they could kill silently from ambush.

"We better be under the protection of your Night Lords," I growled at her.

If I wasn't eaten by a jaguar, a poisonous snake might strike me or an anaconda's coils might crush me.

She refused to tell me where she was taking me.

Ayyo . . . that came as no surprise.

I would have expected the meeting to take place in a large sacred place of priests as it did at Tajin, where we met at the temple in the ceremonial center. But our wilderness trek took us east of the city, into hills, to a small stone pyramidal temple lit ghostly blue by moonlight.

The Guardians were there, seated side by side on thrones at the top of the temple. Looking down at me . . . like gods.

Or demons.

I followed Ixchaal up the steps and stood before the three priests.

Standing at the top, I suddenly realized that I had the battle-axe tightly gripped in my hand, ready to be hurled. Anger boiled in me. They had me running the length of the One-World with killers dogging my every step. And they refused to tell me why—not even what I was searching for.

"What is it that I seek?" I asked.

"The Dark Rift."

I looked to the sky. "It's there, where it always is." The Dark Rift—the Underworld Road to Mictlantecuhtli's hell—was where it was supposed to be.

"You're looking in the wrong place," the Guardian said.

"Where should I be looking?"

"Behind you."

I turned. Uxmal was in the distance. The city was dark except for one area: the great pyramid in the ceremonial center was lit up with hundreds of torches.

Even in the distance, with people on the pyramid appearing to be little more than the size of ants, it wasn't hard for me to understand what was happening: The temple priests were working overtime—collecting heads, hearts, and blood for the gods.

"It's there," the Guardian said.

"What's there?"

"The Dark Rift."

"The Dark Rift is in the House of the Magician," I said, repeating the phrase that was buried deep in my mind.

The Guardian nodded. "The Great Pyramid of Uxmal is the House of the Magician."

"The House of the Magician is a pyramid?" I asked.

"I will explain," Ixchaal whispered.

"Your mother, Ixloom," the Guardian said, "was the Keeper of the Dark Rift. When she passed, it fell to you."

I felt the marks on my belly.

"Yes," the Guardian said. "Stargazer put the marks of the Dark Rift to identify you to us after she passed."

"What happened to my mother?"

"Answers to these questions will come later. You are here to take possession of the Dark Rift."

"What is the Dark Rift?" I asked.

"A codex. One you were born to protect."

"A book? The Dark Rift is a book?"

"A Book of Fates."

"Book of Fates?" I shook my head. The Book of Fates was the 260-day calendar used to divine the fate of people. As far as I knew, it was the only Book of Fates that had ever existed.

The Guardian held up his hand, dismissing my many questions.

"Your duty is to protect the book."

"Is it in danger?"

"Yes. There is no longer a king in Uxmal keeping order in the city, no longer a high priest favored by the gods. The city is in chaos. Fanatical priests, criminal gangs, and mindless mobs control the streets. You must rescue our codex from this violence and safeguard it."

He paused and stared at me.

"This is why you were born; this is why you are the Bearer of the Word. At this moment when the codex is in danger, only you can save it."

"How many warriors do you have to assist me?"

I waited, but the Guardian was silent.

"What happens if I fail?"

"You will begin your journey to Xibalba."

Ayyo . . . Xibalba—the Maya Underworld with nine levels of hell.

68

UXMAL

Ixchaal and I entered Uxmal disguised as beggars. We did not stand out, however. Amid the disorder and mayhem, people feared to wear fine apparel or precious accessories. Yet even amid the chaos and decay, the Maya's former greatness was apparent.

Still one sensed the dynamic Maya spirit and the power of its glorious history. Walking past its magnificent monuments, prodigious palaces, and other elaborately constructed buildings, I could see they were all exquisitely and resiliently crafted out of hard stone. One could feel the eternal grandeur of the Mayan heroes, kings, and gods gracefully carved into the rock itself rather than just painted on. I felt as if I was walking among the gods . . . just as the ancient Maya had done.

"Is it the most splendid of all Maya cities?" I asked her.

She shook her head. "There are others equally marvelous. The Maya were a great civilization, spread over vast territories as the many nations of the north are today. At their height Uxmal and the rest of the Maya world shined brighter than Tula does today. But when the gods deserted them and the Dying commenced, people left the cities, which fell into ruin. Uxmal was the one holdout, but now it falls into ruin."

"I fear I see in Uxmal, Tula's fate," I said.

"I too."

Still there was no superficial similarity between Tula and Uxmal—at least not today. The Toltec capital was bright and beautiful, a brilliantly burnished gemstone, while Uxmal was dying. Still I sensed in her a spirit—venerable and transcendent—that would prevail even after Tula was dust and ashes.

"A strong king is one who controls a city during times of trouble," I finally said.

"In Uxmal's case, when the dark times came, the king was murdered. After his death, anyone capable of fleeing the city left. Not all could leave; the poor had no place to go. A strongman, warlords, and gangs vied for power. The more vicious and murderous the gangs, the more successful they were.

"Some occupied sections of the city, but ultimately resources, rather than physical territory, have counted most. A granary, a water source, the royal armory, the sacred temple with its path to the gods—these resources confer real power, not streets and houses. Some gangs still control districts but their days are numbered."

The countless representations of the Maya rain god, Chaac, evinced the Maya's relentless anxiety over water. While possessing a human body, the god also sported sharp fangs and the scales of a water snake. He carried an axe made of lightning and produced rain and thunder by striking clouds with it.

"Chaac has been as miserly with water in the south as Tlaloc has been in Tula," Ixchaal said.

She explained that despite the enormous amount of jungle vegetation in the Maya lands, the ground beneath their feet—unlike that in many other regions—repelled water.

"Water here collects in large natural stone-lined wells called cenotes. The ground will not hold water, but heavy rains run off into reservoirs that have formed underground. Cities are built around large cenotes, villages near small ones. Like so many others, the cenotes of Uxmal are almost dry. There's just enough water for the small population that still exists in the city."

I thought about Tula and its lack of rain. "The Maya empires were brought down because the rain god didn't give it water?"

She shook her head. "Some areas lacked water, some food, some were torn apart by disease, others by war. But their destruction all had one thing in common."

"Which was?"

"They were abandoned by the gods."

She took me to the ceremonial heart of the city and its most sacred monument. Standing before the tall pyramid, I sensed the same sort of mystery and magic that Ixchaal herself radiated.

"The House of the Magician," Ixchaal said. "No other pyramid in the One-World is like it."

All the sacred pyramids I had seen had four straight sides at the base that swept upward to be narrower at the top than the bottom. The House of the Magician, however, had an oval base, shaped almost like an egg. Narrower than a pyramid, this ovoid edifice was smooth all the way up. She told me the story of how the unusually shaped temple was built by a dwarf:

An old woman who had been childless found an egg that she took home and cared for until it hatched into a baby. The baby grew into a man, but its body remained small and stunted. Though his body was small, the dwarf had tremendous physical powers.

With the old woman's encouragement, the dwarf challenged the king of Uxmal to a trial of strength. After demonstrating that he was stronger than the king, the king ordered him to build the House in a single night. When the king awoke the next morning, the tall pyramidal structure was fully erected.

"The dwarf was a god," I said.

"Yes, that is why they called him a magician. It is said that he was a star that fell from the sky."

The House of the Magician, whatever its genesis, was a stellar achievement. The shape was so intrinsically unique I understood why people attributed to it celestial origins.

It did, however, have one thing in common with other pyramids I had seen: blood. Bloodstains streaked up the steps and down its corner troughs that ran from its flat summit and down the rounded sides.

Ayyo . . . the entire pyramid reminded me of a naked body stained with blood after its head was cut off.

The guards of the high priest of the temple squatted at the bottom, competing at tossing human knuckle bones into a jar. Their clothes were ragged and bloodstained. Some of the blood was still fresh.

Even violent poverty could dim their death-lust.

"How long has the codex been in the House of the Magician?" I asked.

"Beneath the House is another pyramid, an older one, and beneath that one, another built long before that one. The Dark Rift Codex is older than the oldest pyramid, older than Uxmal itself.

"A maze of tunnels is inside, one that snakes down so far it is said it leads to Xibalba itself. That was where the codex was kept, in the deepest pit, as close to Hell as any of the living have ever gotten."

"Is that where the codex is? In Hell?" I asked.

"It's under your feet."

I stared down and realized I was standing on the roof of the cenote, the underground reservoir that held the city's water supply. The roof was almost at street level and was only identifiable as the cenote's cover by the carvings in the stone, all of them tales of the water god Chaac. I estimated the cover to be forty paces wide, making the cenote beneath a large one.

Guards, disreputable and threadbare as the high priest's sentries, were posted at the opening that led down. Besides the absence of bloodstains, their tattered attire differed from that of the temple guards—these cenote protectors wore frayed, faded uniforms of the Royal Guard.

"Are you saying that the codex is in the cenote?" I asked.

"Yes. I told you that when the city was abandoned by all but rats and the poor, there was a battle to control what resources were left. The gang leader who gained control of the cenote calls himself Lord Chaac, the Lord of Water."

I could have guessed that.

"Lord Chaac was a slave who worked as a guard, more of a torturer, for the king. When the king fled, the slave gathered up other warriors who were being left behind and took control of the water."

"Does he have a big army?" I asked. Water was the most important single thing in existence.

"He has a big weapon that keeps other avaricious gangs from attacking him to gain control of the cenote."

"Does he claim to have the god's own lightning rod that he can beat clouds with to bring rain?"

"He has a large bundle of poison hanging in a sisal bag over the water pond."

I groaned in disgust. The poison guaranteed no one would attack him. Kill the water supply, and these human rats and two-legged snakes who occupied the city would be forced to leave—with no place to go, since the land outside was already barely sustaining those on it.

He held hostage what Uxmal held dear—water.

"How did he get the codex?"

"After the king and the high priest left, he led a raid on the temple. Lord Chaac thought that if he could address the gods there and plead his case for the city's leadership, they might lend him their support. When that failed and others contested his control of the temple, he grabbed what he could and retreated with his men into the cenote. Part of his loot was the codex."

"Have you tried buying it from him?"

"No, we tried buying other stolen items to see how he dealt with the offers. He demanded ten times more than we offered. When we met that price, he demanded ten times more. Worse than the price, he haggled for months and we never came to an agreement. Also, he does know this is a sacred book. He would become suspicious, then attempt to kill or dupe us."

"So how do we get the codex from him? I asked.

"That is for the Keeper to decide."

69

To enter the cenote, abscond with the codex, and simultaneously elude Lord Chaac's bloodthirsty cutthroats—formerly royal court torturers—was a challenge to test even the god Quetzalcoatl, the deity of both learning and adventure.

Or a coyotl cur raised by thieving, murdering Aztecs.

"Octli," I said to Ixchaal.

"Octli? Are you planning to trade a jug of octli for a priceless sacred relic? Are you mad?"

"Ixchaal, a temple life—or wherever you and your Guardians were raised—doesn't teach you everything. I believe I know something Lord Chaac will trade for the codex."

"What?"

I locked eyes with her. "Now you get to watch me make magic."

I purchased jugs of octli from a vendor in the square and had the seller's guards deliver them to the guards at the cenote entrance. When the octli vendor tried to give me his usual diluted fare, I handed him a piece of jade that would buy his entire stock several times over.

"I want pure octli, nectar so strong that its smell alone would intoxicate a god."

I took a sniff of what he sold me. Ayyo! Whew. The smell made my eyeballs melt.

Then Ixchaal and I faced the suspicious guards at the entrance. They understood immediately that the octli was meant as a bribe to get their cooperation. For what, they didn't know.

"Take this to Lord Chaac," I told the lead guard.

I handed him a brilliantly burnished, dazzlingly bejeweled obsidian dagger.

He stared at me with mean, greedy eyes.

"Lord Chaac already has a dagger."

He would have liked giving it to me point first.

"Ignore my demand, and he will give the dagger to you—in your avocados. This blade is of the Royal House of Tula. King Quetzalcoatl himself has sent it to Lord Chaac."

The mention of Tula's golden king made the guard's eyes pop. But I could also see that he was tempted to take the knife himself.

"Deliver the dagger to Lord Chaac—now!" I snapped. "Or he will use it to flay you whole."

As he turned to go down the steps, I said, "Tell Lord Chaac that I have another gift for him, something even more valuable."

Ixchaal shot me a glance. I smothered a smirk. I was enjoying leaving her hanging, as she did so often with me. I just hoped I didn't get us killed doing it.

He disappeared down the stairway and I led her away.

"Where are we going?" she asked.

"Just stepping away to give the guards here and down below an extra moment to get some octli in their guts."

A fighter herself, she knew that powerful intoxicants would confound a guard's reflexes and confuse his aim, giving us a chance to foil his swing and take him out. A drunken guard would also be easier to blindside.

"Why do you think the dagger will impress him? He must have others."

"Not like that one. The king himself gave it to me. Like my sword, it has an edge of thick obsidian. Weapons-makers craft such blades exclusively for the royalty and the high lords of Tula. He will recognize it as a royal Toltec blade."

The guard returned and commanded us to follow him back down. His watery eyes and flushed face told me he had already imbibed in the octli. He led us down flights of stone stairways lit by torches, four levels down. When we came out on the bottom, we were on a narrow ledge that ran alongside the pool of water. I first saw the sisal bundle of poison hanging over the water. From there a rope extended to a man on a throne that I took to be a nobleman's chair. It only took a quick slice with a knife from his position to have the poison dumped into the pond.

We went down the ledge to face him, two guards behind us, two guards to our left with their backs to the water, Lord Chaac in front of us.

Lord Chaac was smaller than I expected; my instant thought was about the dwarf who built the House of the Magician, though he was taller than a dwarf. He was more than almost a head shorter than Ixchaal, which put him about my shoulder level. But he was also a thick mass of muscle. Scattered among his many tattoos were battle scars.

A seasoned warrior, he would be no pushover.

His foot was bandaged, either from an illness or a fight.

Loot from the palace, the temple, and wherever else he raided was piled around him. Only one book was there: a codex bound in deerskin.

I gave Ixchaal a subtle look, and her eyes told me it was the Revelation of the Dark Rift.

"I am going to kill you," Lord Chaac said. He spoke without moving from his chair.

The statement didn't require a response. I waited for another one—hopefully friendlier.

"Or I may not kill you if you please me."

"What would please you?" I asked.

"Your blood. All of it. I haven't made a sacrifice to the gods yet today. I give them so much Maya blood, they will be delighted to get Toltec blood."

"My blood is intended for my own gods, and then only in quantities that I can spare."

He leered at me. "Your Toltec gods are whores. Even the male ones sell their bodies to other gods." He held up the dagger. "What else did you steal from the Toltec king?"

"I have other Toltec weapons. Fine ones, made of the best obsidian."

He pursed his lips, nodding, as he ran his finger beside the cutting edge of the blade. "Even the king of Uxmal didn't have a blade this fine. Why have you brought this to me?"

I shrugged. "As an offer in friendship. I gave you something of mine, I want something from you."

"You'll get nothing from me except pain . . . but if you please me, I might kill you quickly. I want more weapons made of royal obsidian."

"I want the codex that is at your right."

He turned and looked at it for a long moment.

"It must be very valuable."

I shook my head. "No, it won't buy you food or kill your enemies. But it is sacred. The gods are angry because you have it. It has to go back to the temple where priests will care for it."

He suddenly laughed. "Priests? We killed all the priests, all the real ones. The Temple's new high priest used to clean the king's bedpan."

"I told you I'm here to trade. You give me the book, and I will give you the most important thing in the world to you."

"What?"

As he spoke the word, I was already twisting and Ixchaal was in motion next to me. The short-handled battle-axe came out from under my mantle and struck the man nearest me in the head. I deliberately twisted the handle so the blade struck him flat, knocking him backward into the water behind him but still continued on its course rather than imbedding itself in him. In the same lethal uninterrupted motion, I decapitated the man standing beside him.

Beside me Ixchaal was spinning on her heels as if infused with the divine ollin, her dagger held out, slitting the throat of the man behind her.

The fourth guard had taken a step back, out of range for her quick swing. As he brought up his axe, she hurled the blade into his throat all the way to its handle. He stumbled backward, but she was on him before he could fall, wrenching the blade free.

We both faced Lord Chaac. He had risen, but was now falling back down. His bad leg wouldn't support his weight.

"I was going to trade your life for the codex," I said, "but now I must take it because you insulted my gods."

His own blade lunged at my stomach, but my axe blade reflexively chopped off his hand, then cleaved his skull down to the shoulders with a powerful two-handed swing.

We grabbed the codex and bounded up the stone steps three at a time to the surface.

All four guards at the entrance were on the ground. Two were not breathing, the other two didn't appear that they would be taking in air for long.

I gave Ixchaal a look.

"I added something to the octli," she said.

"What?"

"My magic."

PART XVII

70

Emilio Luis Carrizo sat in a wicker armchair on his Chiapas patio at his chrome-and-glass breakfast table. He stared out over a lush rainforest of soaring mahogany, sleek ebony, towering teak, and fragrant frangipani. A tall raw-boned man with an immaculately trimmed goatee, an obsidian-hued ponytail, fierce dark eyes, and café leche skin, he carefully spooned sugar into his china coffee mug. He wore beige Zegna trousers of fine Egyptian cotton, black Armani ankle boots, and a white long-sleeved shirt of crisp Thai silk, tight-fitting and athletically cut. Custom tailored in Bangkok, they accentuated his prison-gym muscles, which he'd so painstakingly developed during a five-year bit in Pelican Bay.

"It is hot, patron," said his companion, Raphael Morales. "You'd find short-sleeved shirts, shorts, and sandals more comfortable, no?"

A balding middle-aged man with small mirthless eyes and skin brown as burnt leather, Morales always sported Hawaiian short-sleeved shirts in various shades of yellow, purple, white, and red—this one featuring coconuts, surfers, pineapples, and amply endowed naked women. Barely containing his massive shoulders and behemoth belly, it vividly displayed the jailhouse tats snaking up and down his big-yard biceps and gargantuan forearms, as well as the thirteen Mexican Mafia tattoos semicircling his neck. He'd obviously done time.

"Sí, but then I would have to have my prison tats removed," Carrizo said.

"Why?" his friend asked.

Carrizo shook his head. "I'm supposed to be a respectable businessman, cabron. They project the wrong image."

"Them clothes still demasiado caliente." Too hot, Morales said.

🔯

In truth, Carrizo deliberately kept his tattoos as a reminder that the Pelican Bay Supermax was not an experience he wanted to repeat. To that end he'd never returned to the United States and still swore he'd never make that mistake again. The federales—indeed most of Mexico's most prominent politicians—were far easier to bribe, coerce, and control than their Americano counterparts.

As the years went by, Carrizo had learned to hate Americans—so much so that Morales finally asked him why.

"Americanos officials no take the mordida," Carrizo said, "and I cannot trust a man who no take a bribe."

"Why they no take your money, boss?" Morales had asked.

"They got no ethics."

"What's ethics?" Morales asked.

" 'The Golden Rule.' "

Morales stared at him, silent, his eyes expressionless.

"He who got the gold, rules, no?" Carrizo explained.

"Uno muy bueno rule, boss," Morales agreed.

🔯

"The Apachuros d Huevos—are they part of your 'respectable business'?" asked his friend.

"Not all my investments are in drugs and guns."

"Sí, you also run muchas putas." Many whores, Morales said, grinning.

"A filthy fuckin' business, no." He pronounced *fuckin'* "fockin'."

"Filthy fuckin' lucrative," Morales said, smiling.

"Mucho lucrativo," Carrizo acknowledged.

"Still I understand about the jail tats, boss."

Shrugging, Carrizo glanced at his white-gold Cartier Tank Francaise. Lavishly encrusted with diamonds and sapphires, it read 10:59 A.M.

"This coffee make me nervous." He motioned a servant over. The man wore black charro pants and a white ruffled shirt. "An ice bucket of Coronas to combat the caffeine."

Carrizo was a mean drunk, and Morales viewed early morning inebriants as an ill omen.

"Okay, amigo, tell me about this artifact, this—what you call it?—codex?" Carrizo asked.

"Sí, it's like a book—an eleven-hundred-year-old book. That woman archeologist we grab here in Chiapas, remember? She got it. But the two gringos who took her back?"

"They killed eight of our men."

"Ten—with grenades and automatic weapons."

"They are dead now—the gringos, no?"

"They're back with the woman. She also got another woman with her, another archeologist. They got a second codex, maybe a third. We can't be sure."

"I remember now. I got someone helpin' us up north, remember? We got a man with them too, man on the inside—a mule-packer. We send men to kill them—good men. We got them three different ways, and you say they ain't dead?"

"The mule-packer's disappeared. So's the men we sent after them. I think they *all* may be dead."

Carrizo stared at him, dumbfounded. "They killed a second team *and* the packer?"

"Probablemente, patron."

The chilled bucket of Corona arrived. "Tequila," Carrizo said softly, his rage palpable.

Tequila at 11:00 A.M.—muy malo, Morales thought.

"They kill what? Eight men."

"Ten counting the packer."

"Twenty men dead, and we no got our codexes?"

"Codices—the word ees plural. And them gringos ain't give us nothin' 'cept kill our men and rob us of our shit."

"What's in these cod-i-ces?"

"The packer say a god, Quetzalcoatl, say how the world gonna end in 2012."

Carrizo's face brightened. "When I was in prison I read up on QuetzaWhatchHisShit?"

"You study religion?"

"Naw, just Aztec, Mayan shit. Lotta cholos there study that, wanna bring back the Aztec and Mayan days. They talk about this star-god, this QuetzaMuthafucka—they call him Q—and brag how he gonna come back and save us. Well, I read up on Q. He get into a fight wit' a muy malo hombre name of Tezcatlipoca. God of death, blood, and night, he whup Q's butt—whup it good. Take over all Q's sky, till he run the whole show up there. Now them cholos never say that. They just say Q coming back and we gotta hang wit' him. I say to myself, you ignorant hideputas"—sons of whores—"why you back this bitch? Tezcatlipoca got game."

"But ain't he the god of night and shit?"

"So? I like the night. Day is all work and worry. Night we chingas putas, drink tequila, kick it. And Tez, he got the cojones to git it done."

"Sí, but this Q fucker, he got the books. TexaCatHouse ain't got no books for us."

"And them putas got Q's books?"

"Sí, but TexaCaca—the guy you like—ain't the author."

"Listen, pollo loco. I don't give a shit 'bout no gods. I like dinero, comprende? This QuetzaCockless, he worth muchos dineros. I swing wit' Q."

"So you changin' sides? You ain't backin' TexaDicka no more?"

"We're talkin' millions, tens of millions, hundreds of millions."

"We also losin' twenty men tambien, and we can't let that shit slide."

"Got a rep to sweat," Carrizo agreed.

"Who you wanna send?" Morales asked.

"The packer's kid—that muthafucka mean enough to kill Jesus. Plus them hombres-putas kill his old man. He do it."

Morales nodded. "You still got that norteamericano up there helpin' us?"

"Sí. I tell him we need these motherfuckers bad. Double what we're payin'. Maybe I tell him silver or lead." Silver in the pocket or lead in the head.

"You threatenin' a top dog, boss."

"I want them mutherfuckas."

"Then there it is."

"There it is."

The servant brought a liter of Maestro Dobel Extra-Anejo and rocks-glasses, handcrafted out of 100 percent ten-year-old blue agaves, each bottle was labeled, numbered, and marketed with the name of the ranch where the agave was harvested. Carrizo poured them each four ounces straight-up.

"Salud," Morales offered.

"Y pesatas," Carrizo said, finishing the toast. "Now get that packer's kid. I want Quetzalcoatl's books—codshit, whatever the fuck you call them. And I want them gringo muthafuckas in the ground tambien y pronto."

"Mucho pronto."

"Then vaya con Dios."

"Y pesetas."

"Y putas."

"Y Diabola."

Morales got up. He had to track down the packer's kid, while his boss suborned and if necessary threatened their Washington rat.

And all for some old books?

He preferred running putas.

PART XVIII

71

As I had discovered before, life is a circle. When I asked Ixchaal why I was chosen to join her in tracking down the Guardians' lost codex she said simply:

"The Dark Rift has chosen you to protect and preserve the Words of Quetzalcoatl and the Great Calendar. Who better than the Bearer of the Word to hunt down the Word?"

"All because of the words on my belly."

I had even more unanswered questions than before.

But getting answers from Ixchaal was like sweating blood out of sun-bleached bones.

🌀

This time we had hired a boat that brought us all the way up the coast to a village near Tijan. We then made our way over the mountain. It was too dangerous to return by the Teotihuacán route because of war with Tula.

Before we reached Tula, we learned that the war with Teotihuacán had gone badly. Teotihuacán had attacked Tula first, beating Quetzalcoatl to the punch. Still the king had driven that army all the way back to its city gates. After stripping his supply lines, however,

Quetzacoatl was unable to breach the ramparts. When an army from Cholula reinforced the city, he was forced to retreat. The news of that retreat had spread. Now Cholula, Teotihuacán, and the Aztec clans were banding together to march on Tula.

Ixchaal accurately summarized the military situation.

"Tula is wounded and the vultures are circling to rip off pieces."

Cities that had feared Tula now saw an opportunity to bring the king down—as did the priests who wanted blood for the gods and power for themselves.

Ixchaal and I arrived back at Tula, the codex beneath my mantle and strapped to my back. Entering the east gate, we found chaos reigning. People poured out of the city, carrying all the possessions they could manage. The ones leaving with somewhere to go were wealthy merchants, nobles, and most of the religious elite.

We had heard many different tales as we approached the city, but then I ran into Smoking Shield on my way to the palace. His Jaguar Knight's uniform was dirty, and his face was haggard. He had had no sleep for several nights. Still he was eager to see me. I quickly asked what was happening.

"The king had been cutting the number of human sacrifices for years, and on returning from Teotihuacán, he abolished them altogether along with the priests' incessant wars—the wars they demanded to acquire sacrificial prisoners.

"The priests revolted, whipping up the populace with fiery warnings that their Death God, Tezcatlipoca, would scourge and scorch the land. Our starving masses are in no mood to challenge the gods and have sided with them."

"He should stand his ground and hang all the priests."

"It's too late. The priests have incited so much anarchy, Quetzalcoatl has abdicated. He feels if he leaves Tula, the civil strife might subside enough for the people to unite against the foreign forces coming to sack the city."

"Did his abdication satisfy the priests?" I asked.

"Not in the least. They now accuse Quetzalcoatl of entering his sister's bedroom, while drunk," Shield said, "and violating her."

A king could have a hundred wives, but to force his sister into carnal relations was an unpardonable offense—a taboo punishable by death. The priests clearly wanted Quetzalcoatl's head.

"People say many things about our king, particularly his palace enemies," I said, refusing to credit the rumor.

Smoking Shield nodded. "It's all lies. The night before his abdication, he got so drunk that the next day he had no memory of anything. I believe the priests or his sister doctored his octli. The next morning the clerics started the rumor. Having joined forces with the priests, his sister refuses to refute the rumors, implying he raped her. She clearly plans to assume his throne."

"Maybe she and the clerics feared he would one day reclaim his kingship."

"The rumors would make that hard," Shield agreed.

Glancing at the surrounding chaos, I said, "Tula's out of control. Someone should tell his sister and the priests that soon there will be no throne to assume."

"They were power-mad," Shield said.

"And now they have nothing," I said.

"What do you conclude from all this?" Shield asked me.

"Our king was too learned and too far-seeing for this time and place."

"Too wise for the people?" Shield asked.

"The death priests and the people both wanted blood, and he went against them."

"In other words, the priests and people are getting what they wanted," Shield said.

"In a word, yes."

Glancing around, I suddenly noticed Ixchaal was gone. Nothing she did surprised me any longer. Perhaps she had flown over the wall and up to the stars.

I immediately began to miss her. I cared about her, relied on her, and felt a loss.

Still, wherever she was, I knew we were fated to meet again.

As long as we were alive, we were fated to meet again.

We would meet even if it were in Mictlantecuhtli's hell.

Our destinies, I now believed, were forever intertwined.

72

We went directly to the palace. A large contingent of grim-faced Jaguar Knights defended the palace entrance. Battle-ready, they had packed for a long march.

"The king has asked about you—repeatedly," Shield said as we entered the palace. "You were gone a long time."

"I came a long way."

He stared at me intently. "Did you find . . . the lost codex?"

I nodded.

"And you know your duty?"

"You told me on the temple summit my first night in Tula. As Bearer of the Word, I am to protect and preserve Quetzalcoatl's codices and the Great Calendar."

"Good," he said, nodding somberly and averting his eyes.

"Do you know where the king will go?" I asked.

"He has not said. Many of us would follow him into hell. Are you coming with us to the king?"

I hesitated. "I will join you shortly—after I gather the other codices."

Passing through the great entrance, the vast interior was almost

deserted, a few servants running back and forth. A courtier walked
by me blank-eyed, not even acknowledging my existence.

I did not go immediately to Stargazer's observatory, however. I
headed instead for the king's personal apartments, down dim, deserted corridors in which most of the torches had burned out. Dust
and smudges were so thick that at any other time they would have
caused the royal housekeeper to be whipped.

I thought I saw Zyanya at the end of the hallway. In the corridor
only a single torch still flamed, and in its dim light I could not be
sure it was her. Getting closer, she appeared strangely possessed. I
could see that it wasn't just octli that she had indulged in but something else, perhaps magic mushrooms.

As I got closer she suddenly recognized me and her eyes widened.

I slowed my step. My arms at my sides, I dropped my head before
her.

I saw the blow coming as a blur of motion—her dagger sweeping
up out of her robe at my throat. I deflected it reflexively with my
wrist. Cutting my forearm, however, it still nicked my neck.

When she attacked me with a backhanded thrust, I grabbed her
wrist.

"Why?" I shouted.

"Why did you not die with your mother?" she hissed. "I never
dreamed you'd survive and return to us."

She froze, glaring at me.

"You killed her?" I asked, my voice barely a whisper.

Her features twisted with hate and rage. Butting me in the face,
she broke free from my grip and swung the dagger. I parried it again,
but the obsidian blade glanced off my chest, blood spilling down my
stomach.

Had she been anyone but a royal, I would have killed her. Again,
however, I grabbed at her wrist, seeking to restrain her.

She suddenly tensed and gasped. I looked up from her wrists, which I'd been attempting to restrain. An arm had slipped around her waist and was holding her up.

A obsidian knife-blade protruded through the front of her throat, and I was staring into the king's sad eyes.

Zyanya coughed, and blood slipped down the corner of her mouth.

"Better this way," Quetzalcoatl said. "She would not have survived exile."

"She killed my mother?" I asked hoarsely.

"Yes," he said. "Pregnant with my child, your mother was ready to bear. The thought of a rival child drove my sister insane, and she stabbed your mother in the belly. Assuming you would die with her, she fled. However, Stargazer arrived. His mother had been a midwife, and he knew how to rescue infants from dying mothers. Cutting you out, he found a wet-nurse to secretly wean you. My sister, unfortunately, learned from someone who saw your mother's remains that her belly had been cut open. She knew then the infant had been removed. She eventually tracked down the wet-nurse and tortured your whereabouts out of her. Stargazer got to you first. I was off on some military venture, and having no one to turn to, he tattooed your belly with the Dark Rift's gateway stars and set you adrift in a reed basket."

"And your sister?" I asked.

"She was my royal blood, a princess and allied with the priests. Our father, the king, forbade retaliation. Your mother was a commoner. I was wrong for having violated her. My hands were tied."

"You are my father?" I asked in shocked disbelief.

"A father who abandoned you."

"But you had no choice. You weren't even here at the time. You did not know where I was."

"I loved your mother, and I let her killer live."

"That's over with."

"But it isn't. I must abandon you again . . . I must abandon everyone."

"Everyone?"

"You, Tula, the One-World, all."

"Because of the anarchy outside? Because of the priests?"

"We offered the people life, the priests death, and the priests won. You've seen what the death priests have done to Tula. You saw what they did to the Maya as well."

"Where will you go, my liege?"

"I will set out east toward the rising sun. Like yourself, so many years ago, I shall journey in a reed boat. Smoking Shield will help me build it—just as he helped Stargazer craft yours."

"But you will return?"

"In a boat of resurrection, not death; yes, I shall return."

My father hugged me—for the first and only time in my life.

I thought briefly of the mother who had hugged me in my dreams and at whose breast I thought I'd suckled. A loving maid, who was tortured to death for having nursed and cared for me, was that magical woman. My mother had died *before* I was born.

In sorrow I followed my father up the hall toward the palace doors. He would meet with Smoking Shield and his Jaguar Knights, who would escort him to the sea.

I now had to meet Stargazer and see how his calendar had progressed. I then would collect the rest of the codices and set out on my own journey.

I was the Bearer of the Word.

The Guardians' codex slung in a pack across my back, I headed toward the old man's observatory.

73

I stumbled through the endless palace hallways, numb in mind and body. Its corridors swarmed with Tula's citizens. Deranged by rage and privation, the people exacted their revenge on anything and everything. Looters ransacked everything in sight, bent under huge baskets bursting with maize, beans, chili peppers, cocoa beans, smoked and dried meats; agave-fiber rope-coils, hide sandals, obsidian knives, sheaves of amal paper, fancy feathers, gemstones, and chiseled jade.

At least a dozen despoilers appropriated works of real value—turquoise mosaics of molded gold and silver, embellished with pyrite, shells, and pearls, festooned with feathers, the most valuable of which adorned masks and shields.

A surprising number of brigands staggered out of the palace, their arms piled high with leather-lined human skulls, some of which were also ornamented with turquoise mosaics, the eye sockets glittering with pyrite.

Some of the more musical marauders clutched to their chests conch horns, bells, seed-filled gourds, and calabashes, long reed flutes, big bass drums.

Other freebooters with an eye for high fashion hauled out heaps of gaudily-hued robes embroidered with feathers, fur, and gemstones.

Some of the hungrier pilferers pillaged food. They now poured into the streets loaded down with steaming platters of honeyed maize cakes, stuffed tamales, onions, chili peppers, beans, ears of maize, squash, and tomatoes, whole rabbits, ducks, pitchers of chilled cocoa and octli.

Some animal-lovers meanwhile liberated the courtyard menageries. Starving citizens and wild animals devoured the delicacies side by side without incident, seemingly oblivious to each another.

But on exiting the palace, they quickly discovered they had neither the means to transport their spoils nor a place to safely store them. When this realization hit home, they immediately dropped their plunder where they stood, their bounty soon merging with other booty piles.

As for the liberated jaguars, panthers, bobcats, and deer, they now bounded up and down the thoroughfares in wild-eyed amazement, the frenzied citizens leaping out of their way. Parrots, eagles, falcons, and hawks squawked, swooped, and shrieked just above our ducking heads while anacondas and alligators slithered and scurried underfoot.

I watched the maddening spectacle still speechless with shock. Tula, which had given me so much, was no longer part of my life—nor would it soon be a part of anyone else's. My life and those lives of the panicking people around me would be otherwise defined.

But my past and my parentage were now defined.

My present was also defined—I was to locate Stargazer and help him complete the Great Calendar.

Afterward an odyssey would define my future. The Guardians' codex already on my back, I needed to collect Stargazer's and Quetzalcoatl's codices as well, then search out a safe place far from Tula to cache and preserve them for future peoples and future times. They must not be lost.

Stargazer—my rescuer twice and the wisest man I had ever known—believed the fate of future generations would depend on them.

Quetzalcoatl had said the same.

Everyone knew that the Teotihuacán, Cholula, and Aztec armies would eventually storm the gates. For many years our armies had marched into those lands, seizing prisoners for our bloody priests and their temple-stones, where they had ripped out their hearts and cut off their heads.

No more.

These foreign armies now converged on Tula bent on their own blood vengeance.

Our people—consumed by pillage and revenge against their neighbors—would be defenseless against a common foe.

Not that the barbarians would find riches to plunder or thousands of inhabitants to rape and enslave, to torture and kill. My fellow citizens were doing an amazing job of looting and destroying Tula themselves. To what end I could not fathom. When our citizens fled, none of them would escape with more than they could comfortably carry.

In fact, now that they realized that the immense stores of merchandise would remain behind them in Tula, they put torches to the booty piles, setting them ablaze.

As I headed off toward Stargazer's observatory, stacked goods on all the streets were bursting into flame, eerily illuminating what had been great, golden Tula and its magnificent royal palace.

74

When Stargazer had first taken Desert Flower and me through Tula's vast market, I thought it contained more boundless bounty than existed on all the earth, in the House of the Sun, in the Southern Hereafter and Tlaloc's Eastern Paradise combined—all of it concentrated in a single prodigious plaza.

Looters now ravaged it piecemeal.

The vertiginous pyramidal Sun Temple still loomed over the market. As if to mock that monumental edifice, rioters erected pyramids of plunder by the hundreds—each of them taller than two men, their diameters twice as wide. The rioters heaped everything onto these tottering towers: braided rawhide ropes, maize sheaves, sweet potatoes, onions, peppers, cocoa; skinned and smoked rabbits, peccary pigs, turkeys, ducks, venison, roasting dogs, frogs and fish; maguey and bark paper; agave syrup and fresh honey; indigo and cochineal dyes; obsidian knives, flint spear blades, copper axes; bamboo smoking pipes; chairs and sleeping mats; braziers; pottery; salt; building lumber; charcoal; resin-soaked pine torches; green parrot plumes as well as eagle and falcon feathers; herbal medicines, poultices, oils and ointments; drums, conch trumpets, flutes, calabash rattles; lengths of elaborately dyed, elegantly embroidered cloth; gems, precious stones, shells, even silver and gold; every kind of necklace, earring, bracelet; even the stalls themselves.

In fury and frustration, the lunatic mob quickly put these piles to the torch.

A half dozen slave cages sat at the edge of the market. They were still filled with the prisoners, whom quarry bosses and sacrificial priests had come here to requisition men either for the quarries or the sacrificial stone. The sight of these caged wretches filled the mob with vindictive rage. Aztec Dog People and the captives of other enemies' tribes and states, they were barbarians whose people were about to breach our city gates. The despoilers dragged them into the marketplace, where they and their cages were dropped onto the miniature mountains of loot and set ablaze, the booty piles quickly turned into funeral pyres.

I crossed the chaotic marketplace as quickly as I could.

Thousands of priests and votaries once resided in this neighborhood. All had fled, the only remaining clerics those too old or infirm to run off. They wandered the streets with eyes like saucers, shrieking at the heavens.

Passing the Sun Temple, I saw hysterical citizens on their knees, their faces pointed toward the heavens begging Tezcatlipoca, the lord of the night sky, for forgiveness. Other rioters dragged innocent citizens up the terraced slopes to the temple-summit, spread-eagling them over the stone altars. Playing the role of pretend-priests, they cracked and sawed open their chests, tearing out their hearts. Severing their heads, they flung them over the sides, where their crania bounced and bled down the steps. Slashing open their abdomens, they draped themselves in men's intestines and howled like Mictlantecuhtli's hellhounds.

I hurried on to Stargazer's place of study, my hand on my dagger.

75

I was finally at Stargazer's house and observatory. On entering, I found our few meager possessions untouched, apparently not worth the pillaging and burning. I did not find the old man inside, but I knew where he would be. Entering the hidden wall closet, I located the trapdoor's cord secreted along the wall's edge, a dark thick rug and hard-packed dirt concealing it. Both the rug and the hard dirt adhered to the trapdoor when I lifted it. Closing the closet door and lighting a torch, I lowered myself into the secret tunnel and pulled the trap down over me.

I quickly negotiated the low-ceiling tunnel, picking my way between the badly cracked shoring timbers, which in my absence the old man had not replaced or repaired.

I found Stargazer in his workroom. Kneeling over his writing platform, he jotted down notes and numbers for the last page of his Great Calendar.

In a few moments, he looked up, acknowledging my presence. His computations for the Long Count Calendar were complete. Stargazer had cracked the mystery of the Last Day.

"Here is the last sheet of the Great Calendar, young scribe," he said. "You may translate it into the sacred glyphs."

Taking his place at the platform, I lay out a clean sheet of amal paper and went to work. In an hour I was finished. The glyphs were done, and the Long Count Calendar Codex was finished.

The old man sat slumped in a corner. Always the consummate scientist, he'd refused to give up the ghost until his work was complete. It was, and he was dead.

Finishing his course, his race was done. True to both conscience and king, he had not broken faith.

Why take him upstairs? I thought. *What would you do with him? Hurl him onto a pyre of plunder? He was better off here, where he'd labored so diligently and succeeded so brilliantly.*

Where he had been happy.

One of the shoring timbers would soon collapse, and the rest would fall in tandem. His place of triumph would be his mausoleum, his observatory, his shrine.

I slowly picked my way back through the tunnel, toward the trapdoor and the clandestine closet.

PART XIX

76

As soon as I exited the hidden closet, I knew something was horribly wrong. The heat in the observatory was horrendous, and in the street everyone raced back and forth. Mothers clutched infants and small children, trying to stuff into bags whatever they could grab on their way out of Tula.

The broad avenues were furnace-hot, and the smaller streets were blinding infernos. The buildings lining the big boulevards were now unbroken walls of flame. In the distance a colossal crimson fireball levitated over Tula, and I quickly recognized it as Quetzalcoatl's palace.

Re-entering the observatory, I grabbed a clean loincloth and emptied an olla of water over it, then emptied a second olla into a waterbag. I filled the top of my codex shoulder bag with dried tortillas.

I would be leaving Tula as I had arrived, with little more than the clothes on my back . . . except now I had the extra burden of the calendar and codices.

Leaving the observatory, I headed down the first major thoroughfare I found, the wet loincloth draping my nose and mouth, periodically wiping my smoke-stung eyes with it.

To my amazement, I ran into Smoking Shield, who'd come back toward the observatory searching for me. His uniform was charred and smeared with smoke and soot. The conflagration eerily illuminated his grimacing face. The Jaguar Knight's eyes mirrored those of a deranged jaguar.

"What happened?" I yelled above the hellish din engulfing us.

"The death priests say Tezcatlipoca, the Night Lord, has spoken."

"How?"

"You didn't see it?"

"I was underground with Stargazer."

Smoking Shield stared at me, the grimace turning into a demented grin.

"Tezcatlipoca's fiery fist blazed across the sky. Hurling stars at the earth, the Death God has scorched Tula to the bone. The few remaining priests have taken to the temple summits, where they harangue those still here that Tezcatlipoca has sworn to return. Next time he will kill us all."

"The death priests are madmen," I said.

"Yesterday, I would have agreed. Today, I no longer know."

"Why aren't you with our king?"

"Our lord, Quetzalcoatl, sent me back for you. He wants you with us. He says he cannot abandon you again."

"Then I must forsake him. I have another task. You know that," I said, slapping my shoulder bags.

"I told him you would say that," Smoking Shield said.

"Go to Quetzalcoatl," I said. "Look after him. I must find my own way now."

We stared at each other in motionless silence even as Tula burned.

"And Shield?" I said. "Thank you . . . for everything."

"Go with the gods."

"You too, Jaguar Knight."

He turned and jogged up the red-hot boulevard at a steady clip.

Burdened with my bags, I set out at a slower pace. The air smoked and scorched my lungs, and the horrific heat dried my sopping wet cloth with surprising quickness. Three more avenues, however, and I was at the city wall.

Joining the flood of fleeing refugees, I squeezed through the tunnel that ran beneath the wall.

With Tula behind me, with the calendar and codices across my back, I began my long trek toward the canyonlands, retracing my original path to this fabled city. Perhaps in one of those arroyo walls I could find a repository for the first of my codices.

One last time I stared at the city that had made me a man, taught me to love, and charged me with a hero's quest. I stood there and watched it die.

That life was gone. A new one was beginning, and I was already on my way. I had a mission. I was sworn to reclaim—in the soul's brief blaze, in the Future's final fire—a hint of hope, perhaps even a faint flicker of redemption for our race.

EPILOGUE

77

Once again, Dr. Cardiff was the first to arrive at the conference room. When the three stragglers entered, the president said:

"Sorry we were late. The National Security Council still can't figure out how to handle Gaza."

"You may not have to worry about Gaza much longer. Reets e-mailed me last night, and I printed it up. You'll note she refers to Jamesy and Hargrave as J. and H." She passed around the e-mail. "Return it for shredding when you're done."

The e-mail began:

Dear Cards:

Got some bad news. We got Codex #3 but Apachureros jumped us. J. and H. caught one of them. He said someone at your end informed on us. The guy had no reason to lie, and their catching us made no sense: How else could they have known we'd be in the middle of nowhere in a remote Chihuahua desert canyon? The odds against it being a coincidence are incalculable. Anyway, he showed them the text message that had alerted him, so there's no doubt.

Cards, you got a ringer in your crew, so this will be our last transmission.

Don't worry, though. We have guns, money, mescal—everything we need. We'll get that final codex if it's the last thing we do. In the meantime, we're smashing our sat-phones, busting the GPSs and going to ground. J. calls it "our blood-ground."

"Tell 'em we're pulling the hole in after us," he said.

Don't try finding us. That traitor'll get us killed. If you want to help, nail the hideputa in your midst. Hideputa is Mexican for "son of a whore."

Damn, I'm sick of those 'Pach.

Love,

Reets

PS You were asking if the codices said how Tula got wiped out. Codex #3 may give us that in detail. Coop is working hard on it. Allusive and allegorical, it's tough to translate. If anyone can crack it, though, she can.

So far it looks like Tula got hammered big-time—it wasn't only drought and civil war. They got hit with a devil's arsenal.

So batten down the hatches. Quetzalcoatl says it's coming after us now—2012-style.

"Coop has translated part of Quetzalcoatl's prophesy," Dr. Cardiff said. "I don't know whether this helps us any. The god-king says we're getting it like Tula—the entire 2012 jackpot. Here's his vision—at least part of it."

Dr. Cardiff handed out another sheet of paper.

Quetzalcoatl speaks:

I have seen a vision.

    I have seen the five-fold fiend with eagle wings, rattlesnake fangs, jaguar claws, crocodile jaws, with the hands and brain of man.

I have seen eagle's death-wings, the Dark Rift crashing down, the bottomless pit flung wide, infernal fire, scorched land, rains of fire, blizzards of soot . . .

The rattlesnake above the clouds, his fiery fangs spitting death . . . forests and fields, temples and towers (cloud-capped towers, sun-topping temples) . . . rising fireballs, nothing more.

I have seen the jaguar's claws rake and raze. Deer, dog, rabbit, squirrel, bobcat, bear, wolf, antelope, turkey, fox, dog, coyote, cougar . . . flee. But the fiery god is quick of flame. Charnel and charred, his beasts dream Death.

I have seen the crocodile smile—teeth, seas exploding flame, topless waves like soaring peaks, his rivers of blood . . . his lakes of fire.

I have seen us . . . infinite weapons, infernal death, terse earth, man-made suns detonating death . . .

Cities, farms, industry, science, culture, knowledge, pleasure, art, love, memories, truth, life—gone.

Daring deeds, crowning triumphs—gone.

Life . . . carelessly lost . . . gone.

I have seen the star-gods die, the moon flood blood, the sun die blind and blacken to the heart.

A trillion years of Mictlantecuhtli's hell will not requite the loss.

Hear my words: Blame not the gods and stars, blame . . . us.

Hear my words: Flee not the eagle, the jaguar, snake and croc, flee . . . us.

Eagle . . . farewell.

Jaguar, rattlesnake, and crocodile . . . farewell.

Quetzalcoatl . . . farewell.

Tithing blood, hearts, death, we tithe . . . ourselves.

We tithe the night.

We tithe all to Tezcatlipoca, god of night.

Thus endeth the Vision.

"We wanted to know what happened to Tula," the president said. "I think Quetzalcoatl just told us."

"Thanks a heap, Quetzie," Bradford said.

"What's your interpretation, General?" President Raab asked.

"Fire from the earth, fire from the sky, fire from man," General Hagberg said.

"Dr. Cardiff," President Raab asked, "your take?"

"Tula was the prologue—2012 is the whole nine yards."

"Then may God have mercy on our souls," the president said. "Tezcatlipoca is back."